YOU LEFT ME

SHE WANTS JUSTICE. WILL SHE SETTLE FOR
REVENGE?

SUSAN WILKINS

For Sue Kenyon, who makes it all possible.

PROLOGUE

I might be mad. I'm not sure. But everything feels a little skewed. A tad off kilter. Also, there's the stuff in my head; I'm not stupid. I know it's not normal.

Some people say, 'I heard this voice. I just obeyed it.' Voices are nothing. I have a whole movie in my head. I know what I have to do. And I've imagined in technicolour detail all the ways I can do it. The more I visualise it, the more real it becomes. I'm rehearsing the actions, making sure my mind and body are in synch. So, it is premeditated.

Can that still count as madness?

I haven't lost my capacity for analytical thinking. I know you can't research the ins and outs of this on the internet, because afterwards they'll take your computer and phone, track all the sites you've visited and use it against you in court.

But who's going to remember a middle-aged woman, who walked into a posh kitchen shop in Covent Garden in London two months ago and bought a five-inch Sabatier boning knife, paying for it with cash?

When I did that, was I sane?

A Carbon-Steel knife has exceptional cutting power, but you must never put it in the dishwasher, that's what the sales assistant told me. I didn't tell him that if everything goes according to plan, I intend to throw it in the river.

But am I fooling myself?

Probably. But I don't want to let you down. Not again. I can't.

Part of me knows I'm playing with all this, because it helps distract me from the pain and the grief.

This part keeps telling me I'm not a criminal. This is all just a silly fantasy. Nothing's going to happen. Of course it isn't.

Then there's the other part of me. The dark side. And she's definitely getting stronger. And more insistent.

1

Claire Naylor feels the sweat running down her spine. She lets her gaze drift towards the window. Even with the blinds half-closed, the scorching sun still breaks through, making the classroom unbearably hot. In front of her, thirty Year Sevens are hunched or slumped over their tables. Everyone is waiting for the same thing. The bell.

It's the end of the school day, and nearly the end of the summer term and the school year. The kids are supposedly doing a written quiz, something light to keep their attention. The usual end of term trips have been scrapped this year because the budget is shot, not to mention the worst heatwave for thirty years.

But the kids are quiet. The blistering heat has shut them up. As she watches and waits, Claire wonders how useful her history classes have been to them and the futures they face.

'It's all dead kings and no women, innit?' said one of the more belligerent and outspoken girls.

This term they've been studying the Industrial Revolution. Spinning Jennies, Stephenson's Rocket, it washed over them like code from another planet. Some were diligent and took notes; they tended to be the ones whose parents badgered them, who wanted to see them get up and out.

The school policy is that phones being used during lesson time should be confiscated. But Claire has given up on that; it's too disruptive. The past is irrelevant to these kids, teachers are irrelevant. Only the latest hot social media influencer commands their attention.

The sudden piercing electronic wail echoes down the corridors and the kids erupt into life with the rattling of chairs and thumping of feet.

'No pushing and shoving!' shouts Claire, as they barge en masse towards the narrow doorway.

In less than two minutes, they're all gone and the room settles to the quiet and the dust motes dancing in the sunshine. Claire collects up the quiz papers from the tables and the floor. Someone has drawn a cartoon penis being inserted into what Claire presumes is supposed to be a mouth.

Year Seven! They're twelve years old for Chrissake!

Judy, the teacher from next door, puts her head round the door. She's beaming and sweating. They're a similar age, middle forties, both with a lot of classroom time under their belts and the battle scars to prove it. But Judy is a relentlessly cheery soul, which annoys Claire.

'Thank God it's Friday,' she says.

Claire just nods, hoping she'll go away.

'Have you got anything planned this weekend?' She's persistent, Claire'll give her that. 'Because we're having a barbecue. My old man's obsessed. Thinks if he can char a few sausages and chicken wings, it means he can cook. But quite a few people are coming. It should be a laugh.'

4

Claire scans her. She means well. They all mean well. Come for a drink after work. Come to dinner. Let's meet up in town for a coffee. But she's fed up with their pity. Why can't they just leave her alone?

Claire paints on a smile. 'Sorry,' she says. 'It's my college reunion this weekend. Twenty-five years since graduation. Can you believe it?'

'Oh, that'll be great, seeing old friends. Where did you go to college?'

'In Cambridge. I went to St Peter's College.'

'Wow! I never knew that. So why aren't you teaching in some posh private school that pays you real money and where the kids don't carry knives and throw chairs?'

Claire smiles and shrugs.

Because you used to think you could make a difference?

A couple more minutes of meaningless chit-chat and she escapes. She's walking across the car park when her phone buzzes.

She glances at it. Mum. Her heart sinks. She loves her parents, but everything is a problem for them now. And it's wearisome.

She considers ignoring it. But that would be wrong. She clicks to answer.

'Hello, Mum.'

There's a sigh, followed by her mother's imperious tones. Sandra Naylor still sounds like the posh grammar school Head she once was.

'My God, Claire,' she says. 'This bloody agency, you have got to speak to them. We're paying a small fortune for them to provide carers for your father. And again, they phone me up, barely an hour's notice, to tell me no one's coming. Staff shortages, they say. We're so sorry. Well, not as bloody sorry as me. I can't shower him. I can't lift him.'

'No one expects you to.'

Sandra has just had a double hip replacement. She can barely walk.

'I'm at my wit's end. I argue with them. Some poor untrained girl in the office, it gets me nowhere.'

Claire listens, but inside, where feelings should be, she's numb. That's what grief does, it cauterises the mind.

'I'm coming over, Mum. We'll sort something out.'

'I hate to ask. But what can I do?' Now she sounds defeated and small which rips into Claire.

'I'm sorry,' she adds. More polite and distanced now, as she attempts to regain her dignity.

'Don't be,' says Claire. 'It's fine. I'll be there.'

Derek Naylor has Parkinson's, but neither he nor his wife will countenance him going into residential care, even if they could find a suitable place for him. Claire has looked into it surreptitiously; the only availability is at the luxury end of the market. It would be just about affordable with the sale of their house; but then what would be left for Sandra?

As she unlocks her car, Claire does a rapid calculation. Everything is ready to go. Her bag is packed. She'll just pop home and collect it, make sure Ziggy is fed, then go to her parents. It won't be the first time she's had to step in and bail them out. He'll be embarrassed, but they'll cope.

She's got a room in college booked for two nights for the reunion. Even with this unplanned detour, she can still be in Cambridge by about seven o'clock.

She opens the car door and a whoosh of hot air hits her. Some kind of weather warning has been issued; temperatures are expected to hit forty degrees centigrade in some areas.

Another reason to check on the parents.

The steering wheel is red hot, but she starts the engine and turns on the air-con. She sits in the driver's seat and waits for it to do its work. The car park is partly shaded by trees, but they're already shedding their leaves. Every bit of greenery that surrounds the school is brown and parched.

A small headache is bubbling up behind her eyes. She reaches into her bag and pulls out her water bottle. As she takes a drink, her phone vibrates.

Melissa Rowe's name pops up on the screen. Claire smiles and answers.

'Hey, Mel,' she says.

'Can you believe this bloody weather?' says her friend. 'If I'm on a beach in the Caribbean, fine. Hot is what I'm paying for. But in London?'

'It'll be cooler in Cambridge.'

'You reckon? Anyway, that's why I'm calling. Just wanted to let you know that I'm probably not going to make it to the reunion. It's work. Y'know, deadlines. My editor's being an arse.'

Claire takes another sip of water.

Don't over-react.

'Oh,' she says. 'That's a pity. It's been a while. I was looking forward to seeing you.'

'Yeah, I know. But look, next time you're up in town, we'll do lunch. Somewhere expensive. On me. I promise.'

Don't beg.

'Thing is Mel, I was really hoping you'd come because there's something I need to do. And it has to be this weekend in Cambridge. At the reunion. It's something I have to do for Ella.'

There's a silence on the other end of the line.

Then Mel says, 'That sounds a bit cryptic.'

'It's complicated. I was hoping you'd come, because I need your support.'

Now an audible sigh.

'Well, look,' says Mel. 'I'll talk to my editor. I'll see what I can do. Are you alright?'

She thinks you're crazy. But if it gets her there.

'Yeah, y'know. One day at a time.'

Cliches occupy the space where feelings should be. It's all she has left.

'I'll definitely come if I can. But it won't be until tomorrow morning.'

She won't come.

'That's okay.'

'Right, well, I'll see you then.'

'Thank you.'

Claire hangs up. Driving out of the car park, she can feel the anxiety twisting in her gut. She has to consciously loosen her grip on the steering wheel. It's all under control. Once she gets home, she can take another Ativan. She must ration herself, that's what the doctor told her, because benzodiazepines can become addictive.

Be a good girl. Do as you're told.

She just needs to focus on one thing at a time. Put one foot in front of the other. And stay away from the edge.

2

Friday, 4pm

Melissa Rowe stares at her phone, then at her laptop. Now she feels guilty. Evasion, excuses; okay, be honest, downright lies, are her professional stock in trade. You don't get your boot through some of the doors she has and break the high-profile stories that win awards as an investigative journalist without a degree of cajoling charm coupled with sheer ruthlessness.

She has no intention of going to some stupid college reunion, but judged it best to wait until the last minute to break the news to Claire Naylor.

For some unfathomable reason, Claire has volunteered for the organising committee of this farrago. Mel received the invitation ages ago, which she immediately chucked in the bin. She can't imagine anything more awful than a reunion with all the smug bastards she knew twenty-five years ago. The game of winners and losers, comparing notes, who's made fortunes, who's on their second or third marriages.

Who's dead.

The only reason the college does it is so they can prise open the wallets of their distinguished alumni and fill their overstuffed coffers with even more money. Mel is not about to play that game.

When Claire started hassling her, it was easier to just agree and then invent an excuse to drop out at the last minute. Claire is her oldest friend; the only one she's made an effort to keep in touch with. Sadly, they rarely see each other. Different lives, and for a while, different continents. Still, Mel has no wish to upset her. Especially after what happened to Ella.

She lets her eye travel round the newsroom in its eyrie high above Canary Wharf. It's full for a Friday afternoon. But that's probably down to the quality of the air conditioning. London is sweltering through a record heatwave. The sky is cerulean blue, not the usual comforting grey. Every window on every building, and all their reflective surfaces, have a disturbing sparkle, more like Abu Dhabi or Doha.

She submitted her copy this morning, an Opinion piece for the Saturday edition, which would probably annoy those in power she was hoping to annoy. And, if it wasn't for the bloody heat, she'd be out of town by now, driving down to the coast.

But the awkwardness of the exchange with Claire has unsettled her. She gets up from her desk and strolls over to the water cooler, where two junior reporters are hovering. They fall silent at her approach.

'Don't mind me,' she says, refilling her cup.

They gaze at her in awe; the girl scurries off, but the boy remains. He's pretty, definitely fuckable, and about twenty years her junior. She smiles at him. But nowadays, you have to be extremely careful who you make a pass at. HR has policies, and they don't just apply to the blokes.

She sighs inwardly. Times have changed, and not always for the better.

'Tom, isn't it?' she says. Maybe she can't touch, but at least she can enjoy his proximity and the pheromone buzz.

'Theo,' he replies. 'I know it's cheeky, but can I ask you a favour?'

His hair is dark and curly. Broad shoulders, obviously works out. She can imagine him shirtless. 'Ask away,' she says.

'I'm working on a background piece.'

She knows what's coming next. It's always the same. He wants her to read it and critique it before one of the subs tears it to shreds.

What's it worth, mate?

She tilts her head. Okay, it's a bit flirty.

He smiles. Perfect teeth. Nice package emphasised by his skinny jeans. 'You're the absolute expert on Westminster,' he says. 'It's about some information I've been given that a minister has lied to Parliament about…'

She brushes his upper arm, just with the tips of her fingers. He doesn't seem bothered. Solid muscle.

'Rule of thumb, Theo,' she says. 'Always start from the premise that they're all trying to shaft each other. That's why they're politicians.'

He laughs, giving her the eye. He knows his power.

'My source is a special adviser in the Home Office,' he says. 'But I think he's just trying to play me. He's a guy I went to uni with.'

'Do you trust him?'

'Christ, no. He was always a lying little turd.'

'Then there's your answer. Special political advisers are

the rattlesnakes of Westminster. A SpAds job is to make his minister look good and someone else look bad. Your job is to sift through all the bullshit and identify nuggets of truth. And always double check your sources. That's what makes you a serious journalist instead of a tabloid hack, who just regurgitates the nonsense they're fed.'

He grins and nods. He has his hands on his slim hips and his sleeves rolled up. Downy, muscular forearms, elegant fingers.

'Thank you,' he says. 'And I was wondering...'

'Yeah. I'll look the piece over. Send it to me.' She could suggest they discuss it over a drink.

Don't make a fool of yourself.

She hesitates, then she adds, 'Have you ever been to a college reunion?'

'Yeah. I've been to a couple. They're great. The last one was mad. And quite a lot of fooling around, if you know what I mean.' He gives her a roguish smile.

'My college is having one this weekend. But we're so old, I'm not sure any of my lot will be up to much fooling around.'

He laughs. 'You'd be surprised. And c'mon, you're not old, nowhere near. Go for it. I would.'

He's toying with her. She can feel it. But he's got what he wants. Now he is being cheeky.

She turns on her heel and walks back to her desk. Across from her, Brian, the deputy political editor, gives her a baleful look.

'You need to watch it with all this touchy-feely stuff,' he says.

She glares at him; married, balding, and still five years younger than her.

'I don't know what you mean.'

He rubs his own fingertips over his shirt sleeve in an exaggerated fashion. 'If I did what you do, the boss'd have my nuts in a wringer.'

'Positive discrimination, Bri. It's our turn to be the predators.'

'I don't think she'd see it that way.'

He's right, of course.

She sits down. For a full five minutes, she's managed not to think about Claire Naylor and to keep the guilt at bay. But now it's back.

She glances at Brian. 'I'd tell her it's the heat. Making us horny.'

'Good luck with that,' he says without looking up from his keyboard.

She huffs. 'I've got this old friend trying to guilt trip me into going to my twenty-five-year college reunion this weekend. And I don't want to go.'

'Why not?' says Brian, tapping away.

'I mean, come on, these things are just grim. It was competitive enough back when we were students. Can you imagine it now? Who's made it? Fulfilled all that youthful promise. And who hasn't? The gloating and the pity.'

'Well, I don't know what you're worried about. You're the political editor on a top paper. You've got a shelfful of awards and you've published several books. Surely that's impressive enough?'

'With that lot. Believe me. It isn't.'

'Well, if you've got something better to do.'

He knows she hasn't. She feels fidgety and annoyed. And the damned heat is getting on her nerves. Why can't it rain?

3

Friday, 4.15pm

Leanne Brady checks her emails one last time and closes her laptop. She gets several hundred a day. They have to be triaged into important, the ones she deals with herself, standard, which are passed over to her assistant, and rubbish. She deletes these immediately.

She's a founding partner in a strategic communications consultancy; that's what it says on their glossy website. But although they operate across various sectors, including politics, business and the media, the job remains the same. She's a fixer. The 'hidden hand' is what her husband calls her. And he means it as a compliment.

Her assistant, Caspar, is standing in front of her desk, iPad in hand, ready to take notes.

'And also,' says Leanne. 'Jimmy what's-his-name? The actor that got the BAFTA?'

'Jimmy Adeyemi.'

'Yeah, him. I think he'd be a great face for the new

Breeze campaign. His wife just had a baby. Send flowers.'

Caspar taps his screen.

Leanne takes a breath and exhales. 'I think that's it. I'm off. Can you call my nanny and tell her I'll be home for the children's tea?'

'No problem.' Caspar nods and smiles. 'And I hope you have a great weekend.'

Leanne stands up, slots her laptop in her briefcase and her phone in her Fendi handbag. 'You know what these things are like. Robert's the after-dinner speaker. He's always loved that sort of thing; being invited to high table, impressing the great and the good, getting them onside.'

'Beats a scrap in the House of Commons, I suppose.'

Leanne chuckles. 'On the contrary,' she says. 'It's where they train for it. Have you got anything planned?'

'Just a quiet weekend with Darryl. In the shade, preferably.'

'Good idea. Enjoy yourself.'

As Leanne steps out of the lift into the foyer of the building, the heat hits her like an invisible fog. She hates being hot. Her skin prickles and she feels irritated. Since the menopause hit, it's been worse.

The building is on Farringdon Road, and when the automatic glass doors slide open, she's relieved to see her car is kerbside, waiting. The thing about a great PA like Caspar is all the things you don't have to tell them to do. And with a life like Leanne's, which works to a schedule, that kind of efficiency makes all the difference.

The car is electric, obviously, but the driver has the air-con running and as soon as she gets into the back seat she's cocooned in coolness. She recognises him vaguely. The firm they use only has a small rota of drivers and they're always reliable.

'How are you?' she says. 'Driving round London in this heat must be a pain for you.'

Always be nice. It costs you nothing, and it pays dividends.

'I'm fine, ma'am. I stay inside the vehicle mostly, so I've no complaints. Are we headed for Greenwich?'

'Yes, I'm hoping to be home for my children's tea.'

'I'll see what I can do.'

With the preliminaries over, they lapse into silence. They cross the river at Blackfriars Bridge. The light bounces off the water in dazzling shards. Leanne puts her sunglasses on and leans her head back into the soft leather upholstery.

She went on a course some years ago which extolled the virtues of power napping. Now she swears by it. The psychological benefits are well established. She may look like a knackered, middle-aged woman falling asleep in the back of the car, but there's science behind it.

She wakes just as the car turns into Hyde Vale.

Robert has a good eye for property and once the kids came along, central London was no longer appropriate. The Grade II-listed Georgian townhouse had to be completely renovated. But it's close to Greenwich Park, Blackheath and the right sort of schools.

Leanne lets herself in through the front door and Sybil comes skipping down the hall to greet her. Sybil is her baby and her secret treasure. Six years old, she was premature and delivered by emergency Caesarean. She began her life in an incubator, too tiny and fragile even to be held. The fact they nearly lost her makes her even more precious to Leanne.

Her daughter is frowning. 'Mummy, I'm really worried about Fred. He just sits there in his cage and Valentina says he might be poorly.'

Leanne makes a mental note: add sick guinea pig to

Monday's to-do list.

She follows her daughter down the hall into the spacious kitchen and family room at the back. Valentina is preparing a pasta dish for the children's supper. Allegra, her thirteen-year-old daughter, is already seated at the dining table, scrolling on her phone. No acknowledgement. She is a teenager.

The nanny smiles. She's a cheerful girl and her English is excellent. She also seems happy and satisfied in her work. The last thing any family needs is a disgruntled nanny on the lookout for a stepping-stone to something better. But Valentina is decidedly plain with a homely face, so not much of a temptation for the wandering male gaze. Not that Leanne thinks Robert is likely to stray, but you can't be too careful. Leanne is a planner; she's spent her life being careful.

'Can I get you something, Mrs Gerrish?' says Valentina. 'There's plenty of pasta.' In this area of her life, Leanne uses her married name.

'A cup of tea would be lovely,' says Leanne. 'But Robert and I will eat later in Cambridge.'

Sybil tugs at her sleeve. 'Mummy, what about Fred?'

'Fred's dozy because you feed him too much,' says her older sister in a weary, adult voice.

'Do not!' protests Sybil.

The next five minutes are taken up with a trip to the garden shed, a hands-on examination of Fred, who seems energetic and wriggly enough when released from his cage, and reassuring words to Sybil.

Leanne sits at the table with her daughters and watches Valentina serve them their meal. It smells and looks delicious. Would a couple of spoonfuls do any harm?

Absolutely not!

The memory of her overweight years still haunts Leanne.

In her first year at uni, her nickname was Miss Piggy. All those elegant, privately educated girls with their perfect bodies and their silky manes of hair. She had to starve herself thin and now that she's in her forties, maintaining a good figure is hard work.

'Okay, girls,' she says, folding her hands in front of her. 'Remember that Daddy and I are going to Cambridge this weekend for our college reunion.'

'What's a reunion?' says Sybil.

'It's a special event when you meet all your old friends. We were all students together. It's a chance to catch up with everyone and see what they're up to. I'm really looking forward to it.'

Not strictly true. It'll probably be a nightmare.

Allegra isn't paying attention. She keeps shooting nervous glances at her phone. Some teen melodrama must be unfolding. Sybil is forking pasta and the delicious-smelling tomato sauce into her mouth. Leanne feels her tummy grumbling. She's starving.

'Can I come?' says Sybil.

'No darling. It's not for children. But one day, when you go to university yourself, you'll make lots of friends. Other girls and boys. And you'll all be students together. Working hard but also having fun.'

'Sounds like kindergarten but worse,' says Allegra.

Leanne ignores the comment. When she was thirteen, she'd already figured she had one way out, one shot, and that was school. She slogged her guts out to get the grades. Allegra has it all on a plate, and she doesn't even know it.

Let it go. It's not her fault.

She focuses on Sybil. 'Because what you need to remember, darling, is if you work hard and believe in yourself, you can be whoever you want to be.'

'What if I want to be a pig?' says Sybil. 'Or a pony?'

Allegra gives a snort of derision. Leanne shoots her a warning look.

Fortunately, her phone vibrates. Robert.

She answers it. He sounds breathless, as if he's walking. Now he does need to lose a few pounds. But it doesn't matter as much for men.

'Hello, darling,' he says. 'Listen, bit of a problem this end. You'll have to go up to Cambridge on your own tonight. But I'll be there tomorrow morning. Early. I promise.'

'What sort of problem?'

'It's a security thing. They don't like the risk profile and they're saying they haven't got enough close protection officers to cover me tonight.'

'But they knew this was happening weeks ago.'

Try not to sound peevish.

'It's because of the knife thing. It's made them ultra twitchy. Basically, they don't want me to go at all. But I've put my foot down.'

'Well, I'll wait and we'll go together.'

'Up to you. I know you want to catch up with your chums.'

Face that lot alone? No way.

'Your chums too,' she says. 'I'll think about it. When will you be home?'

'Late. I've got to go. Kiss the girls for me.'

He hangs up. Leanne sighs. Allegra is watching her; that look of total teenage disdain.

She thinks she's so smart. She'll learn. But at least it won't be the hard way, like you did.

Leanne glances at Valentina. 'Maybe I will have some pasta, if there's some left. But just a small portion.'

4

Friday, 5pm

The journey from school to home took Claire twice as long as normal. Traffic was snarled, with a long diversion on her usual route between Luton and Bedford. According to the traffic news, the heat had melted the tarmac.

She stands at her kitchen sink, beads of sweat on her forehead, gulping down half of the glass of water she's just poured. Then she takes one of her tablets. Out of the window, the narrow back garden is a tangle of dying greenery and straw-coloured grass.

She thumbs a quick text to her mother.

Traffic a nightmare. Be there very soon.

Her mother hates texts. She finds the lack of punctuation and verbs offensive. Claire wonders if she'll end up like that, permanently irritated and offended by the unremitting barrage of technological and social change. But maybe it's the constant pain her mother suffers. Her parents dipped into their savings so Sandra could get her hips done privately. But recovery has been slow.

Claire finishes her glass of water and heads upstairs. Her small case is open on the bed. The dress she plans to wear for the dinner is lying next to it, still on its hanger. It's ages old. Blue silk to match her eyes. Ella helped her choose it. She folds it carefully and lays it in the top of the case.

Nowadays, the house is so quiet. The odd pigeon scrabbling on the chimney pot. The estate agent who sold it to them called it a delightful cottage in a semi-rural setting. At the time, it seemed idyllic. The reality is it's a Victorian labourer's two up and two down with a downstairs bathroom added at the back. Ella was only five when they moved in, and she loved the garden. Since then, the suburban sprawl has caught up with them. It's no longer a village. The field that was once their view is now a housing estate.

Claire closes her case and carries it out into the hall. Then she hesitates. She can never pass the other bedroom door without at least glancing inside.

And there he is, curled up on the bed. He opens his eyes and blinks at her.

'How you doing, mate? I thought I'd find you in here.'

Ziggy yawns and stretches. He's getting on in years, and mostly he sleeps. Almost always here. In her room.

'You miss her as much as I do, don't you, Zig?'

He's black and silky, with neat white socks. He extends one paw, curls the pad and claws towards him and licks it.

Claire sits down on the bed and strokes his back.

The room is small and compact with fading wallpaper. But the bookshelf that occupies one whole side of the room remains as ordered as Ella left it. Claire dusts it regularly, launders the duvet on the narrow single bed and vacuums the carpet. She can't bear to change a thing; why would she? But this remains a totally private ritual. A homage to her daughter that no one knows about. Except Ziggy.

As her eye travels round the room, she can feel the knot of anxiety tightening in her stomach. But she's made her daughter a promise, and she plans to keep it.

One way or another.

The drive to her parents' house involves far less traffic hassle. She knows a back route and as she pulls into their driveway, she notices her mother silhouetted in the bay window at the front of the house. Sandra has been on the lookout.

Letting herself in with her key, Claire calls out. 'Just me.'

She can hear the wheels on Sandra's walking frame moving across the polished wooden floor in the sitting room. This is the house her parents retired to; they too were attracted to the semi-rural nature of the area. But development has gobbled the farmland up. It's now a commuter village within spitting distance of the M25 motorway.

Sandra appears in the doorway, leaning heavily on her frame. She's a big woman, tall like Claire, but over time, her lack of mobility has led to her putting on weight. She looks her daughter up and down. The eyes are as fierce as ever, although the face is bone weary.

'Fancy a glass of wine?' she says.

'No thanks,' says Claire. 'I'm driving up to Cambridge later. It's the college reunion this weekend. Remember, I told you?'

Sandra nods. 'Well, I need a glass of wine.'

'How is he?' says Claire.

'Tetchy,' her mother replies.

The progress towards the kitchen is slow. Claire follows her mother.

Finally, Sandra makes it to the Windsor back carver chair

at the head of the kitchen table. She lowers herself into it with some relief.

'Red or white?' says Claire. She tries to ignore her mother's laboured breathing.

'I'll have a glass of the Margaux. It's in the cupboard.'

In Claire's view, her mother drinks far too much. They've talked about it.

'What the hell else am I going to do at this stage of the game?' was her mother's belligerent reply. And it's hard to argue with that.

Claire opens the bottle, pours slowly, the way her father taught her. Then she gets a coaster from the drawer, places it on the table next to her mother and puts the glass of wine on it. The little things matter.

'Thank you,' says Sandra, reaching for the glass. 'I'm sorry about this. I don't want to hold you up.'

'It's fine. I don't need to be there until this evening.'

Sandra takes a mouthful of wine; savours it. Neither of them speaks. Claire directs her gaze out of the window at the scorched lawn and the wilting roses. The sun has moved round, off the back of the house, which is now in shade. But the temperature in the room still borders on oppressive.

'I think about her every day,' says Sandra. 'And I just keep thinking how is it I didn't know, that I didn't realise—'

Here we go.

'Mum, please. Don't!'

'She was such a happy child.' Sandra's eyes brim with tears. 'I'm sorry. I don't want to upset you.'

Upset?

Claire meets her mother's gaze. She's way beyond that. That implies the mild distress that you can recover from. A passing emotion. You just have to pull yourself together. She relies on the tablets to keep everything tamped down, so that the raging inferno beneath doesn't erupt and consume every-thing in its path. It's the only way she can function.

Sandra's chin quivers as she fights back the tears. 'Sorry,' she whispers, and she takes another slug of wine.

Claire puts a hand on her mother's shoulder and squeezes it.

Then she says, 'I assume Dad's upstairs.'

'He is. He's been in his room all day. Even with the stair-lift, I can't get him down here on my own.'

'I'll phone the agency and complain again.'

'Much good it'll do.'

'Well, I'd better get on and give him a shower.'

Sandra holds out her glass. Her hand has a tremor. The arthritic knuckles make it hard to grip. 'Top me up before you go,' she says.

Claire picks up the bottle and pours. She can't think about any of this too much. It's just one foot in front of the other.

5

Saturday, 7am

Detective Sergeant Jo Boden is in a hot sweat. It's still early, but the sun is already high in the sky and blazing. The heat-wave is forecast to continue for the entire weekend. And she was supposed to be off. A trip to the lido?

Fat chance.

Her car is in the garage, the bus didn't turn up, so she ended up walking and now she's late for the early morning briefing. She's hoping to slip unnoticed into the back of the room. It's crowded enough. Unfortunately, her new boss, DCI Rachel Knight, clocks her immediately and gives her the evil eye. Not an auspicious start.

There are about thirty uniformed officers present, because this is a public order operation. The operational commander is Superintendent Hubbard, and he's at the front addressing the troops. Boden has no idea why she's being included. She just got a text from the DCI the previous evening telling her to turn up.

There's a map of the centre of Cambridge projected on a screen at the front of the room. The cursor dances around as Hubbard adjusts it.

'We're expecting two rival demonstrations,' he says. 'And it's likely that they'll try to converge near the front of the college. Our aim is to prevent this from happening. The Minister is scheduled to arrive around midday. He's attending a college reunion and he will be giving an after-dinner speech and spending the night at the college. The reason for the demo is his recent controversial statements on fracking and UK energy security. So, we've got a loose alliance of various green groups who are coming to object. And then a right-wing faction that wants the opposite. What we need to avoid is a punch up. Tempers could become frayed in the heat.'

Boden catches Knight's eye. The boss is standing at the front next to Hubbard, with her arms folded. She looks about as happy to be there as Boden is.

Hardly surprising. It's only a week since she returned from suspension. The general feeling is that she's lucky not to have been booted out. Her old man, who she's divorcing, is awaiting trial on money laundering charges.

The problem is Knight is now the trickiest kind of boss; she's been publicly shamed, and it's obvious to everyone that she has something to prove.

The Independent Office for Police Conduct found her guilty of gross misconduct in the handling of informants. They recommended demotion from her previous rank. But did she know what her old man was up to? Most people assume she did. Boden is reserving judgement.

There's plenty of shuffling and huffing in the room; policing a demo on a boiling hot day is no one's idea of fun. For the next ten minutes, Hubbard uses his map to point out the various deployments. As the briefing ends and the room empties, Boden moves up to the front towards Knight.

'Morning, boss,' she says. 'Sorry I was late.'

'I realise this is your weekend off,' says Knight. Her smile is chilly, but she's trying to be nice. 'I'm sorry to drag you into this.'

'No problem,' says Boden.

What else are you going to say?

'Superintendent Hubbard's got a job for you. We need a local liaison officer to work with the Minister's close protection detail. We need a detective. It should be a DI, but no one suitable is available. I need you to step up. Is that okay with you?'

There's no one suitable, because everyone, including Boden's old boss, has jumped ship. Knight is toxic; working for her will kill your promotion prospects, that's the accepted view. As an outsider, with a cloud over her anyway, Boden has little choice. She and Knight are stuck with each other.

Boden shrugs. 'Surely a firearms officer would fit the bill better than me?'

Knight is about to dismiss that, but Hubbard joins them. 'The DCI tells me you've worked undercover,' he says.

'Yes sir. When I was in the Met.'

'Okay, well, this should be up your street. Here's the situation. Counter Terrorism has informed us that there's a credible threat against the Minister. We have no more detail than that. But he's going to be spending two days in Cambridge at this reunion. In security terms, it's a bit of a nightmare. He'll have his close protection, but he'll be mingling with other guests. A private company will be doing the catering for this event. None of their staff has been vetted.'

'Meaning someone posing as a server could come at him with a knife?' says Boden.

'Exactly,' says Knight. 'Or any of the other college staff.'

'What about the other guests?'

Knight gives her a sour smile. 'They're supposedly all respectable people, alumni of the university, but yes, them too.'

A bit of a nightmare?

Hubbard sighs. 'I don't want a Cabinet Minister attacked on my watch. If anyone tries it, hopefully close protection will deal with it. But we need to identify any potential culprits before they strike. We need to expect the unexpected. It's an eyes and ears job.'

'Take a couple of DCs with you,' says Knight. 'The close protection officers will be from the Met. They'll update you on the situation and tell you what they think is needed.'

Boden nods, but inwardly she's groaning. Spending her weekend off as a minder at some posh college do, and being ordered about by some of the Met's finest boot boys, is not what she had planned. And all this with a possible terrorist on the loose that no one has been able to identify.

'Are you okay with this, Sergeant?' says Hubbard.

Boden catches Rachel Knight's eye. It's clear what she expects.

'Yes, sir,' says Boden. 'I'll take DCs Mackie and Chakra-vorty if that's okay.'

Think of the overtime. We could all do with the extra cash.

'Your choice,' says Knight. 'I'll be in the control room with the Superintendent.'

Boden meets her gaze. There's a fragility in Knight, a tension that wasn't there before. She's desperate to come over as super efficient and super helpful. She has a reputation to rebuild. And it's going to be an uphill struggle. Boden knows only too well that once your colleagues regard you with suspicion, life can be miserable.

She glances at Hubbard. His manner is professional and polite. Boden wonders what he's really thinking. Rachel Knight is tainted. She's probably the last person he wants on this.

He gives Boden a reassuring smile. 'See anything you don't like the look of, Sergeant. I want to know about it. Okay?'

'Yes, sir.'

'You need to report to the close protection team leader. He's a DI called Foley.'

Foley!

Boden can't help smiling. Cal Foley? It can't be.

Knight doesn't miss a trick. 'You know him?' she says.

'Not sure,' says Boden.

'Is it a problem?' Knight's anxiety is palpable. She can't afford for this to go wrong. But all they've got is some vague heads up from Counter Terrorism with no details of what to look for.

It's going to be a total pain.

'No,' says Boden, 'it's fine.' She gives the boss a reassuring smile.

6

Saturday, 11am

The journey to Cambridge proved less of a hassle than Mel expected. She took a cab to King's Cross and spent just over an hour on a cool train, staring out of the window at the parched countryside. And she still didn't know why she was doing this.

A toxic combination of guilt and the prospect of a lonely weekend is probably what tipped the balance. She could've opted to go down to her sister- and brother-in-law's place in Sussex. They keep horses and she often rides with her sister and niece. But somehow, being reminded of the sacrifices she's made for her stellar career, including her disastrous marriage, and the lack of a family of her own, was not something she needed. Not this weekend.

As she gets off the train in Cambridge, there's a vague sense of familiarity but now it feels jaded. Back in her student days, she had such energy and optimism. She remembers walking all the way from the station to the college, dragging a heavy suitcase behind her.

What happened to that girl? Where did she go?

She turned into you, you moron.

The optimism evaporated the first time she visited a refugee camp in the Horn of Africa and watched mothers nursing starving babies. It made her so angry, the look of resignation in those women's eyes. But where does anger get you?

Her fierce ambition to report on the stories that mattered and would change the world had become muted and warped by years of frustration and compromise. The world remained unaffected by her eloquent prose and her pleas for justice and a fairer world. Over the years, one thing became clear to her: most people don't really give a toss. Self-interest and greed rule, particularly amongst those in power.

Her cynicism has grown gradually, turning from a protective shell into full-blown armour. She calls out the bullshit; that's all she can do.

A taxi drops her near the college. It's impossible to drive up to the main gate because the police have closed the road and erected barricades. They seem to be out in force, although only a small gaggle of protesters have gathered across the road. Umbrellas to keep off the sun, a kid with a bullhorn; they don't look threatening.

'Always some bloody demo,' says the cabbie. 'That's the drawback of a town full of students.'

'What's this one about?' says Mel.

'Some Cabinet Minister. The bloke at Energy, who keeps upsetting everyone. He's coming, apparently.'

Of course he is.

Mel has had a few run-ins with Robert Gerrish in her professional capacity. He always treats her like a long-lost pal; same college, same year. But the reality is when they were students, Gerrish was an ugly little slime ball that no one took seriously. They were never friends, not really. God, no. It surprised everyone when he morphed into the most successful and high-profile graduate of his year.

Except Adrian.

But he'll never turn up to a fiasco like this. No way.

As Mel walks through the ancient stone archway and past the Porter's Lodge, she feels a tingle run up her spine. Loathe as she is to admit it, this place still has a peculiar magic. The endless generations of hopeful and gilded youth that have passed through here have left their mark. It's just wealth and privilege, she reminds herself. The elite replicating itself so it can hang on to power.

A long table has been set up on the college lawn with an awning to keep the sun off it. It's covered with rows of name tags; several people are standing behind it, checking off names on a list and handing out the badges. One of them is Claire Naylor. She looks like shit.

Mel joins the short queue. She feels uncomfortable. But then Claire sees her, and wreathed in smiles, she comes rushing round the table to greet her.

'You came!' she exclaims.

'Well, y'know, I didn't want you to feel—'

There's no chance to say more because Claire pulls her into a tight hug. Mel can feel Claire's fingers grasping the material of her shirt.

'Thank you!' she whispers.

The Claire Naylor of twenty-five years ago was tall and willowy, a drop-dead gorgeous beauty. She turned heads wherever she went. She's still thin, but gaunt and stooped. Her shoulders are rounded as if she has the weight of the world on her shoulders.

Losing Ella like that, she probably does.

Her flowing honey blonde hair has faded to a mousy shade of grey and is cut in a short, serviceable bob, which grazes her collar. She looks defeated.

They were best friends once. Claire dazzled, and Mel travelled in her orbit. Over the years, a thread of connection has been maintained; cards, then emails and the odd text. Mel can't remember the last time they actually met.

Claire grasps her hand a little too tightly. 'They're serving coffee in the senior common room. It's lovely and cool in there. Let me just grab your badge and tick you off the list. Did you book a room in college for tonight?'

Mel nods, although she has every intention of being on the last train back to London.

With the housekeeping completed, Claire leads her down the familiar cloistered stone corridors that surround the interior courtyard.

Mel struggles to think of something to say. 'How many are you expecting?'

'Around fifty,' says Claire. 'It's a pretty fair turnout.'

'How did you get roped into organising?'

'I volunteered. It's only an hour's drive from where I live. I was happy to help.' Claire gives her a bright and brittle smile. Her eyes have that glint; she's on medication.

Mel tries to look sympathetic. There's a tension pulsing off her old friend, like a wound spring. Her gaze flickers to Mel's face and then away again. The woman's a complete nervous wreck.

Grief, especially the death of a child, is enough to destroy anyone. Mel knows that theoretically. But she has no idea how it feels.

They walk into the oak-panelled splendour of the senior common room. The walls are lined with gilt framed oil paintings of dead academics. Mel's gaze travels round the room, and stops dead.

Oh fuck!

Her face must say it all, because Claire is looking at her.

'I was as surprised as you,' she says. 'No one thought he'd actually come.'

Adrian Cardello, Hollywood A lister and two times Oscar winner for best actor, is holding a cup and saucer in his hand and talking to a short, stout little man in a three-piece suit, who looks vaguely like the current Master of the college.

Mel has followed his career over the years; it's been hard not to. As a young actor, he moved rapidly from the RSC to films, playing the romantic lead in a string of super successful romcoms. As he's got older, he's pursued a judicious mix of serious dramatic roles and tough guy action heroes. He's currently the lead in a blockbuster spy franchise and has his own production company.

In the flesh, he looks older and shorter than his screen persona. It's amusing to see the Master sucking up to him.

She notices her friend scanning her. 'Do you want to go over and say hello?'

'Christ, no!' says Mel. 'I haven't spoken to him since graduation. He probably won't even recognise me.'

'I'm sure he will. But let's get a coffee, because I need to talk to you.'

Claire leads her to the table where cups and flasks of coffee are laid out on a pristine white cloth. As Mel picks up a cup, she realises her hand is shaking.

This is ridiculous. Get a grip!

She shouldn't have come. This confirms it.

Claire picks up a flask and pours coffee into Mel's cup. It spills into the saucer. Mel can't tell which of them is more neurotic.

What a shitshow?

In her mind, she's already formulating a plan. An urgent call from her editor. A breaking story in wherever; it doesn't matter. She must leave urgently and head back to London.

There's a flurry of activity in the doorway. Several men in dark suits with earpieces walk into the room. They form a semi-circle. In the centre is the short, balding figure of Robert Gerrish, Secretary of State for Energy and Industry, and behind him is his wife, Leanne Brady.

AKA Miss Piggy.

Mel smiles to herself, glances from them across to Adrian. 'This should be funny,' she says. 'Who'll be top dog now?'

'Did you know Gerrish was coming?' says Claire.

'Only when the cabbie told me. Plus, the police appear to be gearing up for a riot. He's nothing if not controversial.'

'It's him I wanted to talk to you about.' Claire puts her cup down carefully. 'Did you know that after Ella graduated, she got a job working in his office as an intern?'

'No, I didn't.' Mel, like everyone else in the room, is staring at Gerrish and his entourage.

'I know this is going to sound crazy,' says Claire. 'And maybe it is. But Ella didn't kill herself for no reason.'

Mel turns to look at her friend. Claire has tears in her eyes and she's visibly shaking.

It was suicide. Oh shit.

'Oh Claire,' she says. 'I wish I could've been more—'

Claire grabs her hand, but her voice is barely audible. 'She was driven to it, Mel. By him. By Gerrish. That man killed my daughter. And if it's the last thing I do, I'm going to make him pay and get justice for Ella.'

7

Claire never intended to just blurt it out like that. She can see from Mel's expression that she's shocked. This has been months in the planning. The chance to volunteer for the reunion organising committee sowed the seed. That's when she realised that if they could persuade Gerrish to come, it would give her the opportunity to confront him. And to expose him. How it played out would depend on him.

Mel is staring at her. 'Wow!' she says. 'That's quite an accusation. Have you got some kind of proof?'

'We can't talk about it here,' says Claire. 'I'll explain later. But I just wanted you to know. And I'm going to need your help.'

'My help?'

'You're a journalist.'

Surely it's obvious what she needs to do?

Mel raises her eyebrows. She'll need time for this to sink in and just springing it on her like this was a mistake.

Claire feels jittery, and it probably shows. Two Ativan so far this morning, but they don't work as well as they used to. She needs to escape for the moment.

'Listen,' she says. 'We'll talk again after lunch. I have to go and make sure that the caterers will be ready on time.'

Mel nods. She seems oddly relieved. Her eyes keep darting in Adrian's direction, unsurprisingly. She's getting distracted.

'I'm not lying to you, Mel,' she says sharply. 'It's eight months since Ella died and this is not just grief. I've considered this from every angle.'

Mel's gaze comes back to her. 'I'm sure you have.'

She thinks you're mad.

Claire checks her watch. The buffet lunch will be served in the Old Refectory. She needs to check that it's all being laid out. There was confusion in the kitchen earlier. Some security issue with the police. Claire is worried it may have put them behind.

The room is filling up with more arrivals. Greetings, hugs, expression of joy and incredulity. Claire puts her head down and snakes through the crowd towards the door. Then she feels a hand grabbing her arm.

She turns to find Leanne Brady beaming at her.

Oh no!

'Claire!' says Leanne. 'I'm really glad to see you looking so well. And you're on the organising committee, which is just splendid.'

She's a good person. It's not her fault she's married to him.

Claire manages to smile. 'Leanne,' she says. 'I have been meaning to call you. But, y'know, I've had my hands full with the parents.'

Leanne's brow creases with concern. 'Must be awful for

you. Parkinson's is such a cruel disease. How's your mother coping?'

'She's just had her other hip done, but it's tough for her.'

Leanne touches her arm. 'And for you, Claire. My god, if you haven't had enough to contend with.'

Claire nods. She can't hold her gaze. She looks for an escape route.

'But listen to me, Claire, if ever you need anything, you must promise to come to me. Are you still looking for a care home for your parents?'

Stop! Please.

'Leanne, I know how busy you are.'

'I can still find the time to support to an old friend. I mean, can you believe it?' She chuckles. 'Twenty-five years. How ridiculous is that? And it all feels so familiar, doesn't it? As if it were yesterday.'

A queasy sense of guilt is seeping up from Claire's gut. In recent years, Leanne has been one of the few friends from the past to remain in regular contact. She was the only one who came to Ella's funeral. Mel sent flowers, but was off on an assignment. This was always going to make things harder. Claire has spent long sleepless nights trying to decide what to do. And, no question about it, her friendship with Leanne got in the way.

In the end, she concluded getting justice for her daughter trumped everything else. If it meant betraying a friendship, or even deceiving a friend, it's a price she's willing to pay.

She gives Leanne her best smile. 'Duty calls,' she says. 'We've been having issues with the caterers. I need to go and check.'

'I don't want to hold you up,' says Leanne.

Claire turns to leave, only to find Robert Gerrish heading straight for her, hand outstretched.

As a young man, Gerrish was skinny with a face like a rat. But ugliness often lessens with age. He's settled into his body, put on weight, lost most of hair, which was always lank and greasy. An expensive, well-cut suit to expand his shoulders and disguise his paunch, the rimless glasses to shorten his nose, and he's morphed into an imposing figure.

'My dear Claire,' he says, seizing her right hand, squeezing it and imprisoning it with his other hand. She still towers over him by several inches. Nowadays he smells of something subtle and expensive, not T-shirts dried on a radiator and bad breath. 'How are you?' Those dark, rodent eyes bore right into her, and he frowns slightly, as if he really cares.

Monster.

His palm is soft, he doesn't squeeze too hard, but the contact with his flesh makes the bile rise in Claire's throat. With supreme effort, she stares right back at him and smiles. 'Robert, we're so pleased you agreed to come.'

He releases her hand and shrugs. His gaze drifts off into the distance. 'This place made me,' he says. 'Made us all. How could I refuse?'

It sounds like he's testing out the opening line from his speech.

Leanne steps forward. 'Darling,' she says. 'We have to let Claire go. She has caterers to organise or we won't be getting our lunch.'

He chuckles. 'Well, we can't have that, can we?'

'No,' says Claire. 'Please excuse me.'

Turning on her heel, she flees.

8

Mel has found herself a quiet corner in the senior common room and she's checking her phone. The fact her old friend Claire appears to have gone batshit crazy makes it more imperative that she manufactures an excuse and heads back to London.

She can imagine that losing a child to suicide must be one of the worst experiences a parent can face. The pain of it must be excruciating. Then there's the guilt that you failed to save them. It would unhinge anyone. And when you mix all that anger and grief with a desperate desire to know why, to understand how such a terrible thing could happen, some kind of serious craziness emerges.

Mel spent the early years of her career as a foreign corre-spondent. Wars, famines, disasters in far-flung places. It was the faces of the survivors that finally did for her. In their eyes, there was always the same question: why? And random chance in a godless universe is not a satisfying answer for most people.

After a stint in Washington, she retreated to the shark-infested pond of domestic politics. At least here, the victims are well fed and usually they know the game they're playing.

Mel is thumbing a text to her deputy, Brian, when she becomes aware of a presence in front of her.

She looks up. He smiles. A few more lines, but the gaze is magnetic. And it still makes her tummy flutter.

Fuck him!

His arms are folded. A defensive stance? At least that's something.

'Of all the gin joints in all the towns in all the world,' he says in those silky tones. 'I was hoping you might be here.'

She raises her eyebrows. 'Still spouting other people's lines, I see.'

He opens his arms. 'At least give me a hug.'

She allows him to wrap his arms around her. They brush cheeks in an air kiss. Her whole body shivers. She has to pull away.

'You're a long way from Rodeo Drive, Cardello,' she says. 'Did you get lost?'

He tilts his head and grins. 'As waspish as ever,' he says. 'I'm glad to see you've lost none of your charm. I flew in last night. Wouldn't have missed this for the world.'

She frowns. 'Are you being serious?'

'Well, semi-serious. I'm also meeting with some investors who are backing my next picture.'

She chuckles. 'Picture?' she says. 'I love this old-style Hollywood speak. You've become quite a mogul.'

'And you've become a crusader for truth and justice. I read all your stuff. And I'm in awe.'

She shakes her head wearily. 'Don't take the piss, Cardello.'

He holds up his hands. The baby blue eyes look incredulous. That classic Celtic look, pale skin, dark hair, blue eyes, is still intact, possibly with a bit of help from a plastic surgeon to keep the jaw chiselled.

'I'm not,' he says. 'I'm dead serious. I read all your articles online. I've also read both your books. Let's face it, Mel, you were always the one who was going to do something serious and worthwhile. Me, I'm just an airhead actor who got lucky. I'm never going to change the world.'

Mel sighs. 'Turns out neither am I,' she says. 'There's not much of a market for serious journalism nowadays. Most people get their news and their opinions from social media. And we all stick to our own silos and don't listen to anyone else.'

'God, I've missed you,' he says.

'Bollocks,' she replies. 'You just want to see if you can still charm me. It's part of your narcissism.'

He grins. 'I depend on the narcissism to keep going. I've got a personal trainer who travels with me and tortures me twice a day. And I can tell you, at my age, it bloody well hurts.'

'You're such a wuss. I wonder if your legion of fans know that. I read somewhere that you still do most of your own stunts. Presumably that's rubbish.'

'Ah ha!' he says. 'You have been following my humble career.'

'It was probably a magazine I picked up at the dentist.'

'I ride the motorbikes, mostly. But apart from that, I have a stunt double. It's the only way we can get insurance for the shoot.'

She smiles. 'You've got an excuse for everything, haven't you?'

'I do miss you,' he says. 'Believe it or not, as I've got older, I have become slightly wiser. Not much, granted.' He holds up his thumb and forefinger, half an inch apart. 'A wee bit. When my last wife divorced me, I thought, why does this keep happening?'

'Don't tell me you came up with some stunning psychological insight?'

'Well, I did. And I am being brutally honest here. I think I keep looking back, trying to replicate the past. The glory days of our youth.'

'Oh, don't give me that shit. The only thing you miss is being young enough and horny enough to shag every girl you meet. Shouldn't you be in therapy for sex addiction by now? Isn't that the usual schtick for blokes like you?'

No! Don't let the bastard see how angry you still are.

He gives her a sheepish look. 'Maybe. You see right through me, don't you?'

'Don't flatter yourself.'

He sighs. 'I've waited a long time to say this. But I want to say I'm sorry, Mel. Sorry for everything.'

The nerve. The barefaced nerve of the man!

'Well, you've said it,' she says. 'Now you can fuck off for the next twenty-five years.'

She glares at him, raises her chin and strides towards the door.

'Hey, Melissa. How are you?' says some woman with a squeaky voice who she doesn't recognise. She ignores her and heads resolutely out into the courtyard. Her heart is thumping in her chest and she feels sick.

It's past midday and already oppressively hot. She walks

across the sun-baked lawn looking for some shade. Part of her just wants to leave. But that would be undignified and anyway, it's far too hot. She heads for the college chapel, opens the heavy oak door and steps inside.

9

Saturday, 12.20pm

DS Boden is watching the comings and goings in the senior common room, where coffee is being served. Positioned at the edge of the room, she has a bottle of water and is doing her best to remain hydrated and alert. But the heat is soporific, and the sea of faces is gradually becoming a blur.

Do your job. It's all anyone can expect.

But is this true? Not in today's police service. If this operation goes pear-shaped, someone will have to carry the can.

But not you.

Gerrish, the Minister, walked in half an hour ago, surrounded by close protection. No one's taken a pop at him yet. But sadly, there's no sign of her old mate. It must be another Foley. She feels a pang of disappointment, but that was her old life. She's moved on.

Taking another sip of water, she does a slow circuit of the room. Nothing much has changed in the last ten minutes. The babble of voices, the array of red, sweaty faces; all of a certain age and a certain class.

She arrived at the college well before nine and found the Bursar in his office. It was small and cluttered, with a fan on the table going at full pelt, and spreadsheets littering the desk and floor. He looked extremely harassed.

'Obviously, anything you need, Sergeant,' he said. He went on to explain the logistics of putting on such a large event, especially during a heatwave. Boden realised he wouldn't be much help. She settled for the key codes to access all the buildings on the college site.

She then spent an hour getting to know every inch of the place. From the kitchens to the cellars to the chapel, she did a recce of the whole complex. Mackie and Chakravorty turned up at about ten.

They counted twenty CCTV cameras, found the pokey backroom next to the Porter's Lodge where the monitors were located, and established that at least five of them weren't working properly. Chakravorty remained there to see if she could sort them out. She's a dab hand with anything electronic.

Once the guests began arriving, Boden positioned Mackie by the main gate in the hope his size and intimidating appearance would be a deterrent.

'An eyes and ears job,' that's what Hubbard said. Boden has made a point of checking in with the control room every half hour. The demo outside has dwindled into two lethargic huddles owing to the heat.

She's staring at her phone, about to give Knight another call, when she hears a familiar voice. 'Does that gorilla on the main gate belong to you?'

She looks up to find him towering over her; bull-necked, head razored to a dark stubble, his trademark pink shirt, silk tie and gold tiepin. But the dark eyes are twinkling with amusement.

Her heart soars.

'You crept up on me, you bastard,' she says.

'Always watch your back, Boden.'

Calvin Foley is grinning from ear to ear. Her impulse is to hug him, but in a public place and on duty?

She scans his face. He still has the sculpted beard tracing the line of his jaw. He still looks like the enforcer for a drug cartel rather than a police officer.

'You made DI,' she says.

He holds up his huge palms. 'What can I tell you? Talent will out.'

'But close protection?' she frowns.

'Don't knock it,' he says. 'I've doubled my salary. Foreign travel, fancy restaurants. I go where they go. But more to the point, what the hell are you doing here?'

'My boss sent me to be liaison officer.'

'I know that,' he says dismissively. 'What the hell are you doing hiding from the world in this backwater?'

Boden raises her eyebrows. 'It's a world-renowned university city, I'll have you know. The Romans settled here.'

Foley chuckles. 'Looks like some of them are still running the place.'

She's beaming. She can't help it.

He shakes his head. 'What the fuck, Jo? No one's seen hide nor hair of you. Not even a bloody Christmas card. You can't still be licking your wounds.'

She sighs. 'Well, y'know. They wanted me out.'

He sighs. 'Don't think you were ever the problem, mate. They've pensioned off Hollingsworth and most of his ilk. You should come back to London where you belong.'

If only.

'Maybe one day,' she says.

He folds his arms. 'Well, it's great to have you onboard, because we have got a bit of a problem here. Don't know what your boss has told you.'

'Not a lot. A non-specific threat to the Minister.'

'Oh, it's very specific. Lots of online chatter. Security services have red flagged it as imminent. While they're chasing it down, his nibs was advised not to attend this event. But the stroppy bastard wasn't having that. As a result, here we are.'

'Why him? Isn't he Minister for Energy? Doesn't sound that controversial.'

'Yes, but before politics he had quite a colourful career in the City. Made shed loads and was, allegedly, a financial fixer for various foreign regimes. Best guess is this is coming out of the Middle East. He did some deals for the Syrians, so it could be Kurdish separatists. That's one theory.'

'And you'd take a bullet for this guy?' says Boden, frowning.

Foley has a deep, rumbling laugh. 'Contrary to popular belief, that's not in the job description.'

'Glad to hear it. So what are we looking for?'

Foley shrugs. 'Probably a determined assailant who doesn't care if they're caught or killed.'

'Well, I've been through the whole college this morning,' she says. 'I've got an up-to-date list from the caterers of all the staff they're bringing in. I've talked to the Bursar; he's running things. All his people are regular employees. If anywhere's a weak spot, I'd say it's the kitchens.'

Foley pulls back his shoulders and inhales. His barrel chest gives him a military appearance as he scans the room of chattering guests. 'Hiding in plain sight,' he says. 'Could be anyone. But if they are here, we need to find them and nick them without causing a rumpus.'

'Piece of piss,' she says.

He grins. 'Chrissake, Boden. I've missed you.'

She smiles awkwardly. Fortunately, DC Chakravorty is hurrying across the room towards them.

She's breathless and excited. 'Have you seen,' she says. 'Adrian Cardello's here. In the flesh. My mum's going to go mental. Do you think I can ask him for a selfie?'

Boden and Foley exchange looks.

'Prish, this is DI Foley from the Met, in charge of the Minister's close protection team. This is my colleague, DC Prisha Chavravorty.'

'Oh, shit,' says Chakravorty. 'Sorry, sir. I got a bit carried away.'

'It happens,' says Foley.

'What about the CCTV?' says Boden.

'I fixed it,' says Chakravorty. 'The wiring had come loose. The equipment's out of the Ark. No one's checked it for ages.'

Foley pulls a pair of aviator shades from his pocket and puts them on. 'I blame the Romans,' he says, and with a nod to Boden, he strolls off.

Chakravorty gives Boden a sheepish look. 'I'm really sorry, Jo,' she says. 'That was unprofessional. I just got carried away. I mean, Adrian Cardello. The DI's going to think I'm a right idiot.'

'He's seen worse,' says Boden.

'You think so?' says Chakravorty.

Boden smiles. 'Yeah. He's seen me. I used to work with him.'

10

Saturday 12.30pm

Leanne is working the room. She's memorised the spread sheet that Caspar prepared for her. It details who will be there, their current occupations and marital status, plus their potential usefulness to Robert in his long-term campaign for the party leadership. Predictably, there's a good smattering of bankers, CEOs and inherited wealth. This, in itself, justifies the trip.

There was a brief lull in the babble of conversation as everyone pretended not to watch the increasingly heated exchange between Adrian Cardello and Melissa Rowe.

Leanne tried to speak to Melissa as she made a beeline for the door, but Melissa cut her dead. Even after all these years, it stings. Except now Leanne is adept at masking her feelings.

It wasn't always the case. She gazes around her. The shabby grandeur of the panelled walls and the vaulted ceiling with its Tudor beams.

This place!

In her first term, she spent a good deal of time just hiding in her room. She was too petrified to speak to anyone. She remembers crying to her mother on the phone and begging to go home.

Buck up! That's what Mum told her. You're as good as any of them.

And she didn't want to let her mother down. She grew a protective carapace and ditched her northern accent. Regional accents have since become quite the vogue, but back then Leanne lacked the confidence to make such a bold statement. Her instinct has always been to keep her head below the parapet.

Melissa has a habit of blanking her or pretending not to remember who she is, although since Robert has been in politics, they've been present at quite a few of the same events and conferences. When confronted directly, she says: oh, Leanne, you've changed so much, I hardly recognise you. The same games, and the same unmistakable sarcasm.

But Leanne gets it. It's about competition and jealousy. Isn't it always? Melissa was never that good at getting on with other girls. She preferred the company of men. She thought girls were silly and superficial. The exception was Claire, and Melissa was always super possessive about their friendship.

Back then, Claire had such an amazing aura; a mixture of beauty and brains, and she was a magnet for men. Melissa was glued to her side from day one. Perhaps she calculated that as the reasonably good-looking sidekick of a dazzling beauty, she'd have her pick of the ones Claire didn't want. And that must be how she got Adrian Cardello. By the end of the first term, they were an item. It was a rocky affair, on, off, then on again. Melissa insisted it was an open relationship, and she was cool with that. But few believed her. Adrian was a serial shagger; he couldn't seem to help himself. Girls threw themselves at him; perhaps he just felt it was rude not to oblige them.

It was when Leanne and Claire shared a tutorial and got closer that Leanne became the victim of Melissa's jealous spite. Melissa christened her Miss Piggy. She never said it to her face. But the whispers, the giggles, the allusions to her weight, and the sneers about the fact Leanne's frumpy clothes came from Marks and Spencers all hit the target.

Leanne has never revealed to anyone that her mum, who was a dinner lady, worked extra shifts to buy her clothes. Leanne had won a scholarship to Cambridge. And Mum was determined that her daughter would have what she assumed were the right outfits for the new world she was entering. Her Mum is long gone now. Cancer at fifty. But thinking about her, the sacrifices she made and the ambition she had for her daughter, still brings a lump to Leanne's throat.

Melissa certainly had no concept of the extent of her own privilege and the confidence that came with it. But looking back on it, Leanne has concluded that Melissa did her a favour. Without the anger and raw misery that her tormenter's cruelty caused, would she have had the motivation to transform herself physically? The dieting. Sweating the pounds off in the gym. Becoming a runner and pounding the pavements. Probably not. Now she has a designer wardrobe, attends catwalk shows and is one of the best dressed political wives.

Slow and steady wins the race. Mum said that too.

She's just finished chatting to some bloke she doesn't remember when she sees her husband approaching. He has a sulky expression.

He shoots a melodramatic glance in Adrian Cardello's direction.

'Did you know the Hollywood heartthrob was going to grace us with his presence?' he whispers.

Robert is feeling upstaged. He entered the room in an Armani suit surrounded by a bevy of tough looking cops. Whereas Adrian Cardello was wearing faded jeans and a relaxed smile, as if he'd gone out for coffee and wandered in by mistake.

But everyone's eyes are on him. They're mesmerised, clustering around him, desperate to shake his hand, as if paying court to a king. A few are even taking selfies. For their kids, they say. No one's interested in a middle-ranking Cabinet Minister.

'Take control of the situation, darling,' she says. 'Go over, shake his hand and tell him how much you like his movies.'

'I've never even seen one of his wretched movies.'

'Doesn't matter.'

Their eyes meet. They're a solid partnership who've morphed into a power couple. They understand each other's needs and weaknesses. Over the years, she's become an expert at nursing him through his insecurities.

Leanne knows she wasn't exactly Robert's first choice. In their student days, he was one of the soppy boys who mooned around after Claire Naylor. Back then, he was competing with the jocks and the public school Hooray Henrys. No chance.

But he and Leanne had a lot in common, and they became friends. He was like her, a boy from a background he never talked about with one thing to recommend him: his brains. In Robert's case, it was maths. He could've had a serious academic career as a mathematician, but investment banking came calling with a highly lucrative offer. They married eighteen months after graduation. For both of them, it was a pragmatic choice.

He looks at her. She can feel the doubt in him, the hesitation.

'Contra mundum,' she whispers and squeezes his hand.

He inhales, strolls across the room slowly, chest out, shoulders back. At least all the media training is paying off. The small gaggle around Cardello falls back. They know the pecking order here.

Robert holds out his hand and beams. 'My dear Adrian,' he says. 'This is such an unexpected pleasure. My Cabinet colleagues will be green with envy.'

Cardello accepts the handshake and grins. 'Hello, Rob,' he says. 'Long time. Last time I saw you, you were wandering around in an Iron Maiden T-shirt.'

Robert laughs. 'And I had a lot more hair.' He rubs his closely shaved, balding pate.

Leanne smiles to herself. She's proud of him. Proud of them.

Job done.

She turns back to the task in hand. Then she notices Claire, across the other side of the room. She should probably speak to her. Now that her youthful beauty has faded, Claire's underlying fragility is all too apparent. But Leanne always knew it was there.

As a student, Leanne had made a careful study of her friend. She wanted to understand how to create that kind of magnetism. But she concluded Claire had no idea why people reacted to her in the way they did. And often it frightened her. The lottery of looks. Everyone came to her with their expectations. They wanted something; a piece of her. Or to use her, as Melissa did.

Leanne soon realised that being the golden girl had its disadvantages. And for Claire Naylor, it certainly turned into a trap. Pregnant at twenty-one by some over-privileged toff, who walked away and left her to it. Claire had always wanted to be a writer, but she became a teacher and a single parent. For Leanne, this contained frighting echoes of her own mother's life. Perhaps that's why she tried to take an interest in Ella.

But their lives took very different trajectories. A couple of times there were men who it seemed Claire might marry. But it never worked out.

Leanne made a point of maintaining the connection. They met for lunch occasionally. Leanne always paid.

Then came the terrible tragedy of Ella taking her own life. Since then, her attempts to reach out to Claire have all been rebuffed. Claire's bereavement has turned her into a hermit. But on the occasions they have spoken, the aggression and anger rippling from her old friend has shocked Leanne. It makes little sense to Leanne. But grief is a strange beast.

She's been watching Claire since they arrived; she looks a wreck. But she's also been observing Robert and the way he keeps glancing surreptitiously in Claire's direction.

Really? After all these years? Does he still carry a torch for her?

When they spoke to her, she saw the look in her husband's eyes. The longing; it was still there. And it cut her to the quick.

But there's nothing to be done about that now. She's here to do a job, and she needs to get on with it.

11

The caterer is short of staff, but she assures Claire that lunch will be served on time. She seems calm and unfazed by the whirlwind in the kitchen. She asks Claire to check if the coffee flasks need refilling; Claire suspects this is a ploy to get rid of her. Returning to the senior common room, she hovers near the tables. This is in order to look busy and to avoid being accosted.

She rearranges the metal coffee flasks on one of the tables. Then she hears a loud guffaw. It snaps her attention across the room to where Robert Gerrish, head tipped back, is laughing loudly at something Adrian Cardello has just said to him.

The blokey bonhomie of it nauseates her. Adrian wouldn't be telling jokes to that monster if he knew.

No, let that thought go.

Claire dithers. She doesn't know what to do with herself. The tension and anxiety inside her threaten to explode. She seizes one of the coffee flasks and heads out of the room.

In the cooler, stone corridor, she stops. But she can't decide which way to run. An oppressive headache has trapped her brain in a vice like grip. She can't think.

This is a mistake! A crazy idea.

In the dead of night, fuelled by grief, it had all seemed simple. As a busy government minister, Gerrish was inaccessible. Claire's friendship is with Leanne. She's never been invited into the Gerrish's social circle. And she knows why. She wouldn't fit. She's a boring schoolteacher with no connections and no money. A nobody. Somehow, she had to bring Robert Gerrish into her orbit. And the reunion fell into her lap like a gift.

At the first meeting of the organising committee, she suggested him as the after-dinner speaker. No one else had a better idea. It was touch and go whether he'd accept. His schedule was packed. He was rising rapidly through the ministerial ranks. It was in the lap of the gods. Claire suspected Leanne persuaded him to come. A triumphant return to their alma mater is something that would probably appeal to both of them. The underdogs who made it.

But the reality, on a baking July afternoon, is it's an absurd plan. What can she say to him? And he'll probably simply deny it. Her complete focus has been on getting him there. Now it's real, it feels impossible. Exposure in the media, forcing his resignation? A public shaming? At the very least, he should go to jail. But he won't. He'll just lie. Mel put her finger on it; can she prove it?

Don't lose your nerve. Not now.

Claire pulls out her phone and rings Mel's number. She answers in one ring.

'Where are you?' says Claire.

'In the chapel. It's the only place that's quiet and cool. I had words with Adrian.'

'I've just been watching him buddying up to Robert Gerrish.'

'The pretty boy versus the nerd. That's a nice photo op,' says Mel. 'Everyone'll be snapping that for their social media feeds.' She sighs. 'Listen, Claire, I'm sorry but I'm going to have to go back to—'

'Can I just talk to you first? I want to explain about Ella.'

Silence on the line. Another sigh, followed by a chuckle.

'Well, you'd better meet me in the chapel. This is like a bad melodrama.'

Claire hangs up. She cuts across the lawn. The college chapel is on the other side of the quad. The heavy oak door is ajar. It squeaks as Claire pushes it open.

Mel is sitting in a pew, phone in hand, smoking a cigarette. She gives Claire a baleful look. 'Why are you carrying a flask of coffee around?'

Claire glances at it.

Why are you?

She sets it down by the door. 'It's empty.'

The chapel is old and monastic. Bare stone walls and hard wooden pews. Claire can't remember the details, but like the original foundation of the college, it probably dates back to Tudor times.

Mel is in the back row. 'Remember when we used to sneak in here and smoke dope?' she says.

'I remember nearly getting caught.'

She was never like Mel, not a risk taker. Stepping out of line, upsetting people, it all petrified her.

And look at you now.

Keep it simple. 'I need your help,' she says.

Mel scans her. 'I can see you're in quite a state about all this. You'd better tell me what happened.'

'I may look like a nervous wreck, but I'm not wrong about this.'

'Just tell me.'

Claire slides into the pew next to her.

'Ella was such an idealist. What we're doing to the planet and to nature; these things really disturbed her. As a teenager she got involved in campaigns.'

'She was right to be disturbed.'

Mel offers her a cigarette; Claire shakes her head.

One chance. Make the most of it. Focus.

'She studied politics and economics at uni. Got a first. She wanted to make a difference. Leanne and I had remained friends. I know you don't like her, but she's been very kind to me.'

Mel grimaces. 'Kind? Doesn't that tell you something?'

Claire shrugs. 'After Ella graduated, Leanne said she could get her an internship in Robert's office.'

Mel gives her a cynical smile. 'I don't really see Robert Gerrish at the forefront of the fight against climate change. Quite the opposite.'

'It was an opportunity to see how government works. Ella was excited.'

'Okay, she went to work in Gerrish's office. Before he was at Energy?'

'He was at Transport. Ella found the work interesting. She learned a lot. Then there was this problem about an email leak. Ella got blamed. But she swore it wasn't her. They just booted her out. No chance to defend herself or to prove her innocence.'

'Claire, emails are always getting leaked, or sent from an

unofficial account or whatever. If it was deliberate, then Ella was probably just the scapegoat.'

She gets it!

'Exactly! That's what she told me. Gerrish had made her the scapegoat!'

Mel shakes her head wearily. 'I'm afraid that's just politics.'

Claire can feel the blood thrumming in veins. She has to make Mel understand. This is all she can do now for her child. Make people understand.

She takes a breath. 'But she was devastated. She worried she wouldn't be able to get another job. That everything was going wrong. And that's when she got depressed. She was so young. Just twenty-four. And it was totally unfair.'

'Yes, but—'

'I called Leanne. Asked her to speak to him. But Ella was just brooding. And in the end, she thought maybe it was her fault. That she had done something wrong. But she was used, Mel. Used. And then dumped like she didn't matter. It destroyed her.'

Mel stubs out her cigarette on the stone floor. She stares at the butt, sighs and tosses it in a corner.

'I'll be honest with you, Claire. I don't really see how you can pin this on Gerrish.'

Pin?

'But don't you see? That's what he did. He decided to put the blame on her. He's the one that's morally responsible.'

'Maybe. But there's not a lot of morality in politics. It's pretty dog eat dog.'

Claire feels the tears erupting. Mostly it's frustration. She can't hold on to them anymore.

Make her understand.

Claire wipes her nose with her fingers. 'You know what she did? She came home to live with me, because she couldn't afford to stay in London. And one morning, she said she was going down to Bristol to see a friend from uni. And I really thought she was getting better. That the tablets were working. I went to work as usual. That evening the police came round. She'd jumped off Clifton Suspension Bridge. There was no friend.'

Just speaking of it gives her a sense of vertigo, as if she's tumbling backwards. That's how Ella must have felt. Just falling and falling. And the fear of it, the absolute terror. In her last moments, did she regret it?

Mel is staring at her. Claire realises her whole body is shaking. Speaking about it all these months later, the pain is as raw as the day it happened. It'll never go away.

Mel flings an arm around her shoulder and pulls her into a hug.

'Oh mate, that is just awful. I am so sorry.'

Claire pulls away, wiping her nose with the back of her hand. 'Now can you see why I have to make him pay? They have to know that people, particularly the young people that work for them, that they can't be treated like this. There has to be a moral reckoning for them. It can't just be a cynical game.'

Mel puffs out her cheeks. 'Well, I agree in principle. But…it's not that simple.'

'Help me, Mel. I don't want to guilt trip you but—'

'But you are. And that's okay. We all do what we have to. And you want justice for your daughter.'

'It's the only thing that's keeping me afloat.'

'Here's the problem. If I wrote this up, as you've just told it to me, with no corroboration, my editor would never publish it. We'd get sued. I'm sorry, but that's the truth.'

'Whose truth?' Claire can feel the energy leaking out of her. 'Not my truth. Not Ella's truth.'

Mel shakes her head. 'I'm sorry.'

Claire nods and dips her head.

Are you surprised?

She feels desolate. 'Well, thank you for listening,' she says.

12

Saturday, 1pm

Lunch is being served in the Old Refectory. Mel isn't hungry, but she definitely needs a drink. The outpouring of Claire's grief was awkward, not to say embarrassing. Mel sympathises. Of course she does. But what the hell can she do about it?

Too many people with their tales of woe. It's knackering.

Fortunately, Claire seemed to realise that what she was asking was impossible. After a few minutes, she did pull herself together. She said she had some task to perform, although Mel suspects it was an excuse to run away.

There's a table at the end of the hall where wine is being served. Mel makes straight for it. She gets herself a large glass of chilled Chablis. Then she pulls her phone out and checks the time of the next train to London. One thirty. If she downs the wine and calls a cab, she might just make it.

'You're looking a bit hot and bothered,' says a squeaky female voice.

She looks up. Or rather down.

Miss Piggy.

'Hello, Leanne,' she says.

Leanne Brady is beaming from ear to ear. Credit where it's due. She's slimmed down from the little lump she once was, but she's still short.

'I wouldn't have thought this was your sort of thing,' says Leanne.

'To be honest, it isn't,' she replies. 'I came for Claire.'

'Yes,' says Leanne, with an exaggerated frown. 'Such a terrible tragedy. I don't know that she'll ever get over it.'

They stare at one another. Mel takes a large mouthful of wine and hopes she'll just go away. But Leanne shows no sign of shifting.

'I was hoping we might run into one another,' says Leanne.

'Why?' says Mel.

'I know we haven't always seen eye to eye. But, y'know, the years pass. We mellow, don't we?'

'Do we? You mean like crappy wine that turns to vinegar?'

Leanne gives an affected chuckle. Her acquired poshness grates. 'You always were a wit,' she says.

What the hell does she want?

'I've always been a huge admirer of your work,' she adds. 'Your special report, a couple of years ago, from Somalia. I thought it was incredibly moving.'

As if.

'I'm glad you were moved, Leanne. Does that mean your husband's party is thinking of increasing the foreign aid budget? Because that's not what I heard.'

Leanne gives her a sad smile, much like a long-suffering primary school teacher. 'Don't you think,' she says. 'That after all these years, it's time we made friends? I know you don't like me, although I've never really understood why. But you're a political journalist, a very fine one, and I have an excellent network of connections in Westminster and beyond. Don't you think we could be of some mutual benefit to each other?'

In your dreams, lady.

Mel drains her glass. Without thinking, she reaches out her hand and picks up another from the table.

'You seem to be confusing me with a tabloid hack you feed copy to,' she says. 'Which, frankly, is insulting.'

'Then I apologise. That was not my intention. All I'm saying is we're two women of a similar age, operating in the same arena. We may agree about more things than you think.'

'Like what for example?'

The wine tastes good. Cool and fresh, it's slipping down a little too fast. But she needs it to cope with this bullshit.

'I'm not just Robert Gerrish's wife,' says Leanne. 'I'm a partner in a highly regarded PR consultancy with a wide range of clients.'

'You mean like private American healthcare providers hoping to buy up the NHS?'

A bit over the top. But she deserves it.

Leanne sighs, as if dealing with a recalcitrant child. 'If you want to know, we don't have any American healthcare providers on our client list, but we do have several firms working in the area of green sustainable energy.'

'Bully for you.'

Mel drains her glass. She can feel her temper rising. It's the middle of the day and the heat is oppressive, even indoors. She's feeling irritable. The desire to put this annoying, sanctimonious little upstart in her place is overwhelming.

'Okay,' says Leanne. 'I thought after all these years, you might take a more mature view. Clearly not.'

Cheeky bitch!

'More mature? What's that supposed to mean? You and I have nothing in common. No interests. Nothing. Never have. Never will.'

Leanne chuckles. 'Come on. We're neither of us eighteen-year-old students anymore, are we? This is just petulance. I'm not sure where it's coming from, although you always saw yourself as Claire's best friend. You didn't want any rivals.'

'You were never my rival. Nowhere close.'

Leanne shrugs. 'Whatever.'

Leave it there.

She can't. 'Claire says you've been very kind to her over the years,' she says. 'Is that right? You've never stopped trying to wheedle your way in, have you?'

Leanne holds up her palm. 'I didn't realise this still bothered you.'

Two large glasses of wine on an empty stomach. Mel can feel the buzz. But it's good; it gives her the shot she needs. She steps a little closer, using her height.

'Bothered?' she says. 'I know you, Leanne. I know what you are. A manipulator, a flatterer; you're always there in the background. The nice little one, the helpful girl, the fixer. Only now you're doing on a much grander stage. But don't try to recruit me into your network of bullshitters. I see you. I see what you are. I always have.'

Leanne takes a step backwards.

She's intimidated. Good!

'Fair enough,' Leanne says. 'That's your view and you're entitled to it.' She smiles. 'What I see is an angry woman who doesn't even know why she's angry. If I were you, Melissa,

I'd get yourself another glass of wine. You look like you need it.'

Tell her! Tell her what Claire really thinks of her nasty little husband.

She's about to, but her head is swimming a bit. It's the heat. She watches Leanne swan off. Stupid little cow. In her fancy designer outfit.

What she needs is some air. She'll miss that one thirty train now, which is annoying.

She makes it to the door and the oppressive fug hits her. Hottest part of the day now. She just needs somewhere cool to sit. She finds a stone bench in the upper garden; it's shaded by an ancient yew tree.

Leanne Brady! What a bloody nerve that woman has!

But a plan is forming; she'll show them some anger. Teach them a lesson they won't forget.

She gets up a little unsteadily and walks back across the lawn. After searching for a bit, and collaring another member of the organising committee, she finds Claire in the kitchens.

Grabbing her friend's arm, she says. 'Okay, I'm on. You want to take that bastard down? We'll do it. You and me.'

Claire stares at her. 'You said we couldn't. There was no corroboration. Your paper would be sued.'

'Trust me. There's more than one way to skin a cat. I'll find a way. Because you're right, it is a question of morality.'

13

Saturday, 1.45pm

Claire is feeling decidedly odd. After her conversation with Mel in the chapel, she took another Ativan. Her mind and body seem to have become detached from one another, and she's light-headed. But it has calmed her down.

The catering staff are overstretched. There's simply not enough of them and they're feeling the heat. Claire is helping by ferrying trays back and forth from the kitchen. She's glad to have a task to focus on.

Then Mel, who seemed drunk, appeared from nowhere and said she would help.

Take that bastard down, isn't that what she said?

You can't rely on her. Stupid to think you could.

Claire suspected the change of heart was fuelled by drink. She got Mel a bottle of water and sat her down on a stool in the shade outside the back door to the kitchens.

Returning to her tasks, her mind meanders. Is this U-turn

genuine? Will it stick once her friend sobers up? Probably not.

Mel has always been volatile; Claire knows this only too well. She reacts and thinks through the consequences later. This has landed her in hot water in her professional life too. Mel has won awards for her bold and fearless reporting. But it seems to Claire that there's a fine line between heroism and recklessness.

As she carries a tray of cold poached salmon into the Old Refectory, a man with a sweaty red face snaps his fingers to get her attention.

'Excuse me!' he says. 'We need more potato salad. I did ask about ten minutes ago.'

'Who did you ask?' says Claire.

'I don't know. One of your lot. Some boy in an apron.'

'I'm not actually part of the catering staff. I'm just helping out.'

He peers at her, his bushy brows puckering. 'Oh, I just assumed…you look like…' Then his expression changes completely. 'Hang on a minute,' he says, beaming. 'Claire Naylor! Of course it is. Oh, I do apologise.'

He looks vaguely familiar and she has a horrible feeling she went on a couple of dates with him.

'I'm on the organising committee, so I'm helping out.'

'Oh, don't worry. Someone else can get the damned potato salad. How the hell are you? You look amazing. But then you always did.'

He's lying. She looks like a mad skivvy. The kind of person he's used to ordering about. That much she does know.

She dredges her memory for a name. But comes up empty. He's big and chubby, hairline receding, small, piggy eyes. He could be anyone.

'So what have you been doing with yourself all these years?'

'Teaching.'

'Jolly good! Splendid!'

She can see from his face what he's thinking. He's adding her to the ranks of those who didn't make it and ended up in boring jobs. The losers.

'Teaching is such an important profession,' he says. 'We can't get enough good teachers.'

The tray is getting heavy. She needs somewhere to put it. She glances around. Then help comes from an unexpected quarter. Adrian Cardello lifts it deftly from her hand.

It takes a moment for her to realise it's him. Her reactions seem to have slowed down.

It's the Ativan.

He smells of sandalwood.

'That's looking heavy,' he says.

'Adrian,' says the red-faced man. 'Good to see you, old chap!'

'And you,' says Adrian. 'But you'll have to excuse us. Hungry people are waiting.' He turns to Claire. 'Where do you want this?'

She points. 'The table over there. Thank you.'

Adrian carries it to the table and sets it down.

She stares at him. He has a lot more crinkles round his eyes; you don't see that on screen.

Say something.

'Thank you for rescuing me,' she says.

He shrugs. 'Rescuing people is my job. Apparently I'm more popular than Batman.'

He still has his roguish twinkle. Nothing is ever totally serious with Adrian.

'He thought I was one of the caterers,' she says. 'I can't remember his name.'

Adrian frowns. 'Richard something-or-other, I think? He was a rower, though it doesn't look like he's done much of that lately. Also, a total dick. You don't want to remember him.'

Claire manages to smile. She's anticipated this moment many times, but she wasn't sure how she'd actually feel. She just feels peculiar. But that's the drugs.

He folds his arms. Perhaps he's nervous too? But how can he be?

'As our dickhead friend would say, how the hell are you Naylor? And why haven't you come over to say hello to me?'

'I was planning to, later. When the crowd around you thinned.'

He sighs. 'I've already spoken to Mel, and got the sharp edge of her tongue. I tried to apologise.'

'What did she say?'

'Told me to fuck off.'

'You must've expected that.'

He sighs and nods. 'Yep,' he says. 'Are you going to tell me to fuck off, too?'

Don't get into this. Not now.

'You know what Mel's like,' she says. 'She speaks her mind.'

'That she does. And it's why we love her.'

Claire considers this statement. After all these years, how can he even say that? They've all become total strangers. But the odd thing is, it doesn't seem that long ago that they weren't.

'What do you make of all this?' he says.

'Why did you even come, Adrian? No one thought you would.'

'I got the invite. I saw you were on the organising committee.'

'You really expect me to believe that?'

He chuckles. 'You see right through me, don't you?'

His old chat up line.

She smiles so as not to upset him. He hasn't changed.

'Why are you smiling?' he says. 'Look, okay, I'll tell you the truth. I was curious. I thought it might be interesting to see how we all turned out.'

Claire glances across the room. 'All your former friends like Richard Dickhead, you mean?'

'Not so much him. Just the important ones.'

'And who are the important ones?'

He tilts his head sideways, like a sad puppy. It's one of his trademark looks. She and millions of others have seen it on the screen. It says: I know I've been a bad boy, but you love me anyway, don't you? It's usually followed by a kiss and a rolling of the end credits.

Run! Now.

'You don't have to answer that,' she says. 'It's nice to catch up with you, Adrian. But I've got a lot to do.'

'But—'

Ignoring him, she turns and walks away without a backward glance.

14

Saturday, 2pm

Boden is hanging around in the narrow alley behind the kitchens. This is where she's focusing her attention. If the threat to the Minister has any substance to it, then the perpetrator is already in place. This has to be the working assumption. Apprehending them without creating a panic is another issue.

Whoever he or she is, unless they're a rank amateur, they'll identify Boden as a cop. There's no time to bring anyone in and secrete them undercover. Foley and his people have a ring of steel round the Minister. Four armed officers. What could possibly go wrong?

Everything.

The CCTV system is rudimentary and covers only entries and exits to residential buildings, the three gates to the outside and the main entrance with the Porter's Lodge. There are no cameras at all in the kitchen.

When Boden asked the Bursar why earlier, he simply shrugged and said, 'Well, it's just a kitchen.'

Just a kitchen?

The catering company brought in for the occasion is run by a couple in their thirties, and dealing with them is proving difficult. He's a chef and bolshy. He began by ordering Boden out of his kitchen. His wife is the catering manager, in charge of everything else and more amenable. But all they've been told, and can be told, is that there are security issues.

'What is this?' said the chef. 'Some government bollocks about illegal immigration? You know how difficult it is to get staff?'

Boden assured him it wasn't that. He didn't believe her.

After some cajoling, they explained they've hired twenty staff for the occasion. Five, they know. An agency has provided the rest. Boden has tried to separate them out and observe each one covertly. A mixture of ages, a mixture of races; the work is hard and hot, and they're probably doing it for a minimum wage.

Needle in a haystack.

Chakravorty is on the CCTV, Mackie is wandering round the grounds on the lookout for any suspicious behaviour. It's all about anomalies.

Are they looking for someone from the Middle East, maybe Kurdish? Or is that just racial profiling? Boden is pondering this when she notices something.

A boy comes scurrying out of the back door to the kitchens with a phone pressed to his ear. She's already noticed him, one of the serving staff. He's scrawny and pale-skinned with a mass of freckles. His head is severely shaved at the sides with a tuft of ginger on the crown.

'Fuck's sake,' he mumbles into the phone. 'I know what I'm doing, right?'

He catches Boden's eye, swivels and moves rapidly away from her down the alley. Not quite out of earshot.

She catches a few snippets of his conversation. 'Yeah…I know…and soon as I…. and filth everywhere…what can I…'

Boden pretends to be scrolling on her own phone as she tries to eavesdrop.

The boy ends his calls and hurries back to the kitchen door. Boden smiles at him. She gets a half-smile in response; but he radiates nerves and tension. He disappears back inside the steamy interior.

She waits a few moments and then follows. A buffet lunch is still being served in the Old Refectory. This involves plates of foods being carried down a narrow corridor to it and dirty dishes being returned by the same route. Tessa, the catering manager, has set up a traffic system of keeping to the left, but it's still chaotic.

The boy picks up two trays of food from the counter and heads off down the corridor. Boden watches him go.

She waits, tucking herself out of the way in a corner. The kitchen is small and tightly packed with tall units: two large range cookers, sinks, preparation and serving areas. Loud and hot, with more than a dozen people rushing around. It's easy for her to be lost in the crowd.

After five minutes, the boy returns carrying a stack of dirty plates. He takes them to the dishwashing area. He hovers. Wound up and anxious. Boden watches him surreptitiously. He's the piece that doesn't fit. He's the one who has some other task or problem on his mind, apart from slogging through a long day's work in a busy kitchen.

Boden adjusts her position to a better vantage point next to a massive freezer cabinet. Thanks to the general chaos of the kitchen, he hasn't noticed her. But he is on high alert. He pulls his phone out and checks it.

Medium height. Age, Boden guesses, early twenties. A long butcher's apron tied round his waist. A white IC1 male, who doesn't match the profile of their suspected perpetrator. If it is him, Boden wonders what she's missing here. What else could be freaking him out?

Tessa, the manager, shouts something at him. She's noticed he's on his phone. He jumps. Goes to the counter, picks up a tray and disappears with it.

Boden moves quickly and intercepts Tessa.

'Quick word,' she says.

The catering manager shoots a look of annoyance at her. She's wearing a white, disposable mob cap, but the sweat is running down her face.

'The boy you just talked to,' says Boden. 'What's his name?'

Tessa frowns. 'Reece, I think?'

'From the agency?'

She huffs. 'Yeah, I think so.'

Boden moves closer to her and meets her gaze. 'I know you're really hassled,' she says. 'But I need his paperwork, his full name, whatever you got from the agency. And I need it now. I wouldn't ask if it wasn't important.'

Tessa inhales. 'I already gave you the list. I mean, this is ridiculous. He's not illegal. Look at him, some white kid with a Brummie accent.'

'As I explained before. This is a security issue.'

'What issue? My husband's right. It's just the bloody police harassing people trying to do an honest day's work.'

Boden stares straight at her. She gets it. The kitchen is roasting. The work is hard. From the catering manager's point of view, this looks like bullshit.

'Listen to me, Tessa,' she says. 'It's not bullshit. Have you got the details on your laptop? Can you just show me?'

Tessa sighs and nods. They snake through the kitchen to the tiny back office. Tessa pulls her laptop from a backpack on the floor. She places it on the tiny desk and opens it up.

'I've got nothing to hide,' she says. 'You can see for yourself. We used a reputable agency. They all have papers.' She gives Boden an earnest look.

'I know that.'

Tessa flaps her hands and wipes her brow with her palm. 'This is the file,' she says. 'I dunno. Just look at what you want.' She frowns. 'Can I trust you?'

'You can,' says Boden.

'Don't tell my husband. He'll go berserk.' With that, she scurries back to the kitchen.

Boden skims the file from the recruitment agency. It contains details and mugshots of the fifteen workers they've provided. Boden takes shots of the screen with her phone.

Then she goes back and looks at Reece Davison's details. There's nothing out of place. His national insurance number is there and looks authentic enough. There's a local address.

Boden closes the laptop, returns it to the backpack. Then she calls Rachel Knight.

'Boss,' she says. 'I'm sending you details of an IC1 male called Reece Davison. I think he needs checking out. I can't explain why, but he's got a vibe about him.'

'I'll go with a vibe,' says Knight. 'You keeping an eye on him?'

'Trying to.'

'I thought the intel was we're looking for IC6? Arab or North African.'

'That's the theory. I've also got details of the other agency staff that've been hired. I can send those too.'

'Good,' says Knight. 'Send them. I'll phone you back.'

Boden hangs up. She returns to the kitchen. No sign of

Reece Davison. She waits several minutes. The place is stifling. She catches Tessa's eye, nods and smiles. Then she heads out into the alley.

All she can do now is keep her eyes open and wait.

15

Mel sits on a rickety plastic stool by the back door to the kitchens. She sips from the bottle of water Claire gave her. She needs to sober up. It's a long time since she's made a fool of herself with booze. Getting drunk is not cool. Nowadays, she relies on a strictly managed weekend cocaine habit to get her through the vicissitudes of life. But, as she never intended to stay, she hasn't brought any with her, which is foolish.

She looks around. Okay, she downed a couple of glasses really quickly. But coming back to this place has made her regress. And the heat's made it worse.

In her three years as a student, this is a part of the college she never visited. In her day, the food was stodgy but filling; she has no idea who cooked it or served it. Back then, they were the chosen ones and everything was new and exciting; the world was their oyster, that's what they were told. And back then, she believed it.

Now, for events like this, a private caterer is brought in

and they have to cope with the shortcomings of an old, institutional building. The staff all look young and inexperienced; Mel suspects they're all on poverty wages and no contract.

There are plenty of comings and goings. The kitchen is steaming and the door is propped open. Two servers on a break come out and sit on the step; she bums a cigarette from them.

She's gone off at a tangent, she knows that. The wine and the unctuousness of Leanne, they combined to tip her over the edge. But what's she supposed to do? Claire's right. There needs to be a moral reckoning. The lies and bullshit need taking down.

Never apologise, never have regrets.

This was her father's mantra, drummed into them as children. He was in the military, third generation. He rose to the rank of Lieutenant Colonel. His father was at Dunkirk. He was a man who needed sons to carry on the family tradition; but what he had was Mel and her younger sister. Mel would've done anything to please him. She tried to be the surrogate son. But he was a hard man to get close to. Then, at the age of sixty, he dumped Mel's mother, married a mousy little woman thirty years younger, and finally got his two darling boys. Nowadays, Mel rarely sees him.

As she stubs out her cigarette, she notices a woman watching her. Tall, smart trousers, hair pinned up and a plain white shirt. She's too young to be part of the reunion, but she looks official. Maybe she works for the Bursar's office, some kind of admin person?

Mel gives her a friendly smile. 'You look like you want to be here about as much as me,' she says.

The young woman shrugs and returns the smile. 'I was just looking for a shady spot.'

'Do you work for the college?'

'No.'

Mel waits. In her experience, most people can't wait to tell you who they are. They want you to know their status and how they rank in the pecking order.

The young woman says nothing. Watchful but also at ease.

Intriguing.

'You look too smart and businesslike to be a guest,' says Mel. 'Do you work for one of the big-wigs here for the reunion?'

The young women chuckles. 'I'm a police officer,' she says.

A cop on the job, now that is interesting.

Mel gets up and walks over to join her. She offers her hand. 'I'm Melissa Rowe. Here for this stupid reunion.'

'Jo Boden.' She accepts the handshake.

'Plain clothes. Part of the Minister's close protection team, I assume?'

'No. I'm local.'

'I saw the demonstrators gathering outside. Gerrish has a talent for polarising opinion wherever he goes.'

'Do you know him personally?'

'We were students here at the same time. But, I'm a journalist, so more recently I've had dealings with him in a professional capacity.'

The cop tilts her head. 'You don't sound like an admirer.'

'Let me tell you something, Jo Boden. Twenty-five years ago, Robert Gerrish was a miserable little toad that no one liked. But he became an investment banker and fixer; made a shedload of money. Several shedloads, in fact. He used this to buy his way into politics. He's still a miserable little toad, but chances are, he could end up at the very pinnacle of government. Unless someone knifes him in the meantime. Sadly, you and your colleagues have the unenviable task of stopping that from happening.'

The cop smiles, but she's not giving anything away. 'That's our job,' she says. 'Do you think someone might try to knife him?'

Mel is warming to her theme. She'd far rather be talking to a cop in a kitchen yard full of stinking dustbins than listening to her former chums bragging about how much money they'd made.

'You know this thing that happened recently,' she says. 'The attack on him at his constituency office. I wouldn't mind betting that was a put-up job.'

'What makes you say that?' says the cop.

'Look at the facts. The attacker evaded security on the way in. One of Gerrish's intrepid political advisers tackles him and he runs away, avoiding most of the CCTV cameras on the way out. Police are looking for a random hoodie. Are you a detective?'

'I'm a DS.'

'Well, what does that tell you?'

The cop shrugs. 'Security should've been tighter?'

'No, it tells you Gerrish wanted to hit all the front pages, posing as the victim of right-wing extremists.'

'How do you know that?'

'It's just a hunch. But, since I'm here, I'm considering digging into it a bit deeper. Seeing if I can build a story. I'm a detective, just like you.'

'Our aim is to find the truth.'

Mel laughs. 'That's rather snippy, Sergeant. But you start with motive, right? I'm guessing the motive here is to make Gerrish look more mainstream and therefore more acceptable. And, guess what, it succeeded. After the so-called attack, his poll ratings went up fifteen per cent.'

'That's a very cynical view,' says the cop. 'It could just be that the CCTV was rubbish. In my experience, that happens a lot.'

Mel smiles. 'I told you. I'm a journalist. It's my job to be cynical.' She drains her water bottle. 'I think maybe I'll go and get a proper drink.'

The cop scans her. 'Perhaps you should get something to eat too?'

Mel puts on an expression of mock surprise. 'Really, officer, are you suggesting I'm tipsy?'

'No, but it's a very hot day. You should pace yourself.'

Mel laughs. 'If you're still here tonight, I can promise you, you'll see some mayhem once this lot let their hair down.'

The cop smiles.

Mel smiles back. 'Thanks for listening to my rant.'

She walks away. One thing has become clear: she'll need a little something extra to get through this shitshow. Finding a cool spot in the garden, she texts her dealer.

Need an urgent delivery. But I'm in Cambridge. Can you accommodate that?

She waits a couple of minutes. Jeremy is reliable and always provides a premium product. She suspects Jeremy is not his real name. But who cares?

A text alert pops up on her phone.

No problem. Give me your exact location and I'll connect you.

Mel smiles to herself. It's an insane world when the most reliable person in your life is your dealer.

16

Saturday, 2.30pm

Claire is collecting dirty plates. She keeps her head down and avoids eye contact. Her encounter with Richard Dickhead has made one thing clear: she doesn't look much like the girl she once was. And that's good. As the day has worn on, her desire to avoid people has increased. Moving around the room, she notices the glances. She can almost hear the whispers and the judgements. 'Apparently, the daughter killed herself. How do you let something like that happen?'

Stop! It's just paranoia.

Why the hell did she agree to do this? She knows why. And the absurdity of it has become more and more apparent to her.

She wants to just disappear. But what she wants most is to turn back the clock to the life she had when Ella was still at school and she was teaching. She remembers when they got Ziggy. Ella chose him from the litter; just a fluffy bundle of fur with enormous eyes.

It's easy now to believe that everything back then was perfect. She knows it wasn't. The job was tough. Money was often tight, even though her parents bailed her out. She had a series of relationships. One even lasted for a couple of years before fizzling out. The men were nice enough, but nothing ever felt quite right. The best times were when it was just the two of them. Her and Ella.

Then you left me.

Her daughter grew up. Obviously she did. It was natural and right. Claire wanted the best life possible for her child; she encouraged her to go to university. The terrible pain of letting her go she kept secret, as every mother must. But she consoled herself with dreams about how their future would be. She could still take Ella on holiday. They would be more like friends than mother and daughter. Theatre visits, films and exhibitions. She remained hopeful.

Her head is fuzzy with the heat; she's had a headache all day that won't shift. She needs to drink more water. This is how her life is now; she takes her medication and she functions. But all she ever thinks about is her daughter.

When Ella returned from London, beaten and depressed, it was frightening. To see her baby suffering like this tore her apart. She nursed her and cared for her. She loved her ferociously, ensured she took her anti-depressants, dragged her out of the house on long walks. She did her very best. And she remained optimistic. Until that terrible day the police came knocking at her door.

Is it your fault? Did she do it because you were a terrible mother?

She suspects she knows the answer.

She's loading plates and dishes onto a trolley when she sees Mel walking across the room towards her. Lunch is more or less over. Guests have retreated to the common rooms. A video compilation is being shown, and there's a photo exhibition.

Mel sighs. 'I thought I'd better have something to eat. Am I too late?'

'No, I'm sure I can get you a plate. How are you feeling now?'

'Oh, I'm okay. Wine on an empty stomach. I missed breakfast. You think I'd learn.'

Claire pushes the trolley towards the kitchen. Mel walks beside her.

They head down a narrow stone passageway between the Old Refectory and the bowels of the building where the kitchens are located.

'I've been thinking,' says Mel. 'About how we should approach this—'

'I thought that was the wine talking.'

Mel shrugs. 'In vino veritas.'

'Forget what I said. It's crazy talk.'

'I thought you wanted justice for Ella.'

'I do. But you were right, it's impossible to prove anything.'

'It's impossible to prove a direct causal connection between Gerrish's actions and Ella's death, but that's not the only way to do this.'

'I'm not sure I follow.'

Mel turns to look at her; the eyes are dark and inscrutable. The expression is unsettling. There was always a part of Melissa Rowe that frightened Claire. She was attracted to trouble. It drew her like a magnet.

'This is about bringing him down, right? Making him pay. Somehow. Isn't that what you want?'

Claire feels a tingle of excitement.

Yes! Of course!

'Can we do that legally, with no evidence?' she says.

Mel chuckles. 'Legally? Jesus, Claire, what planet are you living on? It's all about PR. Reputation and perception.'

Claire can sense her friend's excitement, too. Mel loves to create chaos. It's the risk, the chase, bringing down her prey; these are the things that have always appealed to her. And she likes to win. She hasn't changed.

Claire stops pushing the trolley and turns to face her friend. She hesitates.

You have to be honest. You can't lie.

'If we're really going to do this,' she says. 'There's something else here that you should know. I should've told you years ago. I wish I had.'

Mel scrunches her shoulders. 'Okay, hit me.'

Claire wonders how it will sound when she says it out loud, because she never has.

'Adrian is Ella's father.'

The colour visibly drains from Mel's face. Her mouth opens, but she doesn't speak.

No going back now.

'I promise you, Mel. It was literally a one-night stand.'

Mel exhales. 'You slept with him? You were my best fucking friend! You knew how I felt about him.'

'Which is why I didn't tell you. Or anyone else. I just thought pretend it was some random guy at a party. Because really, that's all it was. It's what I've always told everyone.'

'Does he know?'

'No. And I don't want him to. Please don't tell him.'

Mel shakes her head in disbelief. For several moments, neither of them speak.

Finally, Mel says, 'I never understood why you didn't have an abortion.'

Claire sighs. 'I thought about it.'

'What stopped you?'

What did stop you?

'It's hard to explain. At the time, I was confused. I couldn't seem to decide. I kept the pregnancy secret for as long as I could. Then it was too late.'

Mel gives her head a weary shake.

'What did Ella make of her illustrious parentage? Didn't she want to meet him?'

Claire hesitates. This is the worst part.

Say it.

'She did ask. But I never told her.'

Mel's eyes widen with horror. 'What? You lied to your own daughter too?'

'I did it to protect her. I didn't want her to have unrealistic expectations.'

Mel tuts. 'I'll tell you one thing, Claire. You are fucking weird. Sounds to me like you just wanted to control her. It's no bloody wonder she…'

Mel stops herself, but only just.

Shaking her head again, she turns and walks away. Claire watches her disappear down the narrow corridor back towards the light and the sunshine.

Why did you do that? Idiot.

Claire leans on the trolley. It was impulsive. She just wanted to be honest. Mel was offering to help her, and she blew it.

Crazy.

Again. You let Ella down again.

Did she simply lose her nerve? Standing alone in the narrow stone corridor, she cries. She knows it's self pity, and she's a weak fool.

Then she sees someone come out of the back door to the

kitchen. A woman, but not one of the catering staff. Who is she? As she walks towards Claire, she's checking her phone.

You can't be seen like this. You can't.

Claire abandons the trolley and hurries away.

17

Saturday, 2.45pm

Leanne Brady is weary with the oppressive heat. She sits on a stone bench, in an alcove in one of the long galleried passage-ways. It resembles a medieval cloister and is in the oldest part of the college. But it has the advantage of being quiet and cool.

She's making notes on her phone. A list of the significant people she's spoken to, the ones worth some kind of follow-up.

The lunch was better than she expected. Mass catering, in her experience, is usually disappointing. And she hates buffets. The temptation to go back and refill your plate without really being aware of it is ever present. She's already entered everything she's consumed into her health and fitness app. But it's hard at events like this to estimate what you've actually eaten.

Keeping on top of things. Being organised. These are the cornerstones of her life. Without her phone, she feels naked.

She pauses; her Apple watch vibrates. It's sending her a message: breathe. She exhales, letting her shoulders droop. She's always been good at following instructions. You set out a plan, a strategy, you chunk it down and you follow it. That's how things get done. If there is a recipe for success, that's it.

It's good to have a moment to reflect. She gazes around her at the honey-coloured stone. Worn and ancient, it exudes its own form of calm and reassurance. When she came here as an undergraduate, did she have any concept of how her life would be twenty-five years later? She had ambition, bags of it. But that was mostly about what she didn't want, the life, the people and the places she was determined to leave behind. And she was scared stiff. Back then, she regarded Cambridge as a magic portal to a different world. But was it?

Having money is the thing that changes who you are. Not entirely, but it's the vital ingredient. When you've grown up with a mum, who was a single parent and had to count every penny, you know what money means. Freedom is not having to think constantly how to feed your kids and pay the bills. Freedom is about choice and access to everything you want. Money, serious money, is the only thing that gives you that.

'It's ours by right, because it's our turn.' That's what Robert said when he collected his first million-pound bonus. Empires rise and fall; the study of history teaches you that. And the wheel of fortune turns.

Our turn. Melissa Rowe needs to realise that.

The harsh sunlight is dancing through the leaves on the bushes that surround the quad, and the heat is searing. Her mind must've been drifting because the sudden sound of voices brings her abruptly back to full consciousness.

Further along the gallery, two people have paused for a conversation. They're about twenty metres away. She recognises the man immediately. The tough, slick-looking black guy, who heads Robert's close protection team. His name's Foley; she thinks he's a DI. He's talking to a woman. She's nearly as tall as him, white, hair pinned up, dark trousers, smart and professional. Is she a cop, too? Leanne hasn't seen her before.

Because she's sitting in an alcove, Leanne realises she's out of their line of sight. She should probably get up and make herself known. But something in Foley's manner makes her hesitate. Better to eavesdrop.

'Interesting,' he says. 'You think it's that?'

'He's got two minor convictions as a dealer,' says the woman. 'He's a Brummie. We've got a County Lines gang from Birmingham who've been active round here lately.'

'What about the other temporary staff?'

'Nothing's been flagged up yet. My boss is liaising with counter terrorism on the data we've got.'

'Okay,' he says. 'Security service has still got it red flagged as imminent. All we can do is keep our eyes open.'

'Perhaps we're looking at this all wrong,' says the woman. 'I had an interesting conversation with a journalist. She said she knew Gerrish as a student. She told me the constituency attack on him was a put-up job.'

Leanne feels a shaft of anger shoot through her.

Melissa? Who else could it be?

That evil, conniving bitch.

'That's outlandish,' says Foley.

'Is it?' says the woman. 'This journalist says his popularity's gone up fifteen percent since that attack. He's getting the sympathy vote. Are we just being played?'

Foley chuckles. 'Who knows? Welcome to my world, mate,' he says. 'It's a bit like the weather forecast, security service opts for the worst-case scenario, then if it happens, they can't be blamed. Most of the intel comes to nothing. Until it doesn't. So we have to take everything seriously.'

Leanne sits stock still. She listens to their footsteps receding. When she thinks they're gone, she stands up.

Her husband was nearly killed! And that bitch is going round telling people it was a put-up job. Outrageous! The fury is pumping through her. She doesn't know what to do.

Calm down. Breathe.

Now they think someone is planning to attack Robert again? A red-flag?

Don't go off at a tangent. Think about this. Think!

The police know what they're doing. Foley is a very experienced officer. He's got it covered. They're all armed.

But Melissa and her poison! Why would she do this?

Leanne feels like crying.

Pull yourself together.

She goes back to her breathing. A proper belly breath. Slowly in and out.

18

Saturday, 4pm

Mel lies on the narrow bed dozing fitfully in the afternoon heat. She had every intention of just leaving. That was the plan. She went back to the college room to collect her bag, but she was feeling queasy and decided to lie down. Just for a moment.

Jeremy texted her back earlier. *Local contact has issues.* Emoji of a cop. *But I'm on it.*

This whole thing was a bad idea, as she knew it would be.

A clatter outside somewhere drags her back to full consciousness. With the curtains closed against the fierce sun, the room is yellowy grey. And for a second, she has no idea where she is. A primal panic seizes her. Too many strange hotel rooms in hot, alien places. Then she makes out the shape of the desk, the wardrobe, the washbasin. A student room with Blu Tack stains on the walls and the adolescent desires of generations of occupants.

The conversation with Claire slides immediately into her

head. Claire shafted her; sweet, beautiful Claire. Her best friend, who everyone admired.

Course she did.

Mel doesn't even need to ask how it happened. She knows. Adrian was an equally beautiful boy, full of raging hormones, and he really thought he could just have everything. Why not? He knew how in love with him Mel was. So did Claire. But that was irrelevant. Adrian always got what he wanted.

Twenty-five years ago and it still fucking hurts.

Mel sits up and looks at the time on her phone. Her stomach is growling. No breakfast, no lunch. Just the acidic after-burn of the wine. She needs something to eat.

She checks her texts. Nothing from Jeremy yet. She needs that, too.

She gets up, goes to the washbasin, and rinses her face and hands. Plenty of men have dumped her over the years, and vice versa. Friendships have soured. People are fickle. Mel learned not to care and to move on.

But Adrian was her first love, her first experience of sexual passion. Her feelings for Claire were equally intense. And if she's honest with herself, in the secret recesses of her brain, she always knew those two would betray her. You'd have to be a naïve fool not to realise it was inevitable. And Melissa Rowe is nobody's fool.

She sends another text to Jeremy, hassling him.

Tea and cakes are being served in a marquee on the back lawn next to the Master's Lodge. The enervating heat has slowed everyone and everything down. People are sitting around fanning themselves when Mel wanders in. There's a languid murmur of conversation.

The table is loaded with tiered cake stands. Scones with jam and cream, which is weeping in the heat. Brownies, cheesecake and a mountain of glazed donuts. And reaching out his hand to transfer a second donut to his plate is Adrian Cardello.

Bastard.

Mel watches him as he stuffs both donuts, glancing around him furtively like a naughty boy. No sooner has he consumed the donuts on his plate than he reaches for a third. It seems he's still a man of secret vices.

Walking up behind him, Mel says, 'You'll get fat.'

He starts and turns towards her. He wipes the sugar from his lips and laughs.

'You've caught me,' he says.

'So it would seem.'

'It stops me drinking. Sixty-five days clean and sober.'

'You're a walking cliché, Cardello.'

'Yeah, I've been told.'

Mel picks up a plate and chooses a fruit scone and a little pot of jam.

'Can I get you some tea?' he says.

She scans him. He has such an open, self-deprecating facade, which is totally deceptive.

But aren't we all deceptive?

Claire's betrayal has certainly shocked her. And she really thought no one had the power to hurt her anymore. Clearly, she was wrong.

'That's very gentlemanly of you,' she says. 'I'll have some Earl Grey.'

Mel sits down at an empty table and eats her scone. Adrian goes to the tea table and returns with a pot and two cups on a tray. He's also purloined a tea towel, which he lays over his forearm like a waiter. He stands beside the table, and with a deferential little bow, he says. 'Shall I pour for madam?'

He's playacting for her. He used to do this all the time.

Such a charmer, she thinks sourly, as she watches him pour the tea.

'And lemon for madam?' he says.

She nods.

He picks up a slice of lemon between thumb and forefinger, his little pinky extended, and places it carefully in her cup.

'Tell me something,' she says. 'Did you ever screw Claire Naylor?'

He puts on an expression of exaggerated surprise and sits down at the table opposite her. 'Well, that's a bit out of left field,' he says.

'Did you?'

The clown is gone to be replaced with his earnest face. He is a brilliant actor.

'If you want the honest truth,' he says. 'It's possible, but I can't quite remember.'

'Did it ever occur to you it might upset me?'

'Oh, come on Mel. We had a pretty open relationship.'

'Not because of you, duh-brain. Because of her. She was my best friend.'

He gives her a mystified shrug. 'I adore women,' he says. 'I always have.' As if that justifies everything.

'Like you adore donuts?'

'I'm not just talking about sex. I always prefer their company. Working with women producers and directors has always been better.'

'That's just your narcissism. Because they all think you're gorgeous.'

'I'm being serious.'

'So am I.'

'Women are by far the superior sex. I've always felt that.

Most blokes feel it too, but they fear it. Makes them want to put women down, put them in their place. But I celebrate it.'

'Is that why you've felt the need to screw so many of them? In celebration?'

'You're just mocking me. I mean it. I'm a total feminist.'

'Oh get over yourself, Cardello.'

He sighs and demolishes the third donut. 'I can't win, can I?'

'Win what?'

He always won, and he doesn't even see it.

This is the thing that upsets her. She can feel the worm of spite burrowing through her mind. His ignorance is wilful. He ignores anything that doesn't suit him.

Him and Claire.

'Claire and I had an interesting conversation earlier,' she says. 'You know she had a daughter called Ella?'

He frowns. 'I gather the poor girl killed herself. Terrible.'

'It is terrible. She suffered from depression.'

He sips his tea. 'It's an awful affliction. You may not realise, but I've suffered some pretty dark days myself.'

'You've been depressed? What have you got to be depressed about? The toast of La La land.'

'Come on, Mel,' he says. 'That's not how it works.'

He's like a fish circling the bait. He can't see the hidden hook, but she can. And the power she has in that moment gives her a thrill.

Do it! They deserve it.

'Isn't it?' she says. 'Well, perhaps it's genetic.'

His eyes flicker. The brow puckers. Has he ever wondered? He must've. He's not stupid. That's why he's pretending he can't remember.

'What do you mean exactly?' he says.

She shrugs. She's enjoying this. 'Maybe the disposition is

something you inherit,' she says. 'Perhaps Ella got it from her father.'

Now she can see the doubt in his eyes.

Go on, you bastard. Ask!

'You're talking in riddles,' he says. 'Who is her father?' He's trying to sound casual.

In for the kill.

'Claire's just told me it was you. I never knew. But then why would I? Both of you lied to me. You played me for a sucker.'

She finishes her tea and stands up.

He sits stock still with a look of horror on his face.

'Mel, that's complete nonsense.'

'You just said you can't remember. You can't have it both ways, Cardello.'

'Hang on. Wait a minute. I don't know why she would say that.'

'Then you'd better ask her, hadn't you?'

She walks away. Spite, revenge; call it what you will? There's nothing wrong with it. And we all do it. Because it feels good.

It was worth coming to this stupid reunion just to see the look on his face. In the end, he doesn't get to win. Not him or Claire.

19

Saturday, 4.15pm

So much blood! It oozes through her fingers. He grunts as she withdraws the knife...someone is howling and running. Is it you? Yes, it's you. It is you.

Claire opens her eyes. She's lying in the semi-darkness with a damp flannel across her forehead. Where? How? The fever dream is pulling her back down. She fights it and the splinters of memory slot into place.

She abandoned the trolley of dirty dishes in the corridor behind the kitchens. Gripped by panic, she ran away. From what? She can remember the compulsion, but not the reason. That's gone.

She cut through the gardens. No one accosted her, and she made it back to this room. Set in the gables, it's at the very top of one of the residential blocks. Even with the window wide open, the heat is unrelenting. There's not a whisper of breeze. The dark heavy curtain hangs limply across the window frame, blocking out the sun.

She must've just passed out.

Sitting up slowly, she removes the flannel, reaches over and checks her phone. It's after four. She's bathed in sweat.

She gets up, goes to the sink, fills a tumbler with water and drinks it down.

Her head is a jumble of disparate thoughts. None of this is what she wanted. It's all just spiralled out of control.

Then she remembers. She told Mel. Told her that Adrian was Ella's father. Why on earth did she do that?

Mel was going to help her. They were going to bring Gerrish down; ruin his career. Now that possibility is gone.

But would it have been enough?

In the privacy of her own mind, that question is simple to answer. No. It's not enough. But she can only admit it to herself.

He destroyed Ella. Took her life. And what she wants is a life for a life. That need is deep and visceral. In the end, it's the only thing that will satisfy her. It's what fills her dreams. Her febrile brain won't let go of it.

Revenge is primal.

An eye for an eye.

She goes over to the window, slides back the curtain and looks out. Several stories below, there's a marquee and people taking tea on the sun-baked lawns. Very civilised. Very English. Very Cambridge.

She wants to lean out and shout: 'Vengeance! Why can't I have vengeance? Surely that's my right?'

People would think she's unhinged, and perhaps she is. That's what her daughter's suicide has done to her. It's driven her mad. Only a madwoman would have fantasies about killing someone, wouldn't they?

'Grief has its season,' said her GP, in the seven-minute consultation that was allocated to her. It sounded like something he read in a book. He wrote her a prescription for anti-depressants and referred her to a local bereavement counselling group; she never went.

Now it occurs to her that there was a reason she told Mel about Adrian. It was obvious she'd be upset. And it's driven her away.

It's what you wanted. Secretly.

It was below the surface of consciousness, but now it seems clear to Claire what it was all about. Not some need for honesty. She's been lying about who her daughter's father is for twenty-five years. She's never spoken about Adrian before. He just wasn't relevant to their lives.

When she told Mel the truth, she was burning bridges. And her brain, in its own deranged way, was making perfect sense. Why? Because in her heart, she's always known what she must do. This is just a way of getting to it. Of facing her fears, but being able to overcome them and move forward.

Maybe it's better if the desire to kill is just an impulse. An angry impulse in the heat of the moment. A crime of passion. But she didn't have that luxury. She's had to wait and plan. There were bound to be doubts. Nerves. The pull of conformity. Respectable, educated women like Claire aren't supposed to be violent. She's Sandra Naylor's daughter. It's simply not part of her DNA. But extreme circumstances call for extreme measures. Most people don't have to face the pain of losing a child. And no one knows what they'll do until it happens to them.

She bends down, pulls her overnight case out from under the bed and opens it. The knife is wrapped in a silk scarf and tucked down beside her shoes. She made a special trip to London to purchase it. A secret little adventure. She told her mother she was going to an art exhibition. Sandra Naylor had seemed relieved that she was getting out and about again. But what she was doing was playing out her fantasy. She told herself it was just that. It was a distraction. A bizarre kind of therapy for her grief. She had no actual intention of ever using that knife.

On the same day, she bought a handbag. A black faux silk clutch with a metal chain. The five inch boning knife fitted snuggly in the bottom. With a couple of tissues and her phone on top, it wasn't even visible when the bag was opened. Was this premeditation? Not really. Because back then, she never intended to do anything more. Of course she didn't.

Even when she arrived in Cambridge yesterday, the plan was to confront Gerrish publicly. Accuse him openly of his crime, and hear what he had to say. And then Mel would write about it in her newspaper and expose him.

What kind of stupid idea was that?

She takes the knife out of the case and weighs it in her hand. It fits comfortably; the blade is high grade steel and sharp.

A shiver runs up her spine.

She opens the clutch bag and slips the knife inside. This doesn't mean she'll use it. Almost certainly, she won't. But there's no harm in being prepared, in having that option, is there?

20

Saturday, 7.30pm

Mel sips her wine. Jeremy finally came through. He connected her with some kid who was working in the kitchen. She collected from him. Jeremy would settle with him and bill Mel's card in the usual way. She'd sampled the product in the privacy of her room. It was good stuff. The hit she needed.

She nibbles at the finger food on the bar. Friends will shaft you; that's the way of the world. But she's a journalist, and a bloody good one. She goes out looking for stories, and sometimes they come to you. All you need to do is follow the lead and start digging. This is what she's doing. She gave Theo a call and asked him to do some background checking for her. He was over the moon and only too happy to sacrifice his Saturday night.

The lawn is dotted with her fellow alumni in small clusters. But they've swapped their casual attire for expensive evening gowns and old-fashioned dinner jackets. Casting her eye around, Mel can't pick out a single one with the balls or the imagination to buck the trend. Except her. She's still wearing her jeans and a pair of scuffed cowboy boots she bought in the States. They make her think of all those old country and western songs about lying, cheating men. It's why she's put them on.

One of these days these boots are gonna walk all over you.

Her quarry is wearing a blue satin number which could've been cut from a pair of curtains. It's ruched around the waist; a catwalk model could probably get away with it, but Leanne Brady can't. She looks atrocious. Mel skirts around the group that Leanne is part of, waiting for a lull in the conversation. But Leanne must have a sixth sense; she turns round abruptly to face Mel.

Mel smiles. 'Nice dress,' she says.

'You decided on informal,' says Leanne. Her tone is chilly.

'To be honest,' says Mel. 'It's so bloody hot, I couldn't be bothered.'

They stare at each other for a moment.

'I think perhaps I owe you an apology,' says Mel. 'I was rather rude earlier.'

Reel her in. Nice and slow.

Leanne raises her eyebrows. 'The heat can have an unsettling effect on people.'

'It can,' says Mel. 'And these sorts of events are weird too, aren't they?'

'They can be.'

'I've heard an interesting story doing the rounds.'

She waits, but Leanne doesn't react.

'Aren't you curious to hear the gossip?' says Mel.

'I've got a feeling you're going to tell me, anyway,' says Leanne.

Leanne has become such a smooth operator. Nowadays, it's difficult to get under her skin.

'Well,' says Mel. 'It seems that Claire Naylor blames your husband for her daughter's suicide.'

That hits the target squarely. The look of shock on Leanne's shiny little face says it all. But it's momentary.

She inhales, then she says, 'Claire and I are good friends, and she's said nothing of that nature to me.'

'How can she?' says Mel. 'It's because you are friends. And didn't you get Ella the job in Robert's office in the first place?'

She's wondering what you know. Let her squirm.

Leanne is scrutinising her, those runty eyes caked in make-up. 'Ella was an intern for a short while,' she says. 'After she left, she became depressed. I really don't see what that's got to do with my husband. For a start, as a minister, his everyday contact with the interns was fairly minimal. And I can assure you that Robert doesn't bully his staff.'

'Didn't Ella get blamed for some email leak?'

'I've really no idea.'

Mel is enjoying herself. 'Claire doesn't interest herself in politics,' she says. 'She doesn't understand how the cesspit that is Westminster works. But you and I, Leanne, we do. When Robert was at Transport, as part of his campaign to smear the current Home Secretary in the hope he could nab her job, some emails were leaked. But, it went a bit pear-shaped, didn't it? Robert needed a scapegoat. I've looked it up. This happened last September. Just two months before Ella Naylor died. So blame the intern. Collateral damage. It happens.'

'This is total nonsense,' says Leanne, evenly. 'And if you're thinking of going to your editor with this slanderous rubbish, you'd better be sure to call the lawyers, too.'

Mel raises her palms. 'Hey,' she says. 'I'm just repeating what Ella Naylor told her mother. This is Claire's private opinion. I don't know the truth.' She pauses for effect. 'Yet.'

Leanne shakes her head wearily. 'What do you want, Melissa? What do you hope to gain by this?'

'First, I'd like to think that somehow I can help ease the terrible pain my friend is suffering by getting her some kind of justice. And second, whether or not you like it, holding the powerful to account for their bad behaviour, is part of my job.'

'And what if there is no bad behaviour?'

'Then Robert's got nothing to fear from me. Because you're right, on a story like this, my editor will want corroboration, and the lawyers will oversee everything. We take our reputation seriously.'

Leanne gives her a sad smile. 'Do you?' she says. 'And while you're off on your egotistical crusade, what about Claire?'

'What do you mean?'

'What's she supposed to do until you bring her Robert's head on a platter? Y'know, I actually went to Ella Naylor's funeral. Claire was in pieces. I don't remember seeing you there.'

'I was abroad.'

'Of course you were. I've come across some pretty big egos over the years. Most of them are men. Except you, Melissa. You're up there in the premier league. You are ruthless and then some. Actually, I've always envied that.'

Sarky bitch.

Mel surveys her. Little old Leanne has developed a good

poker face over the years. How much does she know? That's hard to tell. But one thing's for sure. It's game on.

21

Dinner is at eight-thirty, preceded by cocktails on the lawn. Claire has changed into her evening dress; it must be ten years old. It hangs a little loose. In the last few months, she's lost a lot of weight. She glances at her bare arms; white and scrawny. She should've got something with sleeves more suited to her age. She readjusts the gold chain of the clutch bag which is draped over her left shoulder.

The sun may have disappeared behind the buildings, but the temperature is still in the high twenties. The men are sweltering in their dinner jackets; some have already discarded them.

There's no sign of Mel. She was threatening to leave before, and she probably has.

That was never really an option, was it?

Claire has only one thought in her mind now: to get through this. She'll fulfil her obligations to the committee and then it will be over, and her ludicrous plan to confront Gerrish with it. It's a relief.

Because you're a coward. You know you are.

Her head is a jumble of conflicting emotions. Grief distorts the judgement, but not as much as anger. At the root of her desire to harm Robert Gerrish is her fury at the way Ella was treated. Her daughter was used and discarded. It's what caused her death; there's no doubt about that. This will always torment Claire. But what can she do?

Coward. You'll never do it.

How will she deal with this toxic feeling in the years to come? She has no idea.

You're letting her down. Again.

With a glass of sparkling mineral water in her hand, she moves between groups. She stays on the periphery, avoiding all but the most superficial conversations. The other members of the organising committee are a disparate bunch; none of them were friends of hers previously. Now Claire is grateful for that; it makes them safe.

She's listening politely to a fellow committee member, an archaeologist, talk about her latest dig, when she notices Adrian Cardello staring straight at her.

His head is tilted to one side, with a quizzical look. He has a glass of whiskey in his hand, and it doesn't look like his first.

After a couple of moments, he strolls over.

'Ladies,' he says. 'Mind if I join you?'

The archaeologist, who Claire assumed was a sensible woman, blushes and twitters with excitement.

How does he have that effect, Claire wonders? Is it just celebrity?

No.

She knows what it is, but she doesn't have a word for it.

Charisma? Even that sounds wrong. It's a connection that feels genuine and special in the moment. He turns it on you like a laser beam. It's magic. And it's sexual. He generates raw animal magnetism. But like all magic, ultimately it's a trick.

For the next five minutes, the archaeologist talks, and Claire and Adrian pretend to listen. But Claire can feel his eyes on her. It's unnerving. She has to escape. She drinks most of her mineral water and announces she must get a refill. But a moment later, Adrian makes his excuses too and pursues her.

He catches up with her at the bar. Claire can feel herself panicking.

'Right,' he says. 'I'll get us another drink. Mineral water, is it? And then you can tell me about Ella. And don't run off, Claire. Because I'll find you.'

She told him.

Claire's heart sinks. She has a few moments to marshal her scattered thoughts. She could outright lie and blame Mel. But she doubts that will work. Over the years, she has imagined many different scenarios in which Adrian came back into her and Ella's life. But it was never supposed to be like this.

He returns, hands her a fresh glass of iced, sparkling water and says, 'Shall we find somewhere quiet to sit?'

They follow a winding path into a newer part of the college. There's a small sculpture garden, a recent addition that never existed in their time. Adrian selects a concrete bench and invites her to sit.

He looks at her. He seems to be waiting. For what? An explanation?

She sighs. 'I asked Mel not to tell you.'

Adrian chuckles. 'C'mon Claire. This is Mel we're

talking about. She hasn't changed. You upset her. She's going to go for the jugular.'

'I never meant to upset her. It was a complicated situation, and I felt I had to be truthful with her.'

'And is it true?'

What the hell?

'Yes.'

He puffs his cheeks out. 'How did you come to this conclusion?'

'We had sex. It was the party after Finals. Clearly you don't remember.'

He dips his head, stares down at his hands. He's ashamed.

They sit in silence for several moments.

Finally, he looks up and gives her a sorrowful look. 'Why didn't you tell me?'

'I didn't want to be unfair to you.'

'You think not telling me I'd got you pregnant is fair?'

His sanctimonious attitude grates.

'Oh fuck off, Adrian. One drunken night at a party. And as soon as we graduated, you were off to RADA. What were you going to do? Marry me? I don't think so.'

'You didn't give me the option.'

'It would've been a disaster for both of us, and you know it. You'd've left me. And then what? I would've been worse off.'

He frowns and takes a slug of his drink. ' Did…your daughter ever ask about her father?'

'Her name's Ella.'

'Sorry. Did Ella ever ask?'

'Yes.'

'And what did you tell her?'

'Nothing.'

'Nothing?'

'I said I'd had casual sex at a party, which is true. And I didn't know his name.'

'Why? Why would you do that?'

She stands up. 'I don't owe you an explanation. I don't owe anyone an explanation.'

Except Ella. And it's too late for that.

'Don't walk away. Please.'

Claire turns to face him. 'What do you want me to say to you, Adrian? That you're not to blame in any way? Okay, I absolve you. I got pregnant, but I chose not to tell you. Whatever happened to her, it's on me.'

Your fault.

She can feel the tears coming; they ambush her when she doesn't want them to.

He stands, puts his glass down and reaches out to her.

'Come here,' he whispers.

She turns away. 'I don't want your comfort.'

He pulls a tissue from his pocket and offers it to her. She ignores it, wiping her face with her hands. And the tears still come.

He watches her. Neither of them speaks.

Then he says, 'Listen to me, Claire. You had a child, that's one thing. And you're right. Back then, I didn't deserve the truth. I probably wouldn't have done her any good. But you've also lost a child. At the very least, let me be a friend to you now.'

'Why? Why would you even want to?'

'I feel I've let you down. Let her down.'

She sniffs. 'You can't just…I don't know if I can.'

He holds out the tissue again. 'Please.'

She takes it and wipes her nose. The energy is draining out of her to be replaced by lethargy and confusion. She glances at his glass.

'Is that whiskey?'

Alcohol and the tablets she's on don't mix. She knows that. She's been warned.

He picks it up and offers it to her. 'Here. Drink it.'

She takes the glass. 'I haven't drunk alcohol since Ella died. I'm worried if I do, I'll never stop.'

'I've spent years on the wagon, off the wagon. Currently, I'm supposed to be on. But we're all frail creatures. There are times when we need something.'

Claire sips the drink and sinks back down on the concrete bench. Adrian perches next to her, at the end of the bench, not too close.

Her mind is a welter of conflicting thoughts. But now he knows that's one less burden to carry. It leaves her with only one thing to focus on.

How not to let her daughter down.

'Have you ever wanted to kill someone?' she says.

He smiles. 'Most directors I've ever worked with at some point.'

'No, I mean, seriously. Have you ever imagined getting a knife and just going up to them and plunging it into their body? Into their heart. Stabbing them with all your might, until the blood gushes out and they fall down dead.'

He's searching her face and frowning. 'You'd need a lot of anger for that.'

'What if you've got a lot of anger?' She takes another mouthful of whiskey. It burns at first, but then it soothes.

She's forty-seven. The rest of her life stretches out before her like a desert. What the hell is she going to do with it? There won't be a day or an hour that she doesn't think about Ella. If she spends it in jail, does that matter?

No. Nothing matters.

Adrian reaches out and touches her arm. 'Is this how you feel?' he says tentatively.

She takes another drink. 'He killed Ella. I can't prove it. There's no way to bring him to justice or make him pay.'

'I thought she took her own life.'

Why do none of them get it?

'No!' she says emphatically. 'She was driven to it. By him. By what he did to her.'

Adrian furrows his brow. 'Who are you talking about here?'

'Robert Gerrish.'

His jaw slackens. He stares at her in disbelief.

'Are you serious?' he says.

'Yes,' she replies.

A sense of relief floods through her. She's said it. She's put it out there.

Now it's real. You're going to do it.

This is the one chance she'll have to get near enough to that monster. She has to take it. That's clear. It's the only thing she can do now for her child. The consequences are unimportant.

22

Saturday, 7.55pm

Leanne holds up the front of her billowing dress as she hurries up the stone staircase to the suite of rooms set aside for them. They're normally used by visiting fellows, and although it's the oldest part of the college, the interior is modern; a comfortable sitting room with an adjoining kitchen, a bathroom, and bedroom. She nods to the close protection officer standing outside. He smiles and opens the door for her.

Robert is standing at the centre of the sitting room, in shirtsleeves, bow tie hanging loose about his neck, and he's in full flood, rehearsing his speech.

'…but we, my friends, our generation, we are the change makers.' He lowers the sheet of paper he's holding. 'Do you think they'll know what I mean by that?'

Kieran, Robert's special political adviser, is perched on the arm of a chair. 'Trust me, boss. It's a good buzzword. They'll get it.'

Robert frowns, he glances across at Leanne, then he checks his watch. 'Is it time yet? I thought dinner was at eight thirty.'

'It is,' she says. 'I need a word. I think we might have a situation developing.' She shoots a look at Kieran.

Kieran doesn't budge. He just stares at her through his Harry Potter glasses. He may think he's the boy wizard, but Leanne's view of him is somewhat different.

Robert shrugs. 'Let's hear it. Kieran's my man for every situation.'

Unfortunately, Leanne knows this is true. In her opinion, Robert relies on Kieran far too much. He's a wily operator, but can he be trusted? She's yet to meet a special adviser, who can.

'Melissa Rowe has just accosted me,' she says. 'According to her, back when you were at Transport, Ella Naylor was blamed for an email leak. You sacked her and—'

Robert frowns. 'Hang on. Did I? No, I thought she left of her own volition. Stress, wasn't it?' He directs a questioning look at Kieran, who just shrugs.

'Well,' says Leanne. 'Rowe is saying that Claire Naylor thinks this sacking caused Ella's suicide, and she holds you responsible.'

Robert puts his hands on his hips and shakes his head in disbelief. 'What total rot! That's awful. Has Claire said anything to you?'

'Nope.'

He's scowling. He slams his speech down on the table.

'How the hell has she come to that conclusion? I need to talk to her and reassure her—'

'Hang on, Robert. Let's not overact.'

Kieran jumps in. 'She's right, boss. Melissa Rowe's a

toxic hack with more than one axe to grind. And she hates this government.'

'I know, but I can't have Claire thinking something like this about me.'

He shakes his head again; he is genuinely upset, and Leanne knows why.

After all these years, and everything you've done for him.

She says nothing.

Their eyes meet, and he gives her a guilty look. 'It's ridiculous,' he says. 'Claire Naylor is a very old friend. Of both of us,' he adds rapidly. 'Ella's death was a terrible tragedy. Who the hell has been feeding her this nonsense?'

Leanne takes a breath. 'That's what we need to find out. So I don't think you should say anything to Claire.'

Kieran nods vigorously. It's rare for him and Leanne to be on the same page.

'I'll probably see her at dinner. How can I not?' says Robert. 'I don't want her to be upset.'

Her daughter's dead. What does he expect?

Kieran pipes up. 'Best guess, boss. This is Rowe stirring the shit.'

'I agree,' says Leanne.

'She's short of a story,' says Kieran. 'She's doing a bit of cage rattling. If you react in any way, she'll think there's something to it and she'll start digging.'

'But where is this coming from?' says Robert. 'There isn't anything to it, is there?' He's looking directly at Kieran.

Leanne watches the special adviser. He has a decidedly shifty look. She can smell a rat.

Kieran puffs out his cheeks. 'Ella was a nice girl,' he says condescendingly. 'But she was flaky. Y'know what I mean?'

'No, I don't,' says Leanne. 'Explain.'

Kieran's chin goes out, and he gives her a bullish look.

Then he glances at Robert for support. She knows what Kieran's thinking. His breed, special political advisers or SpAds as they're known, hate wives, particularly wives like her, who know this business inside out.

Leanne stares right back at him. And waits.

Arrogant little shit. What's he done?

'Okay,' says Kieran, steepling his fingers. 'I know you brought her in, Leanne. And therefore, you obviously feel responsible. But she was only twenty-four, and somewhat naïve.'

'How old are you, Kieran?' says Leanne. 'Twenty-seven?'

'Yes, but I got my first job in Whitehall at twenty-two.'

The myth of the boy genius.

He sighs. 'Ella was hard-working. No one can deny that. But…' he gives Robert a weary we're-men-of-the-world-aren't-we glance. 'She was out of her depth and easy to manipulate. And if you're asking me, I think that's what happened. Some hack started taking her out for drinks, whispering in her ear. Screwed her probably. And that's when we figured we had a leak.'

'I don't remember any of this,' says Robert. He looks genuinely confused.

'Didn't want to put you in an awkward position, boss. Because of your friendship with the mother.'

'What happened?' says Leanne.

'We had to let her go,' says Kieran.

'How did you know the leak came from her?' says Leanne.

'Process of elimination.'

'Carried out officially?'

'Christ no,' says Kieran. 'I liked the girl. I didn't want to ruin her career prospects. We just told her we were cutting back.' He smiles innocently. 'You know what the press pack is like. Someone took advantage of her. When she realised that, it could've tipped her over the edge, I suppose.'

Someone took advantage, that's clear.

It all sounds ultra-reasonable. And Leanne doesn't buy it for one second.

Robert sighs. 'Oh God, well, we'll just have to come up with something we can say to Claire that's not too hurtful.'

'Yes,' says Leanne. 'We will. But I suggest you leave it to me, darling.'

Kieran nods. 'You're definitely best placed to sort this out, Leanne.'

He's passing the buck.

Leanne studies him. Those damned glasses. The smug expression. He needs to be dealt with. Booted out no question. But that'll have to wait for another day. She'll add that to her to do list.

23

Saturday, 8.45pm

It takes a while for everyone to find their places, but Claire is relieved that the dinner service is starting on time. The seating plan was worked on by the committee. Obviously, Gerrish and Leanne were at the high table next to the Master and his wife. But there was quite a bit of wrangling about who else to place there. Members of the committee felt they should take precedence.

Claire made sure she was as far away as possible. The long tables filling the rest of the hall are placed at right angles to the high table, which is raised on a dais at one end of the room. She insisted she needed to sit at the far end of one of them, to keep an eye on the kitchen, she said. No one argued with her because no one else wanted that job.

Adrian stuck to her side like glue until they entered the Great Hall. But in the crush of people getting through the door, she escaped him. She'd refused to answer any more of his questions.

The whiskey he gave her slid down and miraculously has transformed her mood. She's feeling pleasantly detached and the nattering in her head has been replaced by an odd sense of elation. She knows how this is going to play out.

No more doubts.

As people find their seats, she slips into the kitchen. Tessa has everything in hand. The servers are all lined up, ready to deliver the starter: a salmon mousse with avocado.

She returns to her place to find Adrian standing next to her chair.

'I've swapped the name plates, so we can sit together,' he says.

'That's not really necessary.'

'Oh, I think it is,' he says, pulling her chair out for her. 'Sit down. The Master's about to say grace.'

Claire sits. She has little choice.

A hush falls as the Master gets to his feet.

'Benedic, Domine, dona tua quae de largitate sumus sumpturi…'

The words of the Latin Grace reverberate round the hall and inside Claire's mind. Like a nursery rhyme from long ago, oddly comforting and familiar. She closes her eyes and drifts. The relief is immeasurable. If only she could remain frozen in this moment with no need to go either forward or back.

Once this is done, you'll have peace.

But the grace ends and the clatter of cutlery and the cacophony of voices shatters the moment.

Reluctantly, Claire opens her eyes, only to find a figure looming over her from behind. It takes a second for her to realise it's Mel, and she's dragging a chair along on its two back legs.

'Well, here we are again,' Mel exclaims. 'Just like old times, eh? Hutch up, Cardello. Make some room.'

Adrian shoots her an exasperated look, but he complies. The entire row is forced to move their chairs along so she can insert hers between Adrian and Claire.

'Isn't this cosy?' she says, sitting down. 'The Three Musketeers back in the saddle. Ready to fight for truth and justice.'

She's beaming at them, but her eyes are glassy, the pupils fully dilated.

Adrian sighs. 'Are you on something?' he whispers.

'Am I high, you mean?' she replies. 'Yes, I'm high on the joy of seeing old friends and remembering what great times we had together.'

Claire turns to look at her. 'I thought you'd left,' she says.

Mel has a glass of wine in her hand. She takes a slug. 'Left?' she says. 'Why would I leave when I'm having such a great time? I'm glad you persuaded me to come, Claire. Wouldn't have missed this for the world.'

Even in Claire's odd state of mind, the sarcasm is unmistakable.

Adrian catches her eye and raises his eyebrows. 'She's completely wasted,' he says.

'Oh yes,' says Mel. 'That I am. And if you need a little bump yourself, I've discovered a great source. Right here in the college. Beats donuts, pal. I can tell you that much. But looking at your glass, I'm guessing you've abandoned your latest bout of sobriety. Let's all make merry, eh?'

'You know what I'm wondering, Mel,' says Adrian. 'How much more damage do you intend to do today?'

She tips back her head and laughs. 'Oh, I'm just getting started.'

A server is coming along the row with the starters. An

arm shoots over Claire's shoulder and a plate of salmon mousse lands in front of her. She stares at it.

'What the fuck's this shit?' says Mel loudly. 'Looks like the cat puked.'

She's attracting glances from those seated nearest, some critical, but mostly of amusement. After all, most of them have spent a hot, lazy afternoon getting quietly tanked themselves.

Adrian laughs and shrugs. 'Hey, it's a reunion. She's regressed. But isn't that why we're here? To roll back the clock.'

There's a responsive ripple of laughter down the table.

Then he turns to Mel and says softly, 'You upset Claire any more tonight, I swear I'll break your goddamned neck. I'm not kidding.'

Mel stares back at him, then she chuckles. 'Is that your psycho voice? It's very good. Very sexy.'

'I'm warning you, Mel. Back off.'

Mel shrugs. 'What makes you think Claire's my target? Maybe I want to help Claire. If that's what she wants.'

Claire meets her gaze.

'Isn't that we talked about?' says Mel. 'Isn't that why you wanted me here?'

'It was,' says Claire. Her head is woozy. But she's aware of Adrian's gaze on her. He's watching her like a hawk. She gives him a smile. 'But things have moved on. Forget about it.'

24

Saturday, 9.15pm

The main course is duck. Leanne stares at her plate. She should probably leave the dauphinoise potatoes, definitely loaded with cream. She allows herself a small forkful; they are delicious.

She's seated between her husband and the Master's wife, an uptight and intimidating lady with a reputation as a minor poet. They exhausted most topics of conversation by the time the plates for the starter were cleared. Leanne mixes in the world of billionaires, but the snooty intellectual superiority of this sort of woman still has the power to make her uncomfortable.

She's racking her brains for something to say, but the Master's wife gets to her feet, gives Leanne a tepid smile, mumbles 'excuse me' and leaves the table.

That's a relief.

Leanne glances across at Robert. His face is flushed and

he's hitting the red wine. She pours him a glass of water and touches his arm. He turns to look at her.

'Drink some water,' she says.

He's hyper, eyes over-bright with booze. 'Have you said anything to Claire yet?' he says.

'Not yet. I haven't had a chance.'

He frowns and shakes his head. 'Where is this nonsense coming from?'

He needs to let this go.

'Y'know, Robert, it strikes me Kieran is not being entirely candid here.'

Robert takes another large mouthful of wine. 'I don't think we can blame Kieran if the poor girl was manipulated by some hack in search of a story.'

'I don't think it would be a good idea to say that to Claire, do you?'

'What if it's the truth?'

'What if it isn't?'

Why has he got such a blind spot when it comes to that little shit?

Their eyes meet. He looks away. She surveys her husband. He's twitchy and he has sweat on his upper lip. He may be an experienced political speaker, but coming back here was always going to be unnerving for him. For both of them. It matters too much. His eyes flicker; she can see his anxiety.

'Drink some water and leave the wine alone,' she whispers. 'It's not going to help.'

He huffs, reaches out for his water glass and takes a sip. His gaze travels across the hall. 'Have you noticed?' he says. 'She's at the end of the table there, sitting next to Rowe and Cardello. Who knows what poison she's being fed?'

Leanne lays her hand on his forearm. 'Darling, listen to

me. You need to forget about them and focus on your speech. They're not the important people here.'

But the angst on his face confirms that it still matters to him what these people think. She understands.

It's the wine and the pressure of expectation that's getting to him. He's like her; he still feels as if he has to prove himself. Coming back here is exacerbating that and exposing his soft underbelly. The mantle of the slick politician is peeling back and emotionally, he's regressing to the boy he once was. She can't allow that.

'Robert,' she says quietly. 'You need to pull yourself together. And you need to leave Claire to me.'

'I don't want her to think badly of me.' That's definitely the boy talking.

'She won't. I promise you.'

'It was your idea to give the girl a job,' he says petulantly.

She takes a deep breath. He's right. It was her idea. And no good deed goes unpunished. That's what she's thinking to herself now.

Ella Naylor was a strange girl. She inherited her mother's brains, but not the looks. She was mousy and plain, with an awkwardness about her. It was hard to put a finger on the source of her problems. Claire seemed an affectionate parent, if slightly over-anxious. Ella was shy and lacking in confidence; perhaps she just floundered in the cut-throat world of social media.

Leanne thinks about her own girls and how to protect them. It's already proving a struggle with Allegra, and she's only thirteen.

The funeral was awful. Leanne went on her own; Robert had wanted to come, but it clashed with an important trip to the States. The turnout was sparse. Just family and close friends. Leanne counted a dozen people in the pews at the crematorium. Claire's father was in a wheelchair. There were some random cousins. It was a deeply sad affair.

Glancing again at her husband, Leanne notices half his dinner is uneaten. He suffers with a nervous stomach, especially on big occasions. She catches his eye. He gives her a sheepish look. She reaches in her bag and finds a blister pack of antacids, which she passes to him under the table.

Without a word, he slips one in his mouth.

When they were first together and officially became an item, they had the obligatory conversation about past relationships. From Leanne's side, there wasn't much to tell. The boy at school she first had sex with; she imagined briefly that they were in love. He disabused her of that when he took someone else to the end of term prom. Before Robert, her university relationships were casual and short-lived. But she wasn't stupid. She went to the doctors at the end of fresher's week and got herself on the pill.

Robert's revelations were rather vague. There was one girl, he said, that he was rather keen on. He sort of proposed to her, but she turned him down.

How do you sort of propose to someone?

They've never spoken about his feelings for Claire specifically, or what happened. And now she can see why.

The past is the past, that's what she's always told herself. It doesn't matter. But looking across at her husband's face now, she can see she was fooling herself. It does.

25

Saturday, 10pm

Claire's heart thuds in her chest. Robert Gerrish is on his feet, on the dais, wine glass held aloft '…and I said to the Senator, well sir, I couldn't possibly comment on that.'

Peals of laughter erupt from the audience and roll through the hall from the front to the back, where Claire is sitting. People start to clap and hoot in appreciation.

Gerrish toasts the audience with his glass. He's chuckling. Leanne hands him a tissue and he wipes his face as he waits for the noise to subside. 'Thank you,' he says. 'Who says politics is boring, eh?'

More laughter around the room.

Claire sits stock still; her skin is crawling. Her palms are damp. But she's remained in a bubble throughout the speech. Several times, she was certain he was staring straight at her. That made her want to puke.

Next to her, Mel is banging the table with the flat of her hand. 'Yeh!' she shouts. 'Way to go Robbie!'

No one takes any notice. People are shouting and stomping. They're all mellow with food and booze; jackets and inhibitions have been discarded. Gerrish's speech has gone down a storm.

Except with Adrian. He's calmly sipping his wine and watching her. Not overtly. But it's obvious he's got an eye on her.

This feels peculiar to Claire. After all this time, and now with Ella gone, he's casting himself in the role of her protector.

Mel sits firmly between them. She's making a point. 'Well, that was total bollocks,' says Mel loudly. 'But you've got to give the bloke credit. He's a good rabble-rouser.'

Like Claire, she's eaten almost nothing, but has continued to drink.

Claire stands up. She's a little unsteady on her feet, but she feels much calmer than she has for a long while.

'Are you okay?' says Adrian.

'I'm absolutely fine,' she says. 'I'm just going to the bathroom.'

'I could do with some fresh air myself,' he says, standing up.

She turns on him. 'Adrian, leave me alone. I'm just going to the loo.'

Mel is watching the exchange with interest. 'Don't be stalky, Cardello,' she says. 'Let the woman go and piss in peace.'

He glares at her.

Claire doesn't wait to see what happens next. She slings her bag over her shoulder and walks rapidly away.

There's a queue outside the women's toilet, and Claire joins the end of it. She's glad to escape the heat and the noise of the hall. Out in the open quadrangle, it's cooler. She closes her eyes and tips back her head. Then she hears a familiar voice.

'Claire…'

Her eyes snap open. Leanne Brady is standing in front of her with a concerned smile on her face. 'Can I grab you for a sec?' she says. 'I need a private word.'

Claire sighs.

It's not her fault.

'Come up to our rooms. You can use the loo there.' Leanne doesn't wait for an answer. She takes Claire's arm. There's no choice.

Claire allows herself to be shepherded down the corridor and out across the quad.

'I've heard the most dreadful thing,' says Leanne, once they're out of earshot of anyone else. 'That you think Robert is somehow responsible for the death of Ella. Is this true?'

Claire stops in her tracks, surprised by Leanne's directness.

'This is about something Robert did, not you,' she says. 'I don't blame you at all. We've always been friends.'

Leanne looks distraught. 'Then it is true. I thought it was just Melissa being spiteful. Oh my God, Claire. If you were thinking something like this, why didn't you come to me?'

Claire feels the tears welling. 'She would never have just killed herself. She was driven to it.'

Leanne is shaking her head. 'If this is something that happened while she was working in Robert's office—'

'They blamed her, Leanne. She was totally innocent.'

'Who blamed her? Claire, we need to look at the facts here.'

'She told me. She wasn't lying.'

'I'm not saying she was. But Robert didn't even know—'

'Of course he knew!' Claire realises she's shouting, but she doesn't care.

Of course he did.

Leanne takes a step backwards. She's shocked.

'I know you want a reason for what happened,' she says. 'I get it. You need that. Any mother would.'

A reason? He's always resented you because of what you did. That's the bloody reason.

Leanne has her hands on her hips, head down, and she just keeps talking. 'It's a terrible tragedy. Suicide is hard to grasp and harder to accept.'

'I know the reason,' says Claire. 'It was because of me.'

'What?' Leanne is staring at her, aghast.

That's shut her up.

'He's always resented me.'

'Resented you? No, that's nonsense. He regards you as a friend.'

They're in the middle of the quad. Strings of fairy lights are hanging around them in arcs across the lawn. They cast an eerie glow. And without warning, Robert Gerrish steps out of the shadows. He's frowning, and he looks hot and irritated. He glances at his wife briefly, but he hones in on Claire.

'My dear Claire,' he says, in the pompous tones he's adopted since becoming a public figure. 'There seems to have been a terrible misunderstanding.'

Claire slips her hand into the clutch bag and her fingers find the knife. In seconds, it will all be over. She grasps it firmly. Her body tenses, ready to strike.

This is it. For Ella.

Gerrish is little more than a foot away. She can smell the sweat on him. 'Whatever stories you've heard are just malicious gossip,' he says. 'Ella had some problems. I think we all knew that. But we did nothing to exacerbate them.'

What problems? The bastard's trying to blame Ella!

'All I've ever done is try to help you, Claire. And you throw this at me?' His voice has become a petulant whine. 'Why?'

His jacket is open. The white shirt front has a line of pearl buttons down the middle. Claire focuses her gaze on them.

Aim for the centre. Below the ribs. The soft gut.

It all seems to happen in a flash. Her right hand is holding the knife. She starts to bring it out of the bag in order to strike, when she's barged aside.

Adrian?

His fist is clenched, his arm pulled back, and he takes a swing at Gerrish. The blow misses his face and lands on his shoulder. Gerrish staggers backwards, but rights himself, and rushes at Adrian, seizing him by the throat.

'You fucking bastard!' Gerrish screams.

The two men claw ferociously at one another as two figures appear from nowhere, sprinting across the lawn towards them.

Claire stands immobile, her right hand in the bag, still holding the knife.

26

Boden is running. She's hard on Foley's heels, but he gets there first. They heard an angry shout. On the lawn in the middle of the quad, two men are in a vicious tussle, rocking each other from side to side, like incompetent wrestlers. One of them is the Minister, Robert Gerrish.

Foley weighs in between them, using his bulk to force them apart. He pushes Gerrish backwards towards the wall and contains him with a bear hug. Boden throws her arm round the neck of the other man from behind and drags him backwards. She grabs his arm and forces it up behind his back in an armlock. It's only then that she realises she's got hold of Adrian Cardello, the movie star.

Gerrish is shouting. 'He attacked me! He fucking attacked me! Arrest him!'

'It's okay, sir,' says Foley. 'It's over.'

'You're a piece of shit,' yells Cardello, pulling forward. 'You always were.' It takes all Boden's strength the hang on to him. She jams his arm further up his back to immobilise him.

'Aargh, for Chrissake,' he wails.

'Calm down, sir,' says Boden. 'And I'll let you go.'

'You don't let him go. He's under arrest,' shouts Gerrish. 'And that's a fucking order!'

There are two women hovering, looking totally aghast. Boden recognises one of them: Gerrish's wife. And she steps forward.

'Shut up, Robert,' she says firmly. 'You're behaving like schoolboys and you both need to calm down.'

Foley releases the Minister but keeps him corralled in the corner. 'I want him arrested,' says Gerrish, in a peevish voice.

'No, you don't,' says the wife. 'Because it'll be all over tomorrow's front pages, won't it? And you'll look a complete fool. So it's the last thing you want.'

Boden loosens her grip on Cardello's arm. His shoulders relax and he exhales. 'You should listen to her, Rob,' he says. 'Because she's a million times smarter than you. Should be her in the government, not a dipshit like you.'

Gerrish lunges forward, but Foley grabs him.

'Okay, I'm taking charge of this situation,' says Foley. 'I've no idea what this is about. That's not my business. But it's over. Right? Are we agreed on that?'

Gerrish inhales. His fist is still clenched.

'Are we agreed?' says Foley.

The Minister exhales and nods. He wipes his face with the back of his hand. 'Ask him. He started it.'

Cardello points a threatening finger at the Minister. 'I'm not going to let you hurt Claire,' he says.

Boden and Foley both turn to look at the other woman.

'You're Claire?' says Foley.

The woman is pale and visibly shaking. 'Yes,' she whispers.

'It was a personal matter,' says Gerrish's wife. 'A misunderstanding.'

Something more than that from the look on Claire's face.

Boden turns to Claire. 'Are you alright?' she says.

Claire looks up at her, eyes full of tears. 'I feel a bit…unwell.'

Boden gently takes her arm. 'C'mon, let's go and sort you out,' she says.

As soon as Boden has hold of her, Claire leans in towards her. She's trembling. 'Thank you,' she whispers.

Boden leads her back towards the gallery. Two other close protection officers come hurrying the other way; they're the two who should've had eyes on the Minister. She gives them a nod. Foley is not going to be pleased with them.

As the evening has progressed, things have become far more raucous and unpredictable. It's been dark for about an hour. But the college is a warren of nooks and crannies and ill-lit passageways. Foley decided to keep two officers on the Minister and deploy everyone else on sweeps of the whole site. If there was a threat, it was impossible to determine where it would come from.

Having eyes everywhere was a nightmare.

DC Mackie had been in and out of the kitchens. But the boy whose behaviour had caused concern earlier, Reece Davison, turned out to be a nervous drug dealer, not a nervous would-be assassin. Just as the guests were sitting down to dinner, Mackie caught him red-handed, checking his drugs stash. It was in a backpack, hidden in a store cupboard. Davison was lifted, quietly nicked, and was now out of the equation. But they're no further forward with identifying the supposed threat.

Boden escorts Claire away from the scene of the ludicrous fight. She feels even less sympathy for Gerrish, and she had little before. How can Foley work for these idiots?

'Where are we going?' says Claire.

The Bursar has given the police a suite of rooms on the ground floor near the Porter's Lodge. Boden is heading in that direction.

'Somewhere you can use the bathroom and take some time out. Do you feel like telling me what happened?'

Claire shakes her head emphatically.

'Are you hurt?'

She doesn't reply.

It's clear something has happened to her tonight, and it's not good. She's deathly pale and off-balance as she walks. Boden keeps a hand under her elbow to steady her; Claire doesn't object.

'Has something upset you?' says Boden.

Claire says nothing.

'Maybe I can help you?' says Boden.

'I don't want to talk about it,' says Claire. 'In fact, I just want to go back to my room.'

'Okay. You seem a little unsteady. At least let me escort you there.'

Claire shoots her a nervous glance and nods. 'I'm just a bit dizzy,' she says. 'I'm on some tablets from the doctor. You shouldn't drink alcohol with them. And I have. Stupid really.'

'It's easily done,' says Boden.

They walk on in silence. The room is on the third floor, up a steep flight of stone steps. Claire has to pause for breath several times on the way up.

It strikes Boden, she's suffering some form of shock. But she can't be coerced into speaking and it would be wrong to try.

When they finally get to the door, Boden pulls out one of her business cards.

'Listen,' she says. 'Put this number in your phone. I'm on duty here all night. I don't know the Minister and I'm not part of his team. I'm a local officer. DS Boden. If you need anything, or you just want to talk, ring my mobile. Okay?'

Claire takes the card and looks at it. 'Thank you,' she says. 'You've been very kind. I don't deserve it.'

'Make sure you drink some water. And get some sleep.'

Claire nods. Boden heads back down the stairs.

She doesn't deserve it?

Why the hell would she think that? The detective in Boden can't help wondering.

27

Saturday, 10.18pm

Leanne knows she must get control of the situation and keep control of it. But she's shocked. She can't quite believe what she actually saw.

Claire Naylor reached in her bag and she was pulling something out. Leanne only caught a glimpse, but it looked like a blade.

WTF? A knife? It was a knife.

Plus, she had an eerily detached look on her face. But that's only part of the problem here, and for now, Leanne needs to park that up.

The only thing that's keeping her husband and Adrian Cardello apart is the close protection officer, DI Foley.

Robert is steaming and still intent on some kind of retribution.

He's sneering at Cardello. 'You've always resented me, haven't you?' he says. 'Because I'm smarter than you and you're just an over-entitled pretty boy.'

She needs to close this altercation down now before anyone notices. The last thing they want is footage of Robert and Cardello arguing to pop up online and go viral.

'You're just a greedy wanker banker like all the rest of them,' says Cardello. 'Really nothing more than a thug with a laptop.'

'Okay,' says Leanne, holding up her hand. 'Time out. This has to stop right now.'

'It stops when I say it stops,' snaps Robert. He's still splenetic with fury, which isn't helping.

'I think, sir, you should listen to your wife,' says Foley.

'Really?' says Robert. 'And where were my protection officers when this madman attacked me?'

'I'll be looking into that,' says Foley.

'Yeah, you fucked up,' says Robert. 'And I'll be looking into that too and speaking to the Commissioner personally.'

Leanne glances at the massive police officer. He's staring straight back at Robert; he's inscrutable and unfazed by the threat. Leanne wonders what he thinks of them. She suspects he despises them.

'Shall I escort you back to the suite, sir?' he says calmly.

'That's a good idea. Thank you, Inspector,' says Leanne. Then she turns to her husband. 'Just go with him, Robert, and calm down.'

Her husband meets her gaze. She sees what the others don't, the vulnerability behind the bolshy facade. The fear. He's badly shaken and raw with humiliation. It's obvious he gave close protection the slip in order to have a quiet and private word with Claire. He thought he could explain. That she'd simply accept what he had to say.

How could either of them have known that they were way beyond that?

She had a knife, for Chrissake!

On top of all this, it was Adrian Cardello wading in to protect Claire.

Did he know about the knife?

Robert has always nursed a brooding resentment against Cardello. Leanne isn't sure why. It could be pure jealousy. Cardello was the top alpha male of his year; an actor, a sportsman, and he graduated with a First. Everything seemed to come easily to him. Women fell over themselves to get his attention. It was hard not to rail against the unfairness of that. As far as Leanne is aware, Cardello has never bullied Robert; it's not his style. He's relentlessly nice to everyone. That's the kind of confidence and charisma he has, which in itself is nauseating.

And how can he call them greedy when he earns millions prancing around in front of a camera? He's just a hypocrite.

You can't react. Get control.

She smiles at her husband and puts a gentle hand on his arm. 'It's been a long and stressful day, darling,' she says. 'You've delivered a barnstorming speech; you must be exhausted. Go back to the rooms, put your feet up and have a whiskey. You deserve it.'

What she doesn't say is 'leave me to deal with Cardello.' But he knows her well enough to understand her intention. They're a team. This is how they operate.

Robert gives her a curt nod, wipes his face with his palm and stalks off. DI Foley follows him.

Leanne turns to face Adrian Cardello. 'What the hell was that about?' she says. 'You seem to be getting confused with one of your on-screen personas.'

He gives her a sardonic smile, hands resting on his hips. 'I was trying to protect Claire,' he says.

'From what? From us?'

More like from herself.

She takes a beat, then she sighs. 'How long is it since you've seen Claire?'

'Oh, I dunno,' he replies. 'Years.'

'Exactly. Adrian, listen to me. Claire is deranged with grief. She's got this obsession that Ella was unfairly blamed for something she didn't do, and that drove her to suicide.'

'And did it?' he says.

Leanne throws out her hands. 'I don't know why she killed herself. But I know Robert wasn't involved in whatever happened to her at the office. The idea of giving Ella an internship was to help her. And believe me, she needed it.'

'What do you mean?'

Now you've got his attention.

'I stayed in touch with Claire,' she says. 'Being a single mother was tough for her. I watched Ella grow up, albeit at a distance. She was bright, but she struggled as a teenager.'

His chin is trembling. The adrenaline is still pumping. He tips his head back and inhales. He's calming himself down; she hopes her husband is doing the same.

'You know what Claire told me?' he says. 'She told me I'm Ella's father.'

Wow!

That is news. Leanne tries not to react.

'Really?' she says. 'You think she's telling the truth?'

He wipes his forehead with his palm. 'What do you think? Why would she lie about something like that?'

Leanne can think of several reasons. What better way to get him onside?

She takes the bull by the horns. 'Look, you care about Claire, and so do I. But if she continues with this crazy campaign against Robert, it'll end badly. Very badly.'

She meets his eye. And there's the look.

He knows about the knife.

'I'll make you a promise,' she says. 'If Ella was wrongly accused of some leak, I will find out who's responsible.'

'Can you do that?'

'Yes, and I will. We must stop her, Adrian. Stop the accusations and get her the help and support she needs.'

He dips his head.

'You know I'm right,' she says.

He's about to reply, but Melissa Rowe is strolling down the corridor towards them with a glass in her hand.

'This sounds like a nice little conspiracy you two are cooking up?' she says. 'I was wondering where everyone had got to. I've just seen the big beefy, black cop wrangling poor old Robbie. I have to say, the Minister looked as if he'd got something painful stuck up his arse. What's been going on? And where's Claire? She's not in the toilets, because I looked.'

Leanne takes a deep breath. She needs to keep her temper, but this must be contained.

Adrian glances at Leanne, then he says, 'You're completely bombed, Mel. Go and stick your head in a bucket somewhere.' He turns on his heel and walks off.

Melissa shrugs. 'I guess he doesn't love me anymore. But then did he ever? Just out of interest, Leanne, did you ever shag him?'

Leanne looks at her. Melissa is definitely on some form of narcotic, and coupled with the booze, her capacity to figure any of this out is going to be impaired.

'No,' says Leanne evenly.

'Actually, I believe you,' says Melissa, 'because how do we put this nicely? He's not into bestiality.'

Leanne feels the venom wash over her. It's like acid; it still burns like hell. Not that she's about to let it show.

'Have you got anything specific you want to say to me, Melissa? Because I'd like to rejoin the party.'

Melissa pulls out her phone. 'Yes,' she says. 'I wouldn't mind a comment in your capacity as the Minister's spouse. A colleague of mine in London has been doing a bit of digging at my request. So far he's turned up three shell companies with offshore accounts, that he can connect to the Minister, and which don't appear in the register of interests of members of Parliament.'

She's bluffing.

Leanne sighs. 'I'm not going to comment. You're just on a fishing trip. When he came into government, Robert's financial affairs were closely scrutinised, and by better journalists than you. His investments are in a blind trust and he pays his taxes.'

'And what about the so-called attack at his constituency office?'

'It's being investigated by the police. And there's nothing so-called about it. My husband could've been killed. This is getting ridiculous. Why are you picking on us? Apart from pure spite.'

Melissa drains her glass. 'You think this is spite?' she says. 'Babe, you ain't seen nothing yet.'

She puts her index and middle fingers together to look like a gun, points it at Leanne's head. 'Bam, bam,' she says. Then she laughs. 'I need another drink.'

Leanne watches her saunter off.

She takes a deep breath. She never expected the college reunion to be fun. It was work, for her and for Robert. Now she wishes they could just get in the official car and be whisked back to London and away from this nightmare. She wants desperately to see her children, her two beautiful girls.

She imagines peeping into their rooms, where they'll be sound asleep.

She feels for Claire, she really does. If she lost Allegra or Sybil, it would drive her round the bend too. No doubt about that. She wonders if she should speak to Foley about this, because it is a threat. But if Robert found out Claire Naylor had some kind of mad plan to stab him, what impact would that have? All sorts of old wounds would be reopened. And behind all this, is Kieran and his shenanigans. That's the way out of this. Discover and expose what Kieran actually did to Ella Naylor. Make him carry the can.

Once Melissa sobers up, she'll start thinking like a hack again. Or at least her editor will. Leanne just needs to bide her time. Throw them some red meat, they'll take it.

28

Saturday, 10.30pm

Claire is stretched out on her bed. She kicked off her shoes, but she still has her dress on. The gold chain of her bag snakes across her bare arm, but she has the bag itself firmly clasped against her hip. She's not sure how long she's been like this.

Her brain is numb, with thoughts circling in her head like an echo chamber. Her mind keeps throwing up disjointed flashbacks. The smell of his sweat. The pearl buttons on his white shirt. She wonders if she's going to be sick.

Then she hears a sound. It's coming from far away. Tapping? On the door? There's a voice. She freezes. No one can find her here. She must hide.

'Claire. It's me, Adrian. I know you're there. Let me in.'

She doesn't move.

How does he know? The cop?

'Claire, c'mon. I can help you.'

'Go away,' she shouts.

'No. I won't. So you may as well open the door.'

He's right.

She sits up, swings her legs over the side of the bed and gets slowly to her feet. The bag drops from her shoulder and lands on the floor. She stares at it for a moment. Then she goes to the door and unlocks it.

Adrian steps into the room.

'You okay?' he says.

She sighs. How can she sound less insane that she's feeling?

'Yeah,' she says. 'It's just the tablets I'm on. I shouldn't drink with them.'

He hunches his shoulders and slots his hands in his pockets. 'What the fuck were you about to do, Claire?'

She reels at his tone. 'Nothing,' she says defensively.

He scans the room. 'Where's your bag?'

Her gaze skitters to it; she can't help it.

'Why?' she says, reaching down to pick it up.

But he's there before her. He swoops down and grabs the bag from her outstretched fingers.

'No!' she shouts. 'No, don't!'

He moves away from her. 'Why? What am I going to find? I saw you, Claire. I saw you reach in this bag.'

He puts his hand inside the bag and pulls out the knife. Staring at it, he says, 'You really were going to try to kill him, weren't you?'

Her pulse is thudding in her ears.

Is he right? Were you?

'When you talked about killing Gerrish,' he says, 'I didn't want to believe it. But I've been watching you, the tension in you, and I realised you were psyching yourself up to do something.'

'You should've let me,' she says. 'I don't care if I spend the rest of my life in jail.'

He stares at the knife in his hand. 'Don't be naïve,' he says. He holds the knife up. 'This is a serious blade. As soon as you pulled this out and lunged at him, his protection detail would've shot you dead. They're all armed. They wouldn't have hesitated.'

Is that true?

It's something she's never considered; what anyone would do in response.

Adrian is shaking his head in disbelief. 'You didn't even think of that, did you?'

'No,' she says. 'I didn't.'

'How did you think they'd respond? He's a government minister, a target. That's why he has armed protection.'

It had never occurred to her. But would it have made any difference?

She plonks down on the bed and sighs.

'I feel very confused,' she says.

'And what if you're wrong about Gerrish?'

'I'm not wrong.'

You know exactly what he is.

'But have you considered all the permutations?' he says. 'What exactly did Ella tell you?'

'That they accused her of leaking the email. And sacked her?'

'Who accused her? Rob? What happened? Was she called into his office?'

'I don't know.'

'Claire, it's far more likely that one of his minions did this. And Leanne says she's going to get to the bottom of it.'

It's like a slap across the face.

'You've been speaking to Leanne?'

'Yes, just now.'

He perches on the bed next to her and takes her hand. 'Listen to me. I'm going to help you. And we're going to get to the truth together. But you're caught up in a blind obsession here. Don't you see that? This is craziness. It's not the answer to anything.'

What does he know?

Her head is thumping. It feels as if it might burst. The sweat prickles on her neck. She can feel the bile rising in her throat. She jumps to her feet, rushes over to the washbasin and vomits.

29

Saturday, 10.35pm

Mel pulls the sachet of coke from her pocket. It's nearly empty. She sits on a stone bench in a semi-lit part of the gardens, tips the remains of the powder onto her knuckle and gives herself a little top-up.

The tables have been cleared away in the Great Hall, and a disco is in progress. A terrible selection of grunge and alternative rock is leaking from the open doorway. It sounds odd as it floats across the quad and round the ancient stonework that comprises much of the college. An affront almost to the history of the place. The thrumming base. The ear-splitting electronic whine. This is a place for choirs; madrigals and Gregorian chants. For a short while, Mel was in the college choir. But her voice wasn't really good enough and they booted her out.

Mel put her head into the disco, but only for a couple of minutes. Small gaggles of dark figures were gyrating wildly;

in the red strobe lights they looked like demons trying to escape the fiery pit of hell. She retreated.

Where is everyone?

She tried to find out Claire or Adrian's room numbers, but there was no one sober enough to give her that information.

Dusting the coke from her hand, she feels at a loss. Empty and lonely. These people were once her friends. But like everyone else in her life, it turns out they were not to be relied upon.

Cardello, she gets it. He was a boy led by his dick. But Claire was her best friend. At least, she thought she was. She never understood why Claire became so chummy with Leanne Brady. Leanne was a fright, with her ridiculously uncool M&S outfits and her squeaky voice. Perhaps Claire felt sorry for her? But in their last year, Claire seemed to spend more and more time with Leanne. As if it was a choice, something she wanted to do. She seemed to prefer Leanne to Mel. Not so surprising perhaps, if she was secretly screwing Cardello at the time. Or maybe it wasn't that much of a secret?

She wonders who else knew about it. Everyone probably. Everyone but her. They made her a laughingstock. Maybe Leanne and Claire even joked about it behind her back?

People always let you down. Back then, you were just too young and stupid to see it.

Mel wipes her nose with her fingertips. This is not as good as her usual stuff. Not the strength of hit she's come to rely upon. Probably cut with all kinds of crap. Another reason she should've stayed in London.

Her mind drifts back there. To the job. If she's brutally honest, work is all she has. It's the only thing that gives her life enough shape and purpose to prevent her slipping into the abyss. And when she's not working, she ends up like this. She should probably go to rehab. But what would be the point? Picking over your past to discover why you've made such a car crash of your life.

You know why.

Back in the day, she never intended to be a journalist. Claire was the writer, not her. She studied economics and she wanted to be at the centre of the action, not just a bystander reporting on it. She took part in Student Union debates, and wasn't that bad. She had a sharp brain, and she made people laugh. Then somehow, after it all went shit-shaped with Adrian, she lost her nerve. She decided a career in politics was too hard.

What the hell happened?

Truth is she didn't actually decide; it was more that she wavered. She told herself a few years as a journalist would be a good springboard. Plenty of others had travelled that route. Feminism's all very well, but women in mainstream politics get torn to shreds; you need the hide of a rhino. She saw that and she bottled out. Leanne went for the smart option: the political wife. Power without the exposure.

Women exercising power from behind the scenes, through their man, they get a pass, always have, because they're not a threat. Women who want to be powerful in their own right, they get stoned. In some countries, literally.

Now she can see all those youthful dreams and ambitions about who they'd be and what they'd do were way off the mark. Except perhaps in the case of Cardello.

Rob Gerrish was a maths genius. Everyone knew that. It was assumed he'd stay in academia. But perhaps he just didn't want to be poor. If she'd known back then how things would turn out, she might have made some different choices. Rob was besotted with Claire; he made no secret of it. She wasn't interested. But she was really prissy about sex. She dated, but didn't want to have a full-blown relationship with anyone; it was a distraction from her studies and her writing. That's what she said. Or perhaps that's what she told Mel, because she was secretly shagging her boyfriend?

Mel had a bit of a secret thing with Rob for a while, in retaliation for the infidelities of Cardello that she knew about. But she was Rob's second choice, and she wasn't about to settle for that. No way.

Then he goes from you to Miss Piggy!

That was just rude. Or was it because somewhere, deep in his psyche, he was trying to get as close as he could to Claire? Who can figure the fucked up workings of the human mind?

To add insult to injury, the Gerrishs have morphed into this power couple.

And that could've been you.

Over the years, Mel has wondered how she got everything so spectacularly wrong. Rob was a numbers geek. His grasp of politics was rudimentary; he was a blank canvas. Mel could've educated him, given him a more liberal bent. Together they really could've been change makers, to use the stupid expression from his after-dinner speech.

Why did you never see it?

Marriages that succeed are pragmatic partnerships. She realised that when her own short-lived union went painfully wrong. Her husband was simply a low-rent Cardello clone. He looked a bit like him, although much less handsome. He was a TV writer, and a self-pitying drunk. They had a few memorable times, mostly based around booze. Then it transpired he'd got his script editor pregnant. He left her to 'do the right thing', that's what he said.

What torments her now is why was she was never clear-sighted enough to figure any of this out back when it counted.

Leanne did. Leanne has always had a laser vision of what she wanted.

Mel's mistake was to let immature infatuation grow into an obsessive passion. She loved Adrian Cardello blindly and beyond reason. The obvious lack of reciprocity she ignored. All she ever wanted, ever dreamed of, was for him to recognise the depths of her love for him, and he never did. He could do sexual passion, and initially that fooled her into thinking it was love. But she soon discovered he could do sexual passion with any girl he fancied. Her fixation on him was a compulsion. She couldn't let go of it. She tried so hard to please him, and he still rejected her. Much like her father. And that seems to be a pattern in her life.

You don't need an expensive shrink to tell you that.

But seeing Cardello again has made it worst, because she realises perhaps she never has let it go. Now it's there in front of her, plain as day, the symmetry. Her love for Adrian and her hatred of Leanne. They're the opposite sides of the same stupid coin. The man she wanted. The woman she should've become.

There it is in a nutshell. The epic failure of your useless life.

She knew coming to the reunion would be a mistake. That's why she resisted it. And all it's brought her is a deepening sense of desolation.

And she's about to run out of coke.

She could just go back into the stupid disco and dance with the demons.

Maybe, or maybe not.

30

Saturday, 10.40pm

Leanne is on the phone to Melissa Rowe's editor. They're at opposite ends of the political spectrum, but they have a cordial acquaintance. The editor has clearly been drinking; Saturday night, after all, and that helps loosen her tongue.

'Mel is Mel,' she says. 'This is why she wins awards.'

'She told me she was doing some digging into my husband's financial affairs. But that's old news. And she's asking me about the attack at his constituency office. This is getting very personal.'

There's an audible sigh at the other end of the line. 'What exactly do you want, Leanne?'

'I want you to rein her in.'

'Mel follows her nose,' says the editor breezily. 'Her instincts are usually good.'

Sticks too much coke up her nose, thinks Leanne to herself. But she doesn't say that.

'Anyway,' says the editor. 'I thought you two were old

friends. Talk to her or don't talk to her. It's your choice. Everything will have to be corroborated, you know that. And I'm sure it isn't personal.'

Leanne's sure it is. She hangs up and takes a turn about the gardens. The cooler night air helps clear her head. There's a danger this whole situation could get out of hand. If she tells Foley about the knife she thinks she saw, it could morph into something extremely ugly. However crazy Claire is, arresting her would create more of a nightmare. A grieving mother will always play better in the media than a politician.

But what if Claire and Melissa are in league, which is entirely possible? It could prove a toxic combination and all because bloody Kieran was trying to cover his miserable arse for some stupid play of his that went tits up.

By the time Leanne gets back to the suite of rooms, she's seething. No sign of Foley, but there are two close protection officers on the door and, from the sound of the raised voices within, her husband is safely inside.

She's smiles at the cop, and he opens the door for her.

Robert has taken her at her word and is gesturing with a rather large tumbler of whiskey. As he swings it in front of him, some of the amber liquid sloshes out.

Great! Now you've got to sort him out.

Kieran has his own glass and a sheepish look on his face. It's obvious they've been going at this for a while.

Robert glances at her. No smile. No contrition. But at least he's taking his anger out on Kieran.

'You bloody well need to sort this out!' he shouts. 'I'm not going to be taken down by your incompetence.'

'You won't be, boss,' says Kieran. 'I'll fix it. I promise.'

'Yeah, well, you better had. Because you and I, my friend, are very close to the end of the road here. Sort this or you're gone. And I'll make bloody sure no one else in government gives you a job.'

Robert turns to her, like a little boy looking for Mummy's approval. 'Hello, darling,' he says. He's swaying a little.

Leanne has a sudden memory of her own mother. *Why do you keep calling me darling, Leanne? It just sounds stuck up.*

She bats that away.

Kieran gives her a baleful look as he scurries past her and out of the door.

'Whiskey?' says Robert.

She nods. 'Just a small one.'

He picks up the bottle, pours a good inch into a fresh tumbler, and then tops up his own glass.

'Did you speak to Cardello?' he says.

She settles in one of the leather armchairs. 'Yeah, I don't think he's going to be putting it on his Twitter feed.'

He hands her the glass and she takes a small sip.

'You alright?' he says with a frown. He knows she's angry.

She sighs. 'All these years. All the things we've achieved together, and you've still got a thing about her, haven't you?'

He takes a swallow of whiskey. 'No, course not. That's rubbish.'

'You saying you didn't ditch your close protection, so you could get near to her and have a private conversation?'

'It's not what you think.'

'What am I supposed to think?'

'It's coming back here. Just an attack of youthful nostalgia. Claire was like a mirage. A beautiful girl who bewitched everyone. I was just a stupid boy. But she had loads of blokes after her.'

'Did you ever sleep with her?'

'No!'

'I don't care who else you lie to, but don't lie to me, Robert.'

'I'm not. I swear. She wouldn't have looked twice at me. And thank God for it. Look at her now. She's a total mess. Neurotic as hell. She could never have been the sort of wife I needed, the sort of wife you are to me. She couldn't have coped with any of it.'

Leanne examines her husband's face.

If he only knew just how neurotic.

She decides to leave that alone. There's nothing to be gained by telling him.

She gazes up at him. Drunk and sweaty, a combination of bombast and nerves. He doesn't enjoy dealing with people that much. Feels they're judging him. He's not naturally gregarious. He's had to learn how to do it. But in other ways, he's brilliant. He's proved a wizard at finance. It suits his brain, and it's made them seriously rich. And he wants power as much as she does.

She offers him her hand. 'You mean that?' she says.

He takes her hand and awkwardly gets down on one knee in front of her, his belly straining against the waistband of his trousers. He puts her hand to his lips. 'My darling, I do,' he says. 'From the bottom of my heart.'

She pulls him towards her, and they hug.

'You've drunk too much whiskey,' she says, stroking his bald pate.

'Yeah, I know. But listen. I've found out about this thing with Ella Naylor. Kieran was sleeping with that poor girl.'

'He's admitted that?'

'Yes. The leak came from him. He didn't expect it to be traced back to my office.'

'That's naïve.'

'I told him that. He used Ella. Shafted her to cover his own arse. That's most likely what messed with her head.'

'You knew nothing about it?'

'Course I didn't. The leak was a little black ops of his own. I never sanctioned it. The rest, his involvement with Ella, I knew nothing about.'

'You need to get rid of him.'

'Yeah, I know. You've been right about him all along. But I've told him to shut this thing down and deal with Melissa. Trust me, he's got the message.'

'You think he can sort it out?'

'Yes. He'll find a way. I've left him with no choice.'

Leanne considers this. She's not so sure. Leaving it to Kieran could be risky. He could easily make things worse.

31

Sunday, 12.05am

The official curfew for the disco is midnight. The loud thump of the music has stopped, leaving a disconcerting silence. The air is stagnant and oppressive. Boden is waiting outside the main door to the Great Hall when Foley joins her. Shepherding them all back to their rooms could take a while. But once that's done, the worst part of the night should be over.

Foley hands her a fresh bottle of water. 'Threat's been downgraded to amber,' he says.

Bullshit, then.

Boden cracks the top and takes a long drink. She gives Foley a tired smile. 'Well, no one's killed the Minister, although a movie star tried to break his nose. The demonstrators have all gone home. And we've nicked a drug dealer who was selling the party-goers coke.'

Foley nods and grins. 'I'd call that a good result all round.'

'Would you?'

'Seriously, Jo. When are you going to come home?'

She shrugs. 'My mum wants me to come back to London. Keeps badgering me.'

'All the stuff that happened, you can't be blamed for any of it. You exposed a killer who was also a corrupt cop.'

Boden sighs. 'Get real, Cal. That's why they'll never forgive me. You know what it's like. The omertà.'

'I think things are changing in the Met. They've got to.'

'To tell you the truth, I've got a boss whose old man is about to go on trial as a money launderer. So it's not much different here. I sometimes wonder why I do this job.'

'Because you're bloody good at it. Never forget that. This job attracts the best of people and the worst. That's always been the problem. But you are one of the best.'

Boden finds the compliment uncomfortable. Even in the darkness, she can see the way Foley is looking at her. It's why she's been avoiding him all this time. The attraction between them has never been spoken about, and as far as she's concerned, it never will be.

Why?

She's spent a couple of years now, avoiding that question. Allowing anyone to come close to her has always been a problem. Ever since her sister died. Now it's turned into a way of life. It's the armour that protects her. She needs it.

It looks like Foley is about to say more, but Boden raises her palm as she peers into the darkness.

Across the other side of the quad and the lawn is the college chapel. Boden wandered round it earlier. Compact but still majestic, it had a vaulted ceiling, fluted pilasters and columns, a raised chancel at the end of the nave, and above it a stained glass window.

But a figure has just come out of it and is gesticulating furiously in their direction. It takes a moment for Boden to realise it's Chakravorty. She and Mackie have been out walking the grounds on general surveillance.

'Something's up,' says Boden and she starts to run across the lawn. Foley follows her.

As she gets to Chakravorty, the DC says, 'Woman's been attacked. Head injury. Blood everywhere. Mackie's giving her CPR. She's in here.'

Chakravorty pushes open the heavy oak door and they step inside.

Mackie is on his knees, leaning over a prostrate figure, and administering chest compressions. Foley gets on his phone and calls for medical backup.

Boden scoots round him to the other side. 'I thought I had her for a minute,' says Mackie. 'But she's gone again.'

'Want me to take over?' says Boden. She kneels down on the other side. Foley is still on the phone. 'Head injuries,' he says. 'Looks like she's in cardiac arrest...'

Mackie rocks back on his heels, as Boden takes over the compressions.

Concentrate. Get it right.

She counts in her head. Three rounds, then she checks the pulse in the neck. Three more rounds. Check again. Yes. It's very faint, but it's there.

'I think she's still with us.'

'Paramedics on their way,' says Foley.

The only light in the chapel filters through leaded glass windows. Foley shines his phone torch over the scene.

'Who is she?' he says. 'One of the guests?'

Boden scans her face and then she recognises her. It's the journalist she talked to outside the back of the kitchens.

'I talked to her,' Boden says. 'She told me her name. I think it was Melissa. Yeah, that's it. Melissa Rowe.'

32

Sunday, 12.15am

Claire wakes with a start. The phone is over on the desk, and it's vibrating. Her thoughts are skittish and hard to grasp, but they begin to coalesce. She was sick. She can still taste bile in her mouth. Adrian put her to bed. Then he took the knife and he left. He told her to sleep and that he'd be back later.

She sits up slowly. The nausea has passed, but she's light-headed. She gets up, goes over to the phone and answers it. The call is from one of the organising committee. Garbled and confused, she can hardly make head nor tail of it.

'What?' she says. 'Could you slow down? I don't really understand.'

'Melissa Rowe,' says the disembodied voice. 'She's your friend, isn't she?'

'Yes.'

'They're taking her to hospital. She's in a pretty bad way. You should probably come down.'

Claire hangs up. She scrabbles under the bed for her shoes.

A pretty bad way? What does that mean?

Adrian said Mel was on something. Cocaine? Has she overdosed?

The urgency helps her focus. She still has her dress on. She discards the high heels and grabs a pair of trainers from her case.

Mel needs you.

She hurries down the stone staircase and across the lawn. There are people milling around near the Porter's Lodge. An ambulance is backed up in the gateway. Two paramedics are wheeling someone towards it, strapped to a trolley.

'Mel!' she shouts. It feels like a shout. But her voice is feeble and hoarse. She runs forward.

Adrian steps out of the crowd and moves towards her. He grabs her by the shoulders. The paramedics lift the trolley and slide it into the back of the ambulance.

'What the hell has happened?' she says. 'Is she going to be alright?'

'We don't know,' says Adrian. He looks worried.

The back doors of the ambulance close.

'I don't understand,' wails Claire.

No! You can't lose another one. Mel can't die!

Adrian holds her and rocks her.

The blue lights on the ambulance flash as it pulls out of the gateway and disappears.

'We must go to the hospital,' says Claire.

'Yeah,' he says, although he seems reluctant.

He puts his arm round her shoulder. They head towards the Porter's Lodge, but a woman is blocking their way. She pulls something out of her pocket and holds it up.

'I'm DS Boden,' she says. 'You're friends of Melissa's?'

'Yeah, but we need to get to the hospital,' says Adrian.

'I'll get someone to take you,' the cop says. 'But I just need to ask, when did you last speak to Melissa?'

Why is she asking this?

'Did she OD?' says Claire.

'She has head injuries consistent with an assault,' says the cop.

'What?' says Claire. An assault?

'Oh my god,' says Adrian. 'Last time I saw her was in the gallery. You were the one who dragged me off Gerrish, weren't you?'

'Yes,' says the cop.

'Well, after that, I was talking to Leanne Brady, Gerrish's wife. And Mel appeared.'

'Did you talk to her?'

'Just a couple of words. To be honest, she was pretty jacked up.'

'Jacked up?' says the cop.

Adrian sighs. 'I don't know. Drink? Drugs? Some combination of the two?'

'Was she in the habit of taking drugs?'

'I really couldn't tell you. I haven't seen her for years,' he says.

'What time did you see her?'

'Around ten thirty. I'm guessing. I walked off and left her with Leanne.'

The cop turns to Claire. 'What about you? What time did you last see her?'

The cop's gaze seems fierce, as if she can see right through you. It's unnerving. The tension and anxiety is ramping up inside Claire, and tying her stomach in knots.

'Earlier, I think,' she says. 'At the dinner. I haven't seen her since dinner.'

'Look, we need to get to the hospital,' says Adrian.

He knows we need to escape.

'Yes, of course,' says the cop.

She turns away and speaks to someone.

Adrian pulls Claire towards him. 'Are you alright?' he says.

'I don't understand. What did she mean? Head injuries?'

Adrian sighs. 'Sounds like someone attacked her. That's why the police are in a spin and asking all these questions.'

'Do you think she'll be okay?'

'I don't know. There was a commotion. I was in the bar. I came out and just caught a glimpse of her on the trolley. She had something round her head. Maybe a dressing?'

'Oh, my god. Poor Mel!'

More police are arriving. A car with lights flashing drives in through the gateway. It all looks rather confusing. Claire wishes she had her Ativan with her. She takes several deep breaths to calm her anxiety.

Then she notices Leanne hurrying towards them on the path. She's wearing a silk dressing gown and slippers.

'What on earth's going on?' she says.

'It's Mel,' says Adrian. 'They think someone's attacked her. They've just taken her to hospital.'

'Jesus wept! That's terrible! Did you speak to her?'

'She was unconscious,' says Adrian. 'We're going to the hospital.'

Leanne grasps Claire's hand. She's distraught. 'This is absolutely awful, Claire,' she says. 'You've got my number. Please keep me posted. Mel's tough as old boots. She'll pull through.' She squeezes Claire's hand. 'I'm sure she will.'

'Yes,' says Claire weakly. Being touched by Leanne feels extremely odd after what happened.

You were going to stab her husband.

Fortunately, Adrian is shepherding her away towards the Porter's Lodge. Everything is surreal. The pools of light around the buildings and the blackness behind them in the college grounds. Several of the police officers are heading across the grass towards the chapel.

She turns towards Adrian. 'Why would anyone attack Mel?' she says.

'I don't know,' he says.

'It makes no sense to me.'

Unless…Robert…

33

When Leanne gets back to the room, she finds her husband sitting on the side of the bed with his face in his hands.

'It's true,' she says. 'Melissa's unconscious. They've taken her to hospital.'

Robert raises his palms in exasperation. 'I never thought the stupid sod would take me literally!'

'Well, it looks like he did. Where is he?'

'I've no idea. Haven't seen him since we had words.'

Leanne shakes her head. Then she takes several steadying breaths and repeats a focusing mantra in her head.

Keep calm. Control the narrative.

'If she wakes up, she might be able to identify him,' says Robert.

'It's a horrible thing to say, but we'd better hope she doesn't wake up.'

Put it out there. Why not?

But her husband ignores the comment. 'Everything we've

worked for,' he says. 'Even if I can distance myself…and there's no guarantee that's possible if Kieran talks to the police. And, back against the wall, Kieran's likely to be a squealer.'

He's right about that.

Leanne sits beside him on the bed and takes his hand. 'Listen to me, darling. The important thing is not to panic. Let's be blunt about this. If she dies, we can manage the situation.'

'You think she will die?'

'I don't know. They're saying she's unconscious and the head injuries are serious. Fair chance, I'd say.'

He wipes his face with his palm. Too much alcohol and too much stress. 'I never intended him to do this,' he says.

'Course you didn't.'

'But I'll still be blamed, won't I? Cause he works for me.' He stands up, walks round in a circle like a caged beast.

Robert is a mathematician, supposedly a logical thinker. But when it comes to his emotions, he's impulsive and reactive. He can veer off at a tangent. In this respect, they're polar opposite. Leanne learnt early in life to plan and execute, never to just react.

'I'm cutting him loose. Right now!' Robert says.

'Is that entirely wise?'

He looks at her, and she can see the shadow of his younger self, the nervous boy. The deep uncertainty.

You made him. And only you can rescue him.

He sighs. 'I suppose not.'

'We need to think on our feet. Take one step at a time. And stay calm.'

He smiles at her. 'You're so good at this, aren't you?' he says. 'I don't know what I'd do without you.'

Yeah, now you think that!

She just smiles.

'It'll be alright,' she says. 'Choppy waters, but we'll get through them together. As we always do.'

There's a tap at the door. They exchange looks. Leanne gets up, goes over, and opens it. It's Foley.

'Come in, Inspector,' she says.

He steps into the room, as inscrutable as ever. 'I don't know if you're aware of what's happened,' he says.

Leanne throws up her hands in despair. 'Yes,' she says. 'Melissa. It's terrible. She's one of our oldest friends. Have you any idea what happened?'

'They found her in the chapel. The head injuries are severe. Looks like some kind of blunt force trauma to the skull.'

'Oh my god, that is so awful. Who would do such a terrible thing?'

'My colleagues from the local Major Investigations Team will be looking into it. But, in view of this, we're thinking you might wish to return to London sooner than planned.'

'Tonight, you mean?' says Robert.

'Well, if you think that's wise,' says Leanne.

'In such circumstances, we err on the side of caution,' says Foley.

'Well, I don't know that I can do anything useful here,' says Robert. 'Have you had any updates from the hospital?'

'My understanding is they've taken her straight into surgery,' says Foley.

'Well, we can only hope for the best outcome,' says Leanne.

'Absolutely,' says Robert. 'But, yes, I think we should go.'

'I'll give you some time to get ready,' says Foley.

Foley leaves.

Robert puts his hands on his hips. 'What do you think?' he says.

Leanne shrugs. 'She was pretty drunk. Maybe she flaked out in the chapel and didn't even see who hit her?'

'It's possible, isn't it?' he says.

'Let's just get dressed and packed and out of here.'

'What about Kieran?'

Leanne considers this for a moment. 'Once we're on the road, you send him a text. Say, on security advice, you've gone back to London. But you'll see him in the office on Monday.'

'As if I don't suspect him at all?'

'Exactly.'

Robert nods. 'Yeah, okay. I think you're right. Play this very straight, very cool. We don't know anything. The police'll start questioning people. But that'll take ages. No reason they should suspect Kieran, is there?'

'No,' she says. 'There isn't. She had a row with Adrian Cardello in the senior common room this morning. Plenty of people witnessed that. He'll be much higher up their list than Kieran.'

'You don't think it could be him, do you?'

'Darling, anything's possible.'

34

Sunday, 12.30am

After Melissa Rowe was discovered, Boden immediately reported the situation to DCI Knight on the phone. But it was not her expectation that the boss would turn up in person.

She glances at Foley as the DCI gets out of the back of a squad car.

'The money launderer's wife?' he says wryly.

Boden nods. 'She's got a lot to prove. I'm guessing that's why she's here.'

Knight sees her and heads straight for them.

'Jo,' she says. 'Quite a situation we have here.'

Boden nods. 'This is DI Foley, boss. Head of the Minister's close protection team.'

Rachel Knight gives him a tepid smile. 'Our patch, our case, Inspector,' she says.

'Oh absolutely,' says Foley. 'I'm just waiting to take the Minister back to London.'

'And I gather the victim is a friend of his,' says Knight.

'Well, yes. Sort of,' says Boden.

'Have you got an update on her?'

'Not yet,' says Boden. 'But I've sent DC Chakravorty to the hospital in case she regains consciousness.'

'Do we need armed officers there to protect the victim?' says Knight. 'Could an attack on the Minister's friend relate to the ongoing threat against him?'

'I don't know, boss,' says Boden.

She's been on her feet and on duty since seven am. She's sweated several buckets, changed her shirt twice, caught a drug dealer, and reconnected with the man she's been avoiding for the last two years, because she suspects he may be in love with her. And now she's got Rachel Knight on her back.

'The threat has been downgraded,' says Foley.

'Doesn't mean we should ignore it,' says Knight. 'Okay, you've done a long shift, Jo. But it's a good job I'm here.' She gets out her phone. 'Is the scene properly cordoned?'

Boden nods. 'Yes. And we've got a CSM and a forensics team on the way.'

Knight turns away to make a call.

Boden and Foley exchange looks. 'She's a delight,' he whispers.

'You're headed back to London then?' says Boden.

'Yeah, as soon as his nibs gets his stuff together.'

'It's been good to see you again.'

He shrugs. It's an awkward moment. 'She should let you go home,' he says. 'You're knackered.'

'We're also short-handed. So I'm not holding my breath,' says Boden.

Knight ends her call and turns back towards them. 'Right,' she says. 'That's sorted. We need to start taking witness statements.'

'I've got DC Mackie collecting the names and details of all the attendees at the reunion, so we can follow up,' says Boden.

'And I've got a couple of my lads giving him a hand,' says Foley. 'Just until we're off.'

Rachel Knight stares at Foley. 'Do you consider it a security risk for the Minister to remain here?' she says.

'Well, it depends what you mean,' says Foley. 'The advice to him was not to come. We had a red alert earlier. Now it's amber.'

'Yes, but his friend has been attacked, and is in a critical condition. So we need to interview him. Preferably tonight. Something has happened here. We need to understand what. I want to know if I'm looking for a terrorist, or someone attending this reunion.'

Foley raises his eyebrows. 'Okay,' he says. 'I'll go and give him the good news. I assume you want to talk to his wife as well.'

'Yes,' says Knight. 'Their original intention was to stay overnight, wasn't it?'

'It was,' says Foley.

'Then I don't see the problem,' says Knight.

Boden watches the DCI. She's demonstrating that she's now in the driving seat. And she is the SIO, so she's entitled to do that. This is a complicated and potentially high-profile case and her presence takes a weight off Boden's shoulders.

Foley walks off.

'He's a bit of a sarky bastard,' says Knight. 'Has he given you any trouble?'

That's Cal. Definitely a sarky bastard. It's why you get on with him.

'No,' says Boden, keeping a straight face. She's not about to reveal that they're old mates.

'Okay,' says Knight. 'Well, if this woman dies, this will turn into a media circus.'

'Particularly since she's a journalist,' says Boden.

'How do you know that?' says Knight.

'I talked to her. Or rather, she talked to me. She and Robert Gerrish were students together. But she doesn't like him. She told me she thinks the knife attack at his constituency office was a put-up job. She said she was thinking of digging into it deeper, building a story.'

'Against the Minister?'

'Yes, that's what it sounded like.'

'Umm, that's interesting. Wonder if he knew? All the more reason to talk to him now.'

'Do you want to look at the crime scene?' says Boden. 'We found her in the chapel.'

'What was your initial reading of it?'

In between trying to save her life.

'Well,' says Boden. 'We found her in the aisle. Looks like blunt force trauma to the back of the head. But I'm wondering if she was sitting in a pew and someone came in and attacked her from behind, and she fell sideways into the aisle.'

'It's a good working theory.' Knight hesitates, then she adds, 'I'm glad it's you on the ground. You're a good cop, Jo.'

Two compliments in one day?

'Thanks, boss,' she says.

35

Sunday, 12.35am

'What?' says Robert. 'She's got a bloody cheek. We're ready to go. I will not answer questions tonight. She needs to make an appointment with my office.'

Foley says nothing.

Leanne tilts her head. 'I think we should consider the optics of this, darling,' she says.

'Fucking police are always throwing their weight about. No offence, Foley.'

'None taken.'

'Does she know I'm a bloody Cabinet Minister?'

'Yes,' says Foley. 'But perhaps she's trying to be helpful by talking to you now. Then she won't need to bother you later.'

Leanne scans the DI. He's always a diplomat, but you get the impression he could easily rip your head off if the need arose. He carries that hint of danger, or perhaps it's just that he's a cop with a gun in a holster under his jacket.

'Robert,' she says. 'Law and order. We support the police one hundred per cent.'

'Course we do. Goes without saying,' says her husband.

'Apparently, I do need to say it. You're tired, darling. You've had a bit to drink and you just want to go home. I think everyone understands that. But this is important. We need to do this for Melissa.'

He sighs and flops down in a chair. 'Bring it on, Foley.'

'What's her name again?' says Leanne.

'Detective Chief Inspector Knight. She's just arrived. She'll be the Senior Investigating Officer in the inquiry.'

'Fine. I think we should definitely speak to her,' says Leanne.

Take the bull by the horns. Then you know what you're dealing with.

Foley takes out his phone and makes a quick call.

Robert gives her a sulky look. He's irritated and could easily do something stupid here. She subdues him with a look.

Foley hangs up. 'She's on her way.'

They wait for several minutes in silence. Robert is quietly brooding. But it gives Leanne a chance to order her thoughts. She goes over to the window and stares out into the darkness, mainly to avoid Foley's scrutiny.

The room overlooks the main quad. It's the oldest part of the college. The chapel is directly opposite, across the lawn. The portico is topped with a pediment and a triangular gable. They've opened the double doors wide, and there's a great deal of activity outside and around the entrance. Arc lights have been set up, the entire area cordoned, and police in white suits are unpacking their gear.

She sees two women walking across the lawn towards their staircase. As they get closer, she recognises one of them.

The cop who intervened in the fight and took Claire Naylor away. There's the added complication of that to deal with. She assumes the other one is the DCI. Two women, which may make her task easier.

By the time the tap at the door comes, Leanne is primed and ready. Foley opens it and Leanne steps forward immediately.

'I'm Leanne Brady,' she says. 'The Minister's wife. This is such an awful situation, and we're really glad to have the opportunity to speak to you in person, Chief Inspector.'

The cop accepts the handshake. 'DCI Knight,' she says. 'My colleague, DS Boden.' She's poker-faced, but they're all a bit like that. It's the training.

Robert is on his feet and offers his hand to shake too. 'Robert Gerrish,' he says. 'What can I say? We're in total shock. Do you have any news about Mel?'

He sounds earnest, which is good.

'She's undergoing surgery,' says Knight. 'That's all we know at the moment.'

'Well, since we heard what happened,' says Leanne, 'Robert and I have discussed this. And we feel we absolutely must tell you everything we know.'

'Do you mind if we record this?' says Knight.

'Not at all,' says Leanne. 'Shall we sit down?'

Take control and keep control.

The two police officers sit side by side on the small sofa. They look uncomfortable next to each other. The other officer, Boden, takes out her phone, presses record and sets it on the coffee table. Leanne and Robert take the two armchairs. Foley remains standing by the door.

Leanne steeples her fingers. 'I'm going to keep this simple and straightforward. I don't know if you're film fans, but you probably know who Adrian Cardello is.'

'Yes, and we know he's here for the reunion,' says Knight.

'When we were all students, Adrian and Melissa were involved in what I can only describe as a tempestuous relationship. But it wasn't just a twosome, it was a threesome. Melissa's best friend, Claire Naylor, was the third wheel, so to speak. I'm fairly certain these three haven't seen each other for many years. But when they came back together today, there were fireworks.'

Leanne turns to Boden. 'The fight you had to intervene in earlier was part of that.'

Knight glances at her colleague. A look passes between them.

They haven't discussed it. Good.

This will help keep Leanne in the driving seat. 'Some months ago, Claire Naylor suffered a terrible bereavement,' she says. 'Her daughter took her own life. And it's no exaggeration to say that Claire has been unhinged with grief. I know this because Robert and I have remained friends with her. We knew her daughter, and we've tried our best to give her our support. What Melissa discovered earlier today is that Adrian, who she had been completely in love with, was the father of Claire's daughter.'

'She got pregnant back when you were all students?' says Knight.

'Yes,' says Leanne. 'It happened around the time of graduation, which is twenty-five years ago. Ella Naylor was twenty-four when she took her own life. Adrian didn't know he was the father until today, when Claire told him. Melissa didn't know her best friend and her boyfriend had betrayed her. Until today.'

'You're saying this was a very combustible situation?' says the DCI.

Robert is giving her a sidelong glance. She hopes he has the good sense to keep his mouth shut.

'Exactly,' says Leanne. 'Through the course of the day, Melissa got very drunk and confrontational. So did Adrian. I think she also has a bit of a drug habit. They had a row this morning, in the senior common room, which a number of people witnessed. I don't know why Claire opened this particular can of worms now. But she did. She is not in a good frame of mind.'

The cop nods. She seems to be taking all this seriously, which is essential for the deflection to work.

Leanne sighs. 'When Robert and I attempted to speak to Claire to calm things down, Adrian rushed forward and attacked my husband. He was drunk. I suppose he was feeling guilty and wanted belatedly to be protective. Claire Naylor has had a difficult life as a single parent, and after Ella's death, her resentments seem to have come to a head. I don't know what happened, and I'm not going to speculate. But what I know is Claire blamed Melissa for the fact Adrian in effect abandoned her. And Melissa felt betrayed by Claire, who she now thinks took Adrian away from her. Adrian discovered he had a daughter he didn't know about, but that she was dead.'

Robert is shifting uncomfortably in his seat. She wills him to stay out of it.

'Sounds a very complicated mix,' says Knight.

'It is Chief Inspector. And when you add to that mix lots of alcohol, possibly drugs, and the fact Claire Naylor is in a very unstable frame of mind, frankly, some kind of confrontation seemed likely.'

'Are you suggesting Claire Naylor may have attacked Melissa Rowe, or that they had some kind of fight?'

Leanne raises her palms. 'I'm not suggesting anything.

Really, I have no idea. I'm just trying to provide you with the backstory to some of what's been going on here. I know it all seems a long time ago, but these wounds go deep. And when old jealousies and rivalries resurface, as I already said, you get fireworks.'

'Well, you've certainly provided us with useful context. Thank you,' says Knight. 'I think DS Boden has something else we'd like to ask you both about.'

'By all means,' says Robert. 'As my wife's already said, we just want to help.'

The younger cop smiles. 'This is something that perhaps you could clear up for us,' she says. 'We've heard that Melissa Rowe may have been writing an investigative piece on you, Mr Gerrish.'

Leanne doesn't miss a beat. 'I'm sure she was,' she says. 'More or less, every media outlet has been reporting on the knife attack my husband suffered. And Melissa's angle would be to question the authenticity of it.'

'Why would she do that?' says Boden.

'Because that's her job. She works for a left-leaning publication, and their stance is to be critical of the government. It's what their readers expect.'

'Did you know anything about this, Mr Gerrish?' says the cop.

Robert gives a diffident shrug. 'No, but it doesn't surprise me. As my wife explained, Mel's an excellent journalist. Attacking government Ministers is what her paper pays her to do. It's the cut and thrust of politics and we're used to it.'

'But, apart from that, would you say you're on friendly terms?'

'Oh yes,' says Robert. 'We all swim in the same pond and it's not that big. I quite enjoy my spats with Mel. We're always trying to get one over on each other. Sort of friendly competition. But politics aside, I really am very upset about what's happened to her. It's just terrible.'

Boden nods sympathetically.

'One last thing,' says Knight. 'What sort of time did you last see or speak to Melissa?'

Leanne puckers her brow. 'For me, I think around ten thirty, maybe? What about you, darling?'

Robert shrugs. 'This is really just a guess. I came back to the room at just after ten, with Inspector Foley. And I stayed here, with close protection on the door. I noticed her earlier during the dinner. But we didn't have a chance to talk one to one.'

The DCI gives them a chilly smile. 'Thank you for talking to us, and for your candour,' she says.

'We just pray she pulls through,' says Robert. 'We've known her a long time, haven't we, darling?'

Leanne nods. She looks sorrowful. 'This is just the most awful thing. I hope you find out who was behind it.'

36

Sunday, 12.40am

Boden follows the DCI down the narrow stone stairway. Once they get outside, Knight stops and turns to face her.

She sighs. 'First impressions?'

'Slick,' says Boden. 'I looked her up on the net. She runs a PR consultancy. She definitely wanted to do all the talking.'

'That figures. However, if Melissa Rowe and Gerrish are at opposite ends of the political spectrum, it's unlikely someone after him would attack her.'

'Also boss, terrorists prepare. They come armed. Hit over the back of the head suggests an opportunistic attack.'

'Yes,' says Knight. 'So we need to find the weapon. Could be a rock from the gardens. Or something in the chapel? Has it got any heavy ornaments?'

'We'll get on that,' says Boden, making a note on her phone.

'Opportunists are much more likely to leave prints or

DNA,' says Knight. 'What about this crazy little love triangle?'

Boden shrugs. 'I don't know. We need to talk to the other two. But they've gone to the hospital.'

Knight chuckles. 'Adrian Cardello, eh? My daughter'll be amused.'

She smiles at Boden. It's rare for her to mention anything personal. Boden has never heard her speak of her daughter. This means she's feeling the pressure and wants to get Boden onside.

Don't be so cynical. Maybe she's just being nice.

'Foley and I had to stop him and Gerrish knocking seven bells out of each other. I don't know what it was about. But Gerrish was absolutely steaming. His wife had to talk him down.'

'Strikes me, she's the power behind the scenes,' says the DCI.

'Yeah, and I think what she said about Claire Naylor is accurate. I talked to Claire after the fight and she seemed super-anxious and physically wobbly. But she wouldn't say what it was about. They were all pretty pissed. I offered her support, but she couldn't get rid of me fast enough.'

Knight exhales. 'Okay, best scenario, the victim wakes up and can tell us what happened and who attacked her. Worst case, she doesn't know. Or she never regains consciousness.'

'I've told Prisha to keep me updated.'

'I don't want to dismiss the possibility of an outsider. We need to keep an open mind. But it's possible one of her old chums has attacked Melissa.'

'That's depressing, isn't it?' says Boden.

'Old jealousies and resentments can be pretty toxic,' says Knight. 'They can become obsessional. But this'll be a night-mare if that's what we're looking at here. Adrian Cardello?

Can you imagine what the media will do with that? I don't fancy taking a case like that to trial.'

Mackie is striding towards them across the lawn.

'Got something for you, boss,' he says. 'Looks like the victim could've been involved in a drug deal.'

Knight stares at him with some surprise. 'A drug deal?'

Mackie nods. 'Sounds like she might've been buying. But you need to come to the kitchen and see this for yourself.'

They walk briskly in the direction of the kitchens.

'Buying from the kid we arrested earlier?' says Boden.

'Yeah, but turns out Reece Davison wasn't working on his own. He has a mate. Found him hiding in the kitchen and he's been pretty badly beaten up.'

'Okay,' says the DCI, with a puzzled frown.

'Thing is,' says Mackie. 'I overheard the movie star telling the paramedics the victim may have had both cocaine and alcohol.'

Boden turns to Knight. 'Chimes in with what Gerrish's wife suggested, boss. Melissa has a drug habit.'

Mackie continues. 'This boy seems to be the junior partner in Reece's little operation. Says he's eighteen, but he looks loads younger. And he's a mess. I've called the paramedics.'

They walk through the kitchen where the catering staff are still cleaning up. It's hot and chaotic; pans are being washed and stacked. Surfaces scrubbed.

In the small office next to the kitchen, a boy is propped up against the filing cabinet. His nose is smashed and bloody. His right eye is a swollen mess. The catering manager, Tessa, is kneeling on the floor next to him, holding his hand.

'What happened to him?' says Knight.

Tessa stands up. She's shaking. 'This bloke,' she says. 'He came storming through here. Got hold of Tony and beat him. My husband tried to intervene. Bloke pulled a knife, lunged at him. He kept shouting at Tony, something like 'where is this bitch?' Her cheeks are damp with tears.

Boden takes her arm gently. 'It's okay, Tessa,' she says. 'Just take it slowly. When was this?'

'I don't know. Less than an hour ago, maybe? We've got to be cleaned up and out of here by one. That's in our contract.' She looks exhausted and stressed.

The chef appears in the doorway, hands on hips and sweating. He glares at Boden. 'Oh yeah, now you bloody lot turn up. We got fucking drug dealers coming in here, shouting the odds, like they own the place—'

Mackie moves forward. 'Okay, mate. You need to calm down.'

'Fucker tried to stab me,' says the chef.

'Come with me, mate,' says Mackie. 'Let's talk about this.' He ushers the chef out.

Boden turns to Tessa. 'We'll look after him,' she says. 'You go with your husband and tell DC Mackie exactly what happened.'

Tessa wipes her nose on her sleeve. She gives Boden a pitiful look. 'We didn't know they were drug dealers,' she says. 'I swear. Not Reece or him.' She dips her head and follows Mackie out.

Boden and Knight exchange looks. Boden squats down next to the boy. He's a scrawny mixed raced lad, the first wisps of a downy beard on his chin. A frightened kid caught in the crossfire between the gangs and the police. A victim as much as a perpetrator.

'We're going to get you to hospital, Tony,' Boden says. 'But I just want to ask you a couple of things. Is that okay?'

'No comment,' he mumbles.

'How old are you, Tony?' says Knight. 'I'm guessing fourteen?'

'Eighteen,' says the boy with a hint of belligerence.

'Were you working with Reece?' says Boden. 'Were you his backup man?'

'No comment,' he replies.

'Listen to me, Tony,' says Boden. 'We want to find the man who did this to you. I know you're frightened of him. And you think you'll be arrested too. What if I could arrange for you to go home?'

For the first time, the boy makes eye contact. One eye is a bloody mess, but in his other eye, tears glisten on the dark lashes.

'Where do you come from, Tony?' says Boden.

'Solihull.'

'Live with your mum and dad?'

'My mum.'

Boden shakes her head. 'Hasn't turned out how you expected, has it?'

Tony says nothing.

'They made you loads of promises, didn't they? You work for them, you'll make big money. And here you are. They've done this to you.'

The boy raises a trembling finger to his bloody lips. 'If I snitch, he'll find me and kill me.'

'Not if we find him first,' says Boden. 'Why did he do this to you?'

He hesitates, then he says, 'Cause we gave her the gear and didn't get the money.'

Boden and Knight exchange looks. 'Why didn't you get the money?' says Boden.

The boy sighs. He's obviously in pain. 'Lady said to Reece, that's not how it works. Said she ordered through her dealer in London and paid him. Said she didn't carry cash around. Said if we didn't give her the gear, she'd shop us to you lot.'

Boden gets her phone out. 'I've got a picture I'm going to show you, Tony,' she says. Opening her phone, she clicks to a picture of Melissa Rowe, lifted from her newspaper's website. She shows it to the boy. 'Look at it carefully,' she says. 'Do you recognise this woman?'

The boy nods. 'It's her.'

'Okay,' says Boden. 'This is the lady you're talking about. You're sure?'

'Yeah.'

'You gave her cocaine, but she wouldn't pay you in cash. What happened then?'

'Reece was worried. He had to call them and tell them. Leon went mental.'

'Who's Leon?'

'Reece's brother. Leon said we had to get the money from her. We didn't know what to do.'

'What did you do?'

'Nothing. Then that big copper came snooping round and Reece got nicked. She must've shopped us.'

'And what did you do?' says Boden.

'Phoned Leon and told him. Had to.'

Boden holds up the picture on the phone again. 'Let's be clear about this, Tony,' she says. 'You told Leon that this woman shopped Reece to the police?'

He nods.

'What did he say?' says Boden.

'He was so pissed off. Said he'd deal with the bitch himself.'

A paramedic appears in the doorway. Boden stands up to

allow the paramedic space to come in and treat the boy. 'Alright, mate,' the paramedic says. 'Let's get you sorted.'

Boden follows Knight out of the office. They walk through the kitchen and out into the yard at the back.

The two detectives face each other.

'Well,' says Knight. 'This looks like a promising scenario. Melissa got in some kind of dispute with a drug dealer.'

'Must be a County Lines gang running this,' says Boden. 'Someone connected to the network. A London dealer put her in touch with them.'

'If they thought she was refusing to pay and also she was responsible for Reece's arrest, that's likely to make them furious.'

Mackie joins them.

'What have you got?' says Knight.

'Not sure about the timeframe, boss,' he replies. 'But shortly before Rowe was attacked, an IC1 male, early twenties, comes steaming in, looking for Tony. Gives him a thrashing. Chef tries to intervene. Gets threatened with a knife. He walks out again.'

'This has to be Leon, doesn't it?' says Knight. 'And he came here looking for Melissa Rowe.'

'But did he find her?' says Boden. 'How would he know where to look?'

The DCI ignores this. She's grinning. 'If we can get Reece to talk to us too, and locate the gang, we may be able to wrap this up by morning.'

Boden surveys the DCI. She has a glint in her eye. An impressively quick result could be just what she's looking for here.

37

Sunday, 3am

It seems to Claire that the hospital is busy, considering it's three in the morning. The lights never go off and there's a soft background hum. Air conditioning maybe?

When they arrived in the A&E department earlier, it was a hive of activity. In the waiting area, patients were sitting or lying down and waiting to be triaged. People stared as they walked past, and one woman mumbled: 'Fuck me, in't that Adrian Cardello?'

Behind the triage desk was an area of curtained off cubicles. Doctors, nurses and healthcare assistants were coming and going. Monitors bleeped, trolleys were moving in and out. There was an air of efficient bustle. As the medical staff noticed them, or rather Adrian, they attracted some curious glances.

But Adrian seemed oblivious to the fact he was being gawped at. This is his life, thought Claire. He must be used to it.

He made enquiries and pretty soon an efficient-looking woman, smartly dressed and with a gold name badge, appeared and ushered them into a private waiting room, where they'd *be more comfortable.* It looked like an upmarket dentist, with soft leather sofas and armchairs, and a large potted palm.

The woman went away, came back and told them Mel was in surgery.

Since then, they've just been waiting.

Claire is sitting in an armchair. She can't seem to get her thoughts in any sort of order. The tablets she's on can have this effect. Especially if she takes too many.

Did you take too many?

She can't remember. And she shouldn't drink with them. After the cop took her back to her room, she just wanted to zone out.

Adrian is pacing, but he seems far away. He keeps saying things, but Claire struggles to catch their meaning.

'…she was out to get him…we know that, don't we?'

Gerrish? He's talking about Gerrish.

The woman returns. She speaks to Adrian and he goes off with her.

Pull yourself together. You've got to. For Mel.

There's a carafe of water on the table; she pours herself a glass and drinks it. It helps. Her brain is settling. Her thoughts aren't so fuzzy round the edges. She gets up and walks around a bit.

The door opens and Adrian comes back in. He's smiling. 'I've just been talking to the doctor,' he says. 'They think they've stopped the bleeding in the brain. But she's very poorly. They're moving her to the Intensive Care Unit. We can see her.'

'Is she going to be okay?' her own voice sounds echoey. But all the words are intelligible and they fit together.

'I don't know,' he says. 'I don't think they do.'

He takes her arm and they walk out and down the corridor together. The woman is waiting outside for them, and she leads the way. They're being treated like VIPs and this makes Claire feel awkward. She doesn't like being singled out. But this is because of Adrian.

The corridors all look the same. Long, with off-white walls, vinyl flooring, and harsh strip lightening. They pass through several sets of swing doors. Then the signage announces the Intensive Care Unit. They end up in another corridor, but it has a long window along one side.

Standing beside it, there are two uniformed police officers. They wear heavy Kevlar vests and, strapped to their belts, they each have a side-arm. Next to them and chatting with them is a small Asian woman. All three fall silent when they see Claire and Adrian approach.

Adrian stops in front of the window.

'Here she is,' he says, and Claire notices the tears welling in his eyes.

She peers through the glass. The room is large but arranged in bays. In the nearest one, there's an electronically adjustable bed with a thick air-filled mattress and side rails. On either side of the bed, there are monitors. It's hard to identify the patient lying in it.

Is it really Mel?

The patient's head is swathed in bandages, and she's connected to various tubes and wires. A nurse in scrubs is adjusting something and checking the cardiac monitor.

Oh my god, Mel!

Claire grasps Adrian's hand. 'This is all my fault,' she

whispers. 'I never meant any of this to happen. Everything just got out of hand. It's all my fault, Adrian. I did this.'

He puts his arm round her. 'Sssh,' he says. 'Listen to me, Claire. It's not. We both know what Mel's like.'

Suddenly the cardiac monitor emits a loud electronic wail. The nurse already in the bay immediately begins chest compressions. An alarm goes off at the nurses' station and two more nurses jump into action. Several moments later, the crash team appears. The cops stand back from the door to allow them to enter.

Claire turns away and buries her head in Adrian's shoulder. She just can't watch.

You did this! You did this to her! Put her in harm's way. She didn't even want to come.

38

Sunday, 3.30am

Boden was supposed to go home, but she's in the passenger seat of an unmarked police car, being driven by Mackie. They're bringing up the rear in a small convoy led by armed officers in two X5s, and travelling at some speed along narrow roads into the desolate Fen country to the north of Cambridge.

When questioned by other officers, Reece Davison admitted he was working for a County Lines gang, known as the TZ line. He also provided the location of the hideaway they're using. They've cuckooed an old man living in an isolated lock-keeper's cottage in the Fens. They also discovered his brother Leon Davison has a record of violence as a juvenile and was a suspect in two gang related murders.

The darkness outside envelopes the car, creating an almost claustrophobic feeling. Only the headlights cut through it, revealing patches of mist hanging over the vast fields in a flat landscape. The red taillights of the armed response vehicle ahead drag them in its wake. The occasional dots of light on the horizon from distant farms are the only indications of civilisation.

Mackie is focused on the driving; keeping pace with the ARVs. So they're not speaking much. The phone signal is patchy out here.

Boden is dog tired, but when the DCI asked her to stay on 'to finish this', it was difficult to refuse. Knight is up against a system that has demoted her and would now prefer to see her fail so it can spit her out. Boden knows what that feels like. She also knows being a woman makes it worse.

Her mind drifts to Cal Foley. When they first served in the Met together, he was her Sergeant, and she hated him. But in coming through a blitzkrieg of a case together, they became mates. Foley is a no-prisoners type. His moral code is implacable. You're on the side of the angels or you're not. But once you get beyond the tough carapace, he's loyal to a fault. Boden wonders if he's currently seeing anyone.

Forget it! It wouldn't work.

Mackie exhales. 'This is knackering,' he says. 'But if we nail these bastards, it'll be a great day's work.'

'Do we even think Reece is telling the truth?' says Boden. 'What's in it for him?'

This could all be a rush through the night for nothing. Wanting a result is not the same as getting it.

'Pleads guilty. Lighter sentence,' says Mackie.

Red brake lights flash as the ARV ahead slows. The comms crackle.

'Okay,' says the Team Leader. 'This is it. We're going straight in. Maximum surprise.'

A high embankment looms up ahead. It's part of the earth-works built to carry the canal above the level of the surrounding fields. The ARVs turn to the right and onto a narrow track that runs below and parallel with it for a couple of hundred metres. They switch off their headlights. Mackie follows suit. Dark shapes rise up. These turn into a small copse of trees, heavy with summer foliage. And elevated behind the trees on the side of the canal is a single storey building. The moonlight glints on the white-washed walls. It's an old lock-keeper's cottage which sits on the side of the canal.

Light filters out of two small, rectangular windows. It creates a pool which illuminates two vehicles parked at the back: an old rust bucket with a flat tyre and next to it is a brand new Range Rover Discovery.

The ARVs come to a quiet stop and the armed response teams emerge into the darkness, stealthy as cats. Mackie and Boden wait in their car on the track.

'Looks like someone's definitely home,' says Mackie.

They watch as the teams position themselves to go in. Then Boden's phone lights up with an in-coming call.

'Finally, we've got a signal,' she says.

Chakravorty's name flashes up.

'Hey Prish,' says Boden.

'Melissa Rowe has just died,' says Chakravorty.

'Okay, thanks for the head's up,' says Boden.

Hanging up, she turns to Mackie. 'She's dead.'

'Right,' says Mackie. 'Now they're murderers. Let's have these buggers.'

The armed response team's entrance into the cottage is swift and surgical. The smashing of the front door. Shouts of *Armed Police!*

A couple of minutes pass.

'All clear,' says the Team Leader on the comms. 'Three suspects secured. Plus an old man.'

Boden and Mackie get out of their vehicle and head for the house.

The Team Leader is waiting for them on the doorstep. 'We've got an old man. Looks like he's been cuckooed. I'd say he's got dementia. An IC1 female, an IC3 juvenile male, and another older IC1 male. We've cautioned all three.'

'Great, thanks,' says Boden.

An aroma of nicotine, dope and fried food assails Boden as soon as she enters. The main room has the potential to be cosy, but it's a complete mess. Food cartons, an overflowing ashtray, piles of washing up in the sink, several laptops and a PlayStation.

The suspects all look up at her. They're seated on a battered sofa, with one of the armed officers standing guard behind them.

The woman is in her early forties, hard-faced with a sullen expression and a cruel mouth. The young male is mixed race, a teenager. The other man is in his early twenties, mousy hair styled in a high top fade with patterns shaved into the sides. Boden has seen his mugshot; this is Leon Davison. He has his left hand cradling his right knuckle. To conceal abrasions? Both males wear baggy branded T-shirts, loose fitting cargo shorts and Adidas trainers. It's practically the uniform of any County Lines drug member anywhere in the UK.

But the woman fixes Boden with a steely glare. 'What is this bullshit?' she says. 'You can't come busting in here. You've upset and frightened Norman.'

'Who's Norman?' says Boden.

The woman points to an elderly man slumped in a rocking chair next to the Aga. 'I'm a qualified nurse,' says the woman. 'And I'm his live-in carer.'

'Okay,' says Boden. 'And who are these two?'

The woman picks up a packet of cigarettes from the table, takes one out and lights it. She has an arrogant swagger about her. Inhaling, she wags the cigarette in the direction of the teenager. 'My son,' she says. 'And his friend. Just visiting. Having a bit of a holiday. Not against the law, is it?'

'And you're here because you're Norman's carer. What's your name so we can check that out?'

'It's a private arrangement with Norman's family.'

'What's your name?'

'You can call me Sharon.' The woman stares straight back at Boden, an expression etched with disdain. Boden doesn't buy the story. It's clear Sharon is in charge of this outfit.

'You've been cautioned. Now you're going to be taken in for questioning,' she says.

'What about Norman?' says the woman.

'We're contacting social services.'

The woman gives a gravelly laugh, which erupts into a smoker's cough. 'Good luck with that, love,' she says.

She and the other two exchange smiles.

Boden meets Leon's eye. He glares back with a smug grin.

They're right. This is all going to be a lengthy nightmare. But Mackie appears in the doorway. 'We've found the stash,' he says. 'A sizeable one, too.'

The woman shrugs. 'Don't know what you're talking about.'

Boden takes a deep breath, then regrets it. The whole place stinks. But she's had enough.

'Right, Sharon,' she says. 'You may think this is a routine drug's bust. And even if it sticks and goes to trial, depending on your previous convictions, you'll get two or three years. But I should advise you that this is a murder inquiry. And murder carries a mandatory life sentence.'

Sharon shoots a questioning look at Leon. Boden can see the wheels turning.

'You stupid sod,' she mumbles. She turns to Boden. 'Whatever he's done, it's on him. Not me. Nothing to do with me.'

'You heard of joint enterprise, Sharon?' says Boden. 'I'd wipe the smile off your face, if I were you.'

She turns to the armed officer. 'You can take them in now.'

39

Sunday, 3.45am

Adrian Cardello sits in the back of the taxi. It's a local Uber and it smells of a faint aroma of cleaning fluid and puke. Claire sits beside him. Mel was pronounced dead at 3.26am and since then they've hardly spoken. Claire seems to have gone into a semi-catatonic state. He has no idea what he's supposed to do with her. It feels as if he's stepped out of his normal cocooned world into a time warp. He can't remember the last time he rode in this sort of cab.

He glances across at Claire. She looks worn and defeated, older than her years, and he wonders to what extent he should hold himself responsible for that. Does she really believe he's Ella's father? If only she'd contacted him years ago. He's faced three paternity suits in his career, and regards them as an occupational hazard. Two accepted a pay-out without a DNA test, so he assumed they were fake. The third is his youngest son, who he has acknowledged.

When Mel asked him if he and Claire had ever slept

together, he told her the truth. He couldn't remember. It's a time in his life that he's filed away and forgotten. It was another world, and now it feels like another life. The years after uni were consumed with the struggles of trying to establish an acting career. Yes, he got the breaks, but he bloody well worked for them. And yes, there was a stream of girls, and he can't remember most of their names.

But the party at the end of Finals, he remembers that. How could he forget? It was a wild night. Not his finest hour.

You were just young and stupid.

Back then, Claire Naylor was such a beauty, not to mention a trophy. She had a string of boyfriends, all competing for her attention. The business he's in, he's well aware of how ephemeral looks can be. He's seen plenty of starlets bloom and fade. It's a complete double-standard too. He's had a bit of work to keep the line of his jaw chiselled. But men get away with so much more. His career has gone from strength to strength and now he's cast with female leads who are young enough to be his daughter.

His daughter!

He always wanted a daughter. He loves his three boys, but a girl would've been something special. If he had been involved in Ella's life, could he have saved her?

The cab pulls up at the entrance to the college. Several police cars are parked outside, and Adrian wonders what will happen next.

Claire gets out and walks towards the Porter's Lodge. Adrian falls into step beside her. 'I think the police are going to want to talk to us,' he says. 'And I think we've got to tell them about Rob. What you think he did to Ella and the fact that Mel was out to expose him.'

'I can't,' says Claire. 'I'm going home.'

'Well, at least let me take you.'

'No.'

'But—'

'Go back to your life, Adrian. And I'll go back to mine. There's nothing we can do for Mel now. Or Ella.'

Adrian watches her walk away. Such a fragile figure with hunched shoulders. There's a uniformed police officer at the gate. Claire speaks to him briefly and then disappears inside.

What an absolute train wreck!

He pulls out his phone and rings his PA. 'Yeah, get a car to collect me asap. Get something local. I need to get back to London tonight. I'll be at the college.' He hesitates. 'No, scrub that. Get it to collect me on the Silver Street Bridge. Phone me back with an ETA.'

Adrian walks through town towards the Backs, an open area behind the colleges on the east bank of the River Cam. He needs to stretch his legs, clear his head and to think. On reflection, getting involved in talking to the police tonight is probably a mistake. He's had quite a bit to drink and he's emotionally hyped. He can have someone collect his stuff. Walking away is the smart move. He has his reputation and image to consider.

And there are a lot of issues to weigh up here.

He certainly intends to point the finger at Rob Gerrish. But he needs to rehearse and perfect his pitch before he does that. Let the cops come looking for him.

The lawns and gardens of the Backs are picturesque in the daytime. At four in the morning, it's a slightly different proposition. Adrian briefly considers whether someone will try to mug him for his phone or even the Rolex Oyster on his wrist. But on a warm night, the area is far from deserted. A few homeless people sleeping rough. A group of revellers who've probably emerged from a club and who are sitting around in a semi-circle drinking. They hail him, inviting him to join them. He's far enough away to avoid recognition.

He finds himself on a familiar path and his mind drifts back to those summers long ago when he came down here to smoke dope, or more frequently to have sex with girls. Back then, everything seemed so easy and carefree; or is that just a trick of memory, colouring the past?

His relationship with Mel was certainly a rollercoaster ride. Even back then, she was a spiteful and vindictive bitch. If things didn't go her way, then look out. She wasn't the sort of girl who got on with other girls. But her friendship with Claire was sacrosanct. He was never sure why.

'Shag Claire and I'll cut your balls off,' she said to him on one memorable occasion.

Seeing her again was interesting and irritating in equal parts. She hadn't changed. The same acid tongue. The same malevolent ball breaker. But now she seemed suffused with the bitterness of disappointment. It was sad to see. He wondered what she'd got to be disappointed about; her career was pretty successful.

And she still went straight for the throat, like a rabid attack dog. He's sorry she's dead. Obviously he is. But stuff happens that you can't predict. He's found that in life. You just have to deal with it and move on.

His phone buzzes with an incoming text. The car is waiting for him.

40

Claire drives home as the sun is rising. It looks like being another scorching day. When she got back to the college, she was still reeling and it took her nearly an hour to gather her things and slip away; she hopes unnoticed.

There was a large police presence in the college grounds. People in white suits and a little tent in front of the entrance to the chapel. Her car was parked at the multi-storey in the centre of town. She left by the back gate and no one attempted to stop her.

She feels shaky but traffic is light because it's early, and she gets home with no mishaps.

Watching her dying friend through a window, as medical staff tried desperately to resuscitate her, has left a sense of hollow despair. The shock of it sent something akin to a jolt of electricity through her brain.

Mel is dead. Mel is dead because of you.

It's feels surreal, like a bad dream. But she can't wake up.

The only parking space she can find near her house is at the end of the street. It's Sunday morning. All her neighbours are home and asleep in their beds. She takes her overnight bag from the boot and walks towards her cottage.

The first thing she sees is Ziggy, hunkered down on the front wall, soaking up the first rays of sunshine. There's a cat flap in the back door for him to enter and exit. But it's as if he's there waiting for her. Somehow expecting her.

She strokes his head. 'Hey, Zig,' she whispers. He rubs his soft muzzle against her hand. He's getting on; his face used to be jet black, now there are strands of grey around his whiskers.

The quiet of the early morning is soothing. She notices the birdsong. When she was a child, Ella could list all the summer birds that visited. The numbers have dwindled. Now they're lucky if they get a few house martins.

As she unlocks her front door and steps inside, relief floods her veins. Nowadays, this is the only place she feels remotely comfortable. This is because the tiny house is still infused with her daughter's presence. She'll never move. She can't. Ziggy jumps down from the wall and strolls in after her.

The door opens straight into the open plan sitting room. It's long and rectangular and runs into the kitchen area at the back of the house. Dumping her bag next to the door, Claire walks through to the kitchen, tops up the kettle and switches it on.

Ziggy has a special cat feeder with a timer attached. It can be set to open at intervals over a couple of days when she's not around. His water bowl sits beside it, but that's nearly empty.

Claire picks it up. 'Sorry, mate,' she says. 'This heat. I should've left you extra water.'

While she washes it and refills it, he rubs round her legs with his tail straight up and just the tip bent.

'Okay,' she says. 'I hear you. Food too.'

She gets a sachet of his food from the fridge and puts it in a clean bowl. Because of his advanced age, she buys a special preparation online. He's picky for a cat, but definitely eats less than he used to.

As she places the bowl on the floor for him, he goes straight to it.

She strokes his back. He eats.

'Don't you die on me too, Zig,' she says. 'I don't think I could cope with that.'

For a moment, she just stands there and watches him. He's a delicate eater and takes his time.

Adrian said the police would want to speak to them, and he's probably right. So she will get a chance to tell them what she thinks happened.

Robert Gerrish killed Mel. His motive is obvious. Mel intended to expose his treatment of Ella. When he discovered this, he had to stop her. It's the only explanation that makes sense.

But will they believe her? Will they see who he really is? Probably not. He's too powerful.

As she waits for the kettle to boil, she unlocks the French doors at the back and steps out onto the small patio. She's immediately embraced by the scent of lavender. The bees are already hard at work gathering nectar. The large terracotta pot of pink and purple petunias is looking a little sad. She goes back into the house and fills her watering can at the sink.

The simplest, everyday rituals of life are the threads that hold her together. Caring for the garden is part of her homage to her daughter. Ella loved the natural world and wanted to do all she could to save it. They'd planted the garden together years ago; chosen the lavender to attract the bees.

Claire goes round all the pots in turn, watering them. The vibrant geraniums, the tall daisies. And for the few moments it takes, the nattering in her brain quietens.

Then she makes some green tea in a ceramic pot, takes it and a mug out onto the patio and sits down at the little wrought-iron table. She should probably eat something herself. She hardly touched her dinner last night, but she can't face the prospect of food.

Last night. Were you really going to do it?

Adrian stopped her. How did he even know? Was she that transparent? He took the knife. She doesn't know what he did with it.

But then she watched Mel die. Watched her friend disappear before her eyes.

Your fault. You put her in harm's way.

Witnessed up close, death is chilling. She realises that now. The reality of it is not how she imagined it would be. She's never seen anyone die before. Ella's death was remote. She wanted to see her daughter's body but was talked out of it. She knew why. It was because a fall from such a great height…

Even now, the thought of what happened to her little girl it is unbearable.

If she'd stabbed Gerrish, what would she have seen? Would it have happened there in front of her? The horror and the emptiness of it. The staring into the abyss.

How could that bring you peace?

It would've haunted her forever, the taking of another's life. And certainly wouldn't have brought the relief she craves; she can see that now. The killing would've dragged her down into the void, too. It would've been revenge born of madness and anger. It would've destroyed her too.

Ziggy sits in the doorway, licking his paw and using it to clean his mouth and whiskers. She glances across at him. He looks back at her.

'Yeah, I know what you're thinking,' she says. 'I'm certifiable. I really was going to kill him. How completely insane is that? It wouldn't have brought Ella back to us, would it? And Mel was just trying to help me. That's what got her killed. And I am responsible. What the hell have I done?'

Glancing through the open doorway, she notices her phone is vibrating on the counter. If she ignores it, it'll stop. It does. She sips her tea. It vibrates again.

She gets up wearily, goes into the kitchen and picks it up. Six o'clock on Sunday morning?

Mum. A shaft of fear shoots through her.

She answers.

'Mum?'

'Claire?' says an anguished voice. 'I know you're in Cambridge. But I didn't know what else to do. Your father has fallen. He tried to get out of bed in the night. I phoned the ambulance. But we're still waiting. I think he might've broken something. He's just there on the floor. I'm at my wit's end.'

'It's alright, Mum. I'm back. I'll come straight over.'

41

Sunday, 9.30am

Leanne sips her coffee and scrolls on her phone. The news feeds and social media are full of it. *Prominent political journalist murdered.*

This is one advantage of a twenty-four-hour news cycle. There's no waiting around and worrying. The confirmation that Melissa is deceased is obviously a relief.

Robert is still asleep, which is probably just as well. He drank far too much and he'll probably have a hangover. But he hasn't questioned the line she took with the police; he seemed relieved. The official car dropped them home at about five in the morning. He dozed most of the way back. With Foley in the front seat next to the driver, they weren't going to talk about anything.

Leanne didn't waste the opportunity though, and by the time they turned into Hyde Vale, she had several scenarios mapped out in her head.

Now she's settled in the kitchen with her laptop, her

phone and her coffee. Sybil has been demanding attention since about six am. Allegra is a teenager, so she'll be crashed out until midday.

Leanne accepted Valentina's offer to make her a fruit bowl for breakfast, and she's just finished it. The task now is to monitor and track how the narrative unfolds. But with Melissa gone, the most problematic hurdle has been cleared. Everything now becomes speculation, and that's manageable.

'Mummy,' says Sybil, from her position on the floor amongst a pile of toys. 'Can we get another guinea pig?'

'Another one?' says Leanne, without removing her eyes from the screen. 'Why?'

'I think Fred might be lonely.'

'He's got you.'

'Yes, but I'm not always here. I have to go to school. And didn't you say it's important for everyone to have friends?'

'Did I?' says Leanne, looking up from the screen and smiling.

Friends?

Such a woolly concept. There are only two types of people: those you can rely and those you can't. The rest is social noise. She'll have to explain this to her daughter one day. Fortunately, not yet. She goes back to scrolling the news feeds.

The front doorbell rings. Leanne looks at the time.

Already?

Sybil leaps to her feet. 'I'll get it!' she cries.

'No, Sybil,' says Leanne emphatically. 'Leave it to Valentina.'

'Why?'

'Because I say so.'

Sybil scans her to see if she's serious. Sharp as a tack and she's only six. It makes Leanne smile inwardly.

Leanne gives her daughter a stern look. Sybil returns to her toys.

There's the sound of Valentina's footsteps in the hall and the front door opening. Leanne has already briefed her; there may be some press attention today, so she needs to be on the alert. Valentina's used to this and knows how to stonewall. But there's the drift of muffled voices, and a moment later Kieran appears in the kitchen doorway.

They stare at one another. He looks dishevelled.

'I just got the train back,' he says.

'Didn't you get Robert's text?' says Leanne.

'Well, yeah,' says Kieran, pulling off his Harry Potter glasses and cleaning them on his shirttail. 'But, shit, Leanne. She's dead.'

'I am aware.'

'There's this guy from her paper, Theo Webber. He's been on my case since about seven this morning. Says he was working with Rowe to investigate the boss.'

'And what did you say?'

'Just that I, we, had no idea about that. And that the Minister is devastated at the loss of an old friend.'

Leanne scans him. As liars go, he's fairly plausible. But if Melissa's colleagues are already digging, that's not a good sign. She needs to get ahead of this.

'I'll phone her editor.'

Kieran huffs. 'Leanne, I handled it.'

'To express our condolences,' she says.

He's such a loser.

But she smiles. 'Kieran, you must be exhausted. We're grateful for the update, but you could've done it on the phone. Go home. Get some sleep.'

He gives her a sheepish look. 'I was hoping to touch base with Robert.'

'Robert is asleep.'

'Not anymore,' says a grumpy voice from the hallway. Her husband walks into the kitchen in pyjama pants and a T-shirt. 'God, I need coffee.'

Now it could get complicated.

Leanne goes over to Sybil. 'Run upstairs, darling,' she says. 'And see what Valentina's doing.'

Sybil gets up and trots obediently to the door. Leanne closes it carefully behind her. Then she goes over to the coffee machine and refills the reservoir.

'Can I get one of those too?' says Kieran.

Little shit doesn't have the manners to say please.

But Leanne makes two cups of coffee.

Robert slumps on a stool at the counter. Kieran perches next to him.

'Just wanted to bring you up to speed, boss,' says Kieran. 'One of her colleagues has been sniffing around, but I think I've got it under control.'

'Under control?' says Robert sourly. 'You dare to come here and say that. It's totally fucking out of control, thanks to you.'

'What?' says Kieran. 'I don't know what you mean.'

Leanne decides to just let this play out.

Robert turns and glares at him. 'I told you to sort it out. I did not tell you to do something like this.'

Kieran's jaw slackens. He goes as white as a sheet. 'You think I...that I had something to do with this? My God!'

'Well, it's a bit of a bloody co-incidence, isn't it?' says Robert.

'Yeah, but I would never...I'm not a...'

Robert shakes his head. 'Oh, save the bloody performance for the police.'

Kieran looks as if he might cry.

'I tried to have a word with her,' he says. 'But she was completely bladdered and just told me to fuck off.'

Robert exhales. 'And did anyone see this exchange?'

Kieran dips his head, like a schoolboy caught sending dick pics. 'I really don't know,' he says. 'It was outside the disco. There were people around.'

'Listen to me, Kieran,' says Robert, raising his index finger threateningly. 'You let my wife handle this. Stay the fuck out of it. Go home. And tomorrow you go to the office, act as if nothing out of the ordinary has occurred. And you keep a very low profile.'

Kieran wipes his nose with the back of his hand.

'I am telling the truth,' he mumbles. 'I didn't—'

'I don't give a flying fuck,' says Robert. 'Don't tell me what you did. I don't want to know. And you and I will not speak about this again. This conversation never happened.'

Kieran stares at him. He's frozen with shock.

'Now go,' says Robert.

Kieran gets off the stool and disappears into the hall, shoulders hunched. The front door opens and then slams shut.

Leanne puts a coffee down in front of her husband.

Robert rubs his face and exhales.

'What do you think?' he says.

Leanne sighs. 'He's always been slippery as an eel. I suspect it will turn on whether the police have forensic evidence or CCTV.'

'You think he did it?'

Leanne ponders. 'Hard to call it,' she says. 'I'd say sixty forty in favour. So yes, probably.'

'Then we are in deep shit,' says Robert, putting his face in his hands.

You've just got to hold this together. Hold him together.

'Don't be so pessimistic, darling,' she says. 'As long as we keep our nerve, I still think we can handle it.'

'Jesus wept!' says Robert. 'I hope you're right.'

She comes round the counter and kisses him on the cheek. 'You worry too much,' she says. 'It'll be fine.'

42

Sunday, 12.05pm

Boden got about five hours' sleep; as soon as her head touched the pillow, she was out. She and Mackie had dropped Norman off at a respite care facility north of Cambridge. He seemed oblivious to everything around him. Specialist officers would come to interview him, but Boden doubted he'd be able to provide much information about the TZ gang.

The team briefing is scheduled for midday. As Boden arrives, the room is filling up. Reinforcements have been drafted in, including a DI from Hertfordshire, who is standing next to the DCI at the front.

Rachel Knight looks like she has had no sleep. But it's clear she intends to keep her hand firmly on the tiller. Probably running on adrenaline and coffee.

Chakravorty appears in the doorway, catches Boden's eye and comes to join her.

'How you doing?' says Boden. 'Get any sleep?'

'Not much,' says Chakravorty. She frowns. 'I'm worried. It's kept me awake.'

'Worried about what?' says Boden.

'I think I overhead something,' says Chakravorty. She sounds nervous. 'But I'm not sure. I might have got it wrong or misunderstood, because I was quite far away.'

'Okay, back up here,' says Boden. 'Where were you and what did you overhear?'

Chakravorty speaks in a fast whisper. 'At the hospital. It was when the victim went into cardiac arrest. Adrian Cardello was there and her other friend. A woman. We were outside, but we could all see the resus team through the window. And when the doctor called it and said she was dead, her friend really lost it. Obviously, she was upset. And she seemed to blame herself. I couldn't catch everything she said. But I think she said something like 'everything got out of hand... it's all my fault...I did this.'

Chakravorty exhales. It's a weight off her chest.

'Implying she was the attacker?' says Boden.

'I think so.'

'The other friend?' says Boden. 'This is Claire? Claire Naylor?'

'I don't know. But, yeah, he called her Claire, I think.'

At the front of the room, DCI Knight raises her voice. 'Right everyone,' she says. 'Can I have your attention, please?'

'Okay, Prish,' whispers Boden, patting the DC's shoulder. 'Leave it with me.'

'This is a very fast-moving investigation,' says Knight. 'And we've had a number of developments overnight. We've taken three more members of the TZ gang into custody. Well done to everyone involved in this.'

A mugshot of you-can-call-me-Sharon pops up on the

screen at the front of the room. 'Here we have Sharon Kenley-Smith,' says the DCI. 'Married to Roy Kenley-Smith, believed to be the current leader of the TZs. They're Birmingham-based but obviously spreading their wings. She's been arrested on a number of occasions but has never come to trial. But this is the individual we're interested in, Leon Davison.'

A second mugshot pops up.

'We found a burner in his possession with a series of texts. The recipient of the texts is the victim, Melissa Rowe. To summarise, the texts are threatening in nature. Rowe appears to be insisting that she's got an account with a London dealer and pays for her drugs through him. Leon doesn't accept this. Tells her that's not the arrangement. Later in the string, he accuses her of reporting Reece Davison, his brother, who actually supplied the drugs to her to the police. She denies this and tells him to fuck off. I'll read you his last text to her.'

Knight reads from her iPad. *No one shafts us, you skanky bitch. You fucking gonna pay. We coming for you.*

The DCI lets her eye travel round the room. 'The threat is explicit. It's clear Leon arrived to carry it out, because shortly before Rowe was attacked, he was in the kitchens. He beat up one of his own gang and threatened the chef with a knife. Now what we need to do is to place him at the scene. Forensics are working on it and we're looking at all the CCTV to try to trace his path through the college. But he's our prime suspect.'

'She's cracking on,' whispers Mackie.

Boden isn't surprised. A fast result on a high-profile murder inquiry has got to be her priority.

She raises her hand. 'Just wondering, boss. He's a drug dealer, carries a knife, and threatened the chef with a knife.

But Rowe was killed by blunt force trauma to the back of the head. Why didn't he knife her?'

Knight throws her a frosty look. 'Good point, Jo. And one we'll endeavour to answer. Perhaps he preferred to take her by surprise?'

'The tone of his texts suggests he was looking to confront her and punish her,' says Boden.

The DCI glares at her. It's clear she doesn't welcome this intervention. 'Well,' she says sourly, 'we might be in a better position with all this if any of the officers on duty at the college on Saturday night noticed there was a drug dealer wandering around the place. But I suppose it was getting late and you didn't have your eyes and ears open, did you?'

Ouch!

Boden and Chakravorty exchange glances.

'Harsh,' mutters Mackie.

This was brutal and designed to shut Boden up. It has the opposite effect.

She takes a deep breath and says calmly, 'So are we continuing with other lines of inquiry, boss?'

'As you know, it's my policy to always keep an open mind,' says Knight.

'Well,' says Boden. 'DC Chakravorty has some intel which you should be aware of.'

'Okay,' says Knight. 'Come to my office. But I think we can wrap up here. Actions will be issued. Thank you, everyone.'

Chakravorty turns to Boden. 'It'll be okay,' says Boden. 'Ignore the sarcasm. She wasn't on the ground, doing a double shift, and looking for a terrorist in a haystack.'

By the time Boden and Chakravorty reach the DCI's office, Knight is behind the desk looking knackered but fierce.

'Right,' she says. 'Make this succinct because I want to get home and get a change of clothes. DC Chakravorty?'

This confirms what Boden is already thinking. The boss is hoping to assemble enough of a case to charge Leon Davison and make a statement to the press by the end of the day. That is fast.

'Okay, well, um, I think I overheard something, boss,' says Chakravorty. 'But I can't really be sure.'

Knight exhales. She's about to launch into the DC, but Boden intervenes.

'Long story short, boss,' Boden says. 'This relates to what the Minister's wife told us about Claire Naylor, Melissa Rowe's friend. Naylor and Cardello were at the hospital when Rowe died. Prisha thinks she overheard Naylor telling Cardello that everything got out of hand and it was all her fault.'

Knight puffs out her cheeks. She shoots a look at Chakravorty. 'Naylor appeared to be taking the blame for Rowe's death?' she says.

'She was upset and crying,' says Chakravorty. 'But yeah, I think she said 'it's all my fault. I did this.'

Knight exhales and throws out her palms. 'Right, well, go and get her. Bring her in for questioning.'

43

Sunday, 12.30pm

Claire has put together a plate of cold chicken and some salad. She carries it out through the patio doors on a tray. Her parents' garden is large and rambling, the opposite of her own. Her mother used to attend the Chelsea Flower Show every year and could boast she had ten different varieties of roses. Now they employ a gardener to keep it tidy.

Her mother is settled in a reclining garden chair in the shade of a large umbrella, eyes closed behind her ancient Jackie O sunglasses. She looks haggard. Exhaustion probably.

When Claire got there shortly after six thirty, the ambulance had finally turned up. But the paramedics were efficient and kind. They told Claire that her father would probably be admitted. She followed them to A&E and waited a couple of hours beside him in the cubicle until he was.

Being back in a hospital again was unsettling. But this time there was no VIP treatment, no special attention. And oddly, that helped. It was familiar. She sat with her dad and held his hand, as she'd done on many previous occasions.

She was back to operating on autopilot, and that was a relief. Going through the motions of life with the minimum of feeling. Sometimes, when she's teaching, she can manage this for hours at a time. It's as if she has a split personality. One self occupies the shell of her body. It functions adequately. But inside, the emotions are frozen. They drift somewhere in the back of her mind like a mist, or the hint of a distant memory she can't quite recall. The other core self remains packed away where it can't trouble her. And the two don't connect. It's much better when they don't.

This isn't normal. She knows that. Nothing in her life has been normal since she lost her daughter.

Placing the tray on the garden table, she arranges the cutlery and the linen napkin and the plate of food. She can tell from her mother's breathing that she's dozing.

'Mum,' she says softly. 'I got you something to eat.'

An intake of breath and Sandra Naylor wakes. She removes her sunglasses and blinks at her daughter.

'Oh,' she says. 'Thank you. Have you phoned the hospital?'

'They only admitted him an hour ago.'

'Yes, but you need to keep on at them, you know that.' Claire is well aware the acerbic tone is to cover her mother's fear; this time she thinks she's going to lose him. That he'll just never come home.

'I call them in a bit,' Claire says. 'Just eat your lunch.'

Sandra needs some help to adjust the back of the chair into a more upright position.

'Aren't you having anything?' she says.

'I'm not that hungry.'

Sandra frowns. 'Look at you, you're skin and bone. Have you got a hangover?'

'Don't go all headteacher on me, Mum.'

'You're a grown woman. You make your own choices. But, as a mother, I worry. Surely that allowed?'

Claire gives her the ghost of a smile. 'He'll be alright, y'know. He will come home.'

Sandra gives her a sharp glance. 'You can't say that. Because we never known what's round the corner, do we?'

Claire dips her head and accepts the rebuke. At times, her mother can be rather brisk.

Sandra picks up her knife and fork. 'We all get old,' she says. 'Your father and I have had a good life. I'm not about to engage in self-pity. And I know him, nor is he.'

She eats in ladylike mouthfuls. Claire sits down on the garden chair opposite and watches her. The heat haze sits like an invisible blanket over the trees and shrubs. The sky is relentlessly blue.

'Well,' says her mother. 'How was the reunion?'

'Fine,' says Claire.

Just don't go there.

'Did Melissa come?' says Sandra. 'I always thought she was a lovely girl. Very lively and bright.'

Claire finds she can't speak. She picks up her phone to distract herself. It's on silent. Three missed calls. And they keep coming. The police have been trying to get in touch with her. DS Boden? Wasn't that the cop who took her back to her room? She left a voice message saying they need to speak with her as a matter of urgency.

It can only mean one thing. Adrian has talked to them, told them about the knife, or maybe even given it to them. They must know she tried to stab Robert Gerrish.

If she's honest, it's a relief. Now it can all be over. They'll lock her up and she won't have to go through the motions any longer.

She wonders who'll look after her parents when she goes to jail. Her dad will have to go into care. Sandra will resist this, but there'll be little choice. Claire just hopes she'll have time to make the arrangements before the trial. She'll plead guilty. Obviously. She wonders how long she'll get. And what about Ziggy?

'Are you alright?' says her mother.

'Just a bit tired.'

Sandra puts her knife and fork down and dabs her mouth with the napkin.

'I'm not a fool,' she says. 'Something has happened. You look like…I don't know…a zombie. As if someone has stolen your soul.'

Claire meets her mother's searching gaze.

'Oh Mum,' she says. 'Mel's dead. It happened on Saturday night. And it's all my fault.'

Sandra shakes her head abruptly to shove the idea aside. 'No! How can that be? What happened? Some kind of accident? Not this getting drunk and jumping in the river like when you were undergraduates.'

'It's…it was the thing with Ella. I told her about it.'

'About Gerrish? And I told you we must speak to a lawyer. If that man bullied my granddaughter, I don't care who he is. We must get the police involved. Demand a proper inquiry. I don't care what it costs. We can mortgage this place. We can—'

'Mum, the police are involved. They want to question me.'

'Why?'

'Because I…took a knife to the reunion to try to stab him. I'm sorry Mum. I realise now how completely deranged…'

She shakes her head wearily.

Sandra's jaw slackens. 'Oh my god, Claire.' She opens her arms. 'My poor, poor girl. Come here!'

Claire gets up, goes over to her mother's chair, kneels beside it, and lays her head on Sandra's chest.

Her mother's arms close around her protectively. 'I didn't realise you were still thinking about that,' she says. 'You haven't mentioned it for a while.'

'It's insane. I've just become more and more obsessed. I couldn't seem to get him out of my head. It just feels like he's this monster. And I had so much anger. And I don't understand where it's all coming from. I just wanted to kill him.'

Sandra strokes her hair. 'Sssh. We lost our precious little girl. It's coming from that.'

'It's made me crazy.'

'Well, you must talk to the police. Tell them your suspicions about Gerrish. And they will understand. We'll get you a good lawyer. And, in the end, it might not be as bad as you think.'

'I wish I could believe that.'

44

Sunday, 2.30pm

Adrian Cardello sips a green smoothie and gazes down at the River Thames from the balcony of his penthouse apartment in the Battersea Power Station complex. It's a hazy, hot afternoon, light shimmers off the river like a pane of glass, and he's just completed a workout with his personal trainer, Jermaine. He was in Cambridge for less than twenty-four hours, but it wrecked his diet and his routine. Alcohol, processed sugar and carbs. He admitted the binge to Jermaine, and that he'd woken up feeling crap.

The tall, perfectly toned former NFL player and committed vegan had given him a sardonic look and said, 'Is what it is, man.'

You could say that about the entire weekend. A total balls-up.

When Adrian was at drama school, he'd been taught that his body was his instrument. That sounded really arty and airy-fairy at the time. The reality is it's a million-dollar investment on which his career depends, not to mention the careers of a number of others.

But Jermaine was gentle. For Jermaine.

Every muscle in Adrian's body is now humming and on the cusp of being painful. Jermaine is an expert at pushing him just to the edge. But Adrian knows that now he's on the wrong side of forty, maintaining his star power depends on this. His next movie is due to start filming in a month; it's an action adventure with a dash of wisecracking romance. The hope is to turn it into a multi-million-dollar franchise and they're trying out an unknown female lead, so he's got to carry the movie.

He finishes his smoothie, takes a long shower, ending with a thirty-second cold blast. He hates that bit.

As he dresses, he thinks about the phone call. Leanne Brady called him this morning. Completely random. He has no idea how she got his private number. And she was insistent. They needed to talk about Claire.

Did Leanne see the knife? She must've done. That's the only conclusion he can come to. He could've just refused. In fact, that was probably the sensible option. Why is he letting himself get dragged into this?

Rob Gerrish needs taking down a peg or two.

Now he's annoyed with himself. That's ancient history. An old grudge and he needs to let it go. But part of him is simply curious. And there's no harm in just listening to what Leanne has to say, is there?

He checks his watch. She's due at three, and the doorbell rings right on time.

Adrian answers it himself. He's given his assistant the afternoon off.

Leanne is small, and no one would call her good looking. She has an odd, lop-sided mouth. But it's obvious she's worked hard on herself over the years. A complete makeover, and that takes discipline. Adrian can certainly respect that.

'Oh Adrian!' she says with a tragic tilt of the head. Her hair is immaculate, a soft honey blonde bob. 'I can't believe what's happened. It's awful beyond belief.'

'Come in, Leanne,' he says. 'It is awful.'

'I gather you went to the hospital.' She follows him into the apartment. An elegant, silky summer dress and open-toed sandals. She's certainly learned how to dress since her frumpy cardigan student days.

'Yes,' he says. He frowns and dips his head, although he has a sense that they're both just play-acting here. Leanne and Mel were never friends. Mel hated her.

The weekend reunion certainly stirred up all the slime from the bottom of the pond. For him, it exhumed a toxic romance and reminded him that love and hate can be close companions. Mel always had a talent for bringing out the worst in him. And he should've anticipated that. But now she's dead, and there's no point dwelling on it.

'Can I get you…some tea?' he says.

'Thank you.' She surveys the room. 'Now don't tell me, this place is so wabi-sabi. I'm going to say Axel Vervoordt. He designed an apartment here for a friend of ours.'

Little Leanne Brady from a council estate somewhere grim and northern?

Her transformation is amusing, if nothing else. He smiles to himself. 'I'm useless at all that,' he says. 'I just bought the place, furniture and furnishings included. I chose this apartment because of the view of the river.'

Leanne walks to the open balcony door. 'Yes,' she says. 'It is pretty perfect.'

They stare at each other for a moment, like two players on a stage.

'Right,' he says. 'Earl Grey?'

'Lovely,' she replies.

He busies himself making tea, while Leanne goes out on the balcony and looks at the river. It gives him a chance to adjust to the fact this could be a delicate encounter. But what does she want? There's no way Leanne gives a stuff about Mel.

He has a Japanese-looking tea service that came with the place. He's never used it. But he arranges the delicate ceramic cups on a tray and fills the pot with boiling water. He carries it over to the glass coffee table in the centre of the room.

Leanne returns from the balcony and they perch on opposite sofas.

'Well, you're probably wondering what this is about,' says Leanne.

He shrugs and tries to look mystified.

'I find myself in a very awkward position,' she says.

She saw the knife.

'The police spoke to Robert and I shortly after the attack on Melissa.'

'I haven't spoken to them yet,' he says.

'The problem is, I think I know what happened.'

'Really? My goodness.'

Does she?

He pours the tea into the two little cups and offers her one. There are some coloured glass coasters on the table. Leanne sets her cup on one of them and then makes a slight adjustment, turning it through forty-five degrees. Adrian finds the precision of it fascinating. It's as if she's an actor, feeling her way into a role, looking for little bits of business to express her character. This gesture speaks is about a need to control.

'After you and Robert had your little altercation,' she says. 'I made you a promise.'

'Yes, you said you'd find out who was responsible for wrongly accusing Ella of some leak.'

'I did. But circumstances have rather overtaken us, don't you think?'

He meets her gaze.

'That's one way of putting it.'

'I think the real problem here is with Claire herself. She's just not the person you remember.'

He's already figured that out for himself.

'In what way?' he says.

'She hates us, Adrian. You, me, and also Melissa. She hates us because we're the ones who made it. And she didn't.'

No mention of Robert.

'That's quite a bold assertion,' he says.

'I'm the one who kept in touch with her over the years. Her life was rather boring and ordinary.'

'Maybe that's what she wanted.'

Leanne shrugs, as if this is a mystifying concept. Then she says, 'Claire desperately needed a reason to explain why Ella took her own life, which, as a parent, I totally understand. I'm sure you do too.'

He nods. 'Well, yeah.'

'So she created this tale.'

'You saying none of it's true?'

'Something may have happened to upset Ella. But Robert had nothing to do with it. Ella worked for a few months as an intern in Robert's department. It's a large government department. He's the Minister. He had virtually no contact with her. It's a conspiracy theory that only works in Claire's head.'

Where's she going with this?

Adrian watches Leanne's face. She holds firm eye contact and exudes earnest conviction. If this is an act, she's better at it that most of the performers he works with.

'And speaking frankly, between old friends,' she says. 'You know how crazily obsessed she is with it, because you rushed in and took a swing at Robert to stop her stabbing him, didn't you?'

Bam! There it is. Delivered like a pro.

He meets her gaze. She raises her eyebrows.

'Didn't you? Come on, Adrian. I was there. I saw the knife.'

He exhales and steeples his fingers.

'Did you tell the police?' he says.

'No, I didn't. And now I wish I had. Because what does she do in her crazy, possibly psychotic state? She turns on Melissa. Some kind of row ensues and in a rage she hits her over the head.'

He stares at her.

Wow! She wants to blame Claire for Mel?

She's monitoring his reaction; he goes for wide-eyed surprise.

'And we both know what Melissa and Claire most likely rowed about, don't we?' she says. 'You.'

He gets up, rakes his fingers through his hair. 'I don't know what to say. What do you intend to do about this?'

'I don't know,' says Leanne. 'That's why I thought I'd come and speak to you.'

He puts his hands on his hips. 'That was probably the right thing.'

'I don't think Claire's in her right mind,' says Leanne. 'But, as her oldest friends, I think we should help her.'

'How?'

'Obviously, justice needs to be done. For Mel. But I think

we need to find a way to ensure that Claire gets proper treatment, and not just blame for what she's done. As I've already said, I don't think she was in her right mind.'

'You think I can help with this?'

'Well, yes. I think she trusts you. She's become much more wary of me lately. I suppose because I'm Robert's wife.'

She wants to use you, so she remains at arm's length.

'Okay,' he says. 'I think you're probably right. We can't just stand back and do nothing.'

45

Sunday, 3.05pm

Claire drives home from her parents' house in a trance. Talking to her mother has helped her gain some clarity. She is calmer. The chance to confess and explain is something she welcomes. Maybe the police will unravel the craziness of all this. She owes it to Ella. And to Mel.

The panic she felt when she got the first message from DS Boden has lessened. She's taken a couple of her tablets, and that's helping. She cruises along, her brain in a detached reverie. The heat shimmers on the tarmac like puddles of water in the road. Perhaps her mother is right. It might not be as bad as she thinks.

As she drives up to her house and parks, she sees two women sitting outside in a car. They get out. And one of them is the woman who took her back to her room in college.

Claire tries not to panic.

Take a couple more Ativan. Just in case.

She pops two out of their bubble pack and swigs them

down with the water she has in the car. Then she gets out and clicks the key fob, wondering when she'll get a chance to drive it again. Can they just lock her up? She must ask her neighbour to take care of Ziggy.

The police officers walk towards her. The woman she recognises holds up her warrant card. 'Hello Claire. Remember me? DS Boden.'

Claire nods. 'You're going to arrest me, aren't you? Can we do it inside?'

Boden nods. She follows Claire up the short path and into the house.

'Adrian's got the knife,' she says.

'The knife?' says DS Boden with a frown.

'Adrian Cardello,' says Claire.

'Okay,' says Boden. 'We want to question you in connection with the death of Melissa Rowe. So I'm going to caution you.'

This stops Claire in her tracks.

Mel?

'I don't understand,' she says.

'You do not have to say anything. But, it may harm your defence if you do not mention when questioned something you later rely on in court. Anything you do say may be given in evidence. Do you understand what I'm saying, Claire?'

What is she talking about?

'No,' she says. 'No, I don't understand. You're saying this is about Mel? Mel's death?'

'Yes. What did you think it was about?'

Claire feels the bile rising in her throat. She swallows it back. It stings. 'What are you saying? You think I killed Mel?'

A whirlwind of panic engulfs her. No, this is ridiculous. It makes no sense.

'We want to talk to you about your movements and what happened that night. And it's probably best if we do that at a police station and you can have a lawyer present.'

Claire slumps down on a chair. 'This is absurd. Mel was my friend. I didn't kill her. Why would I kill her?'

The interview room is small and boxy, just four walls and no windows. There's a lot of hanging about. It's all rather cold and formal; a set of procedures that have to be followed. Or perhaps they just want to make you feel like a criminal? And that will make you more likely to spill your guts and tell them everything.

But it has the opposite effect on Claire. She's retreating into herself.

The cascade of panicky thoughts has ebbed. The tablets are doing their work. There's a lawyer who's turned up. They called him. He's young and seems extremely hassled. He roots in his briefcase for a pen. She watches him. It's clear he's just going through the motions.

You can't confess to these people about Gerrish.

He glances at her and asks if she's okay. She just nods.

She's feeling rather drowsy. She'd like to just sleep.

Finally, Boden comes in and sits down. The other officer who came to the house is with her. A small Asian girl; she looks too young to be a police officer. More like some of Claire's A level students.

They remind her she's still under caution. They say their names. The lawyer says his. Darryl something-or-other.

'Do you recognise my colleague, DC Chakravorty?' says Boden.

Claire looks at the other officer and smiles. It's a reflex

action. The polite thing to do. The girl doesn't smile back. Claire shakes her head.

'Can you answer for the recording?' says Boden.

'No,' says Claire.

'DC Chakravorty was at the hospital when Melissa went into cardiac arrest and died. She overheard you speaking to Adrian Cardello. Do you remember what you said?'

Claire shakes her head again. Her brain is scrambling to catch up. Why are they talking about this? What did she say? She has no idea. All she remembers is crying and being really upset.

'I don't remember,' she says. 'But I didn't kill Mel.'

They need to get this into their heads. The ridiculousness of it. She may be crazy, but not that crazy.

'Okay,' says Boden. 'When did you last see Mel?'

'At dinner. She sat with me and Adrian. Well, that was to talk to. I saw her on a stretcher, being put in an ambulance. And I saw her in ICU...' her voice trails off.

'And when you were at the hospital,' says Boden, 'you don't remember saying to Adrian Cardello that what had happened to Melissa was your fault?'

'Maybe I said that. But I didn't mean that I killed her.'

'What did you mean, Claire?'

'I persuaded her to come to the reunion to help me prove Rob Gerrish drove my daughter to suicide. And she said she would. And if you want to know my opinion, that's what got her killed.'

You said it! Now it's out there. They know.

'Okay,' says Boden. 'I think we'll take a break there.'

Claire meets the cop's eye. She wants to be sure that they know she's telling the truth.

46

Boden and Chakravorty walk across the office to their desks.

'Robert Gerrish, the Cabinet Minister?' says Chakravorty with a disbelieving frown. 'That's really going to cheer the boss up. Do you think it's true?'

'Who knows?' says Boden. She picks up a half-drunk cup of coffee from her desk. It's cold. She drinks it anyway.

'What are we going to do with Claire?' says Chakravorty.

'I'll ask the boss. I suspect release her under investigation. We'll need to ask Cardello what he thinks Claire said. Also, when I arrested her she said Adrian's got the knife.'

'That doesn't fit with blunt force trauma to the head,' says Chakravorty.

'No,' says Boden with a sigh. 'And I believe her. I don't think she did it.'

If the DCI is still fixated on a fast result, it certainly won't be coming from this lead.

Boden drains her cup. 'Wish me luck,' she says, and heads for the DCI's office.

Rachel Knight is on her feet, hands resting on the desk and staring intently at the screen of her laptop. Mackie is standing beside her, looking over her shoulder. He points at the screen.

'…there you go, boss,' he says. 'Footage is terrible. We've enhanced it as much as we can.'

She shakes her head. 'Could be him,' she says. 'It's possible.'

For most of the day, the DCI has had three analysts working with Mackie to pull apart every shred of CCTV they've collected from the college. The purpose of the exercise is to establish if and when Leon Davison, the drug dealer, located Melissa Rowe in the chapel. Now, it looks as if they've come up with something.

If Knight has got the evidence she needs, and the CPS agrees, then she'll be going ahead with a charge. In which case, she won't be that interested in Claire Naylor.

Boden hovers in the doorway, waiting for the DCI to notice her.

'I think you're right, Scott,' Knight says. 'Interesting.' She looks up at Boden. Her eyes are underscored with deep purple shadows, knackered and then some, but she has a smile on her face. 'Jo,' she says. 'Come and look at this. Tell us what you think.'

Boden steps forward.

'This is the view of the front of the chapel from across the lawn,' says Mackie. 'Time is 11.43. Which is fifteen minutes before me and Prisha found her.'

He turns the laptop round to face Boden and presses play.

The picture quality is grainy with patches of deep shadow

and pools of light from different sources. The door to the chapel appears to be ajar.

A figure crosses the lawn diagonally. At first he's a silhouette with his back towards the camera. Then he stops in the archway of the door to the chapel and turns sideways, as if to check the coast is clear. His profile is illuminated, but only for a second. Then he pushes the door and enters.

'Well,' says Boden. 'Doesn't look like Leon to me. We know from witnesses he was wearing a baseball cap. This looks like an older man.'

'Exactly,' says Mackie.

'Could be anyone,' says Boden.

'Look again,' says Mackie. 'The way he walks and holds himself. Like an actor maybe?'

Boden peers at the screen.

'Shit,' she says. 'You think it's Adrian Cardello?'

47

Leanne is a huge fan of breakfast meetings. Her energy levels are at their highest and it makes her feel she has a jump on the day. She usually conducts them in her firm's boardroom, with an array of pastries from the artisan bakery round the corner for her guests. She never touches these herself. Well, almost never. But this morning, as she waits, she decides she could perhaps do with the sugar hit to sharpen up her thought processes. She selects an apricot Danish and takes a bite. Delicious.

As she waits, she savours the gooey pastry and reflects on her encounter with Adrian Cardello. He's as tricky as he is charming. But she thinks it went well.

Her overall plan is to place Claire in the frame and, therefore, neutralise any threat to Robert. That's not quite how she put it to Adrian, of course. But he seemed open the notion that Claire could be the culprit and conceded that their old friend needed help. If anything, he agreed a little too easily. And this has made Leanne wary.

Climbing to the very top of the Hollywood pile takes more than good looks and acting ability. It requires a ruthless nature. As a young man, Adrian had always seemed rather happy-go-lucky, maybe even a bit flaky. Yet, from the outside, his ascent looks seamless. He's turned into a powerful man, and it wouldn't do to underestimate him.

He immediately volunteered to cover all Claire's medical and legal bills. And they agreed that with a top-notch legal team, the right doctors and a plea of diminished responsibility, they could probably minimise the time she would have to spend in jail. But pinning the blame on Claire is the longer term strategy. This morning she has to park that up and deal with more immediate issues.

She licks her fingers and checks her nails. They've suffered a little over the weekend and she's booked an urgent appointment at the nail salon.

Her assistant, Caspar, is approaching. She sees him through the glass door to the boardroom. He's sashaying and swinging his hips, which he only does when he's with a bloke he really fancies. And Theo Webber is hot. The tall, lean physique of an athlete, but with floppy romantic dark curls. Right up Caspar's street. Her assistant opens the door and ushers the journalist inside with a flourish.

Leanne stands up, beams, and holds out her hand. 'Theo,' she says. 'Thank you for coming.'

He accepts the handshake warily. Typical lefty hack who thinks everyone's trying to steal his lunch.

'I was curious,' he says.

Leanne offers him a seat. He dumps his retro satchel style bag on the table and pulls out a chair.

'The first thing I want to say,' says Leanne, 'is that,

although we had our political difference, Melissa was one of my oldest friends. I feel her loss keenly and personally. I talked to your editor yesterday, and I told her as much.'

'Yeah, she said.'

A short, polite exchange. A box ticker for her as much as you.

'And I gather you were working on a story with Mel. Which, I have to say, makes you a very lucky young journalist, to have had the opportunity to learn from one of the best.'

He sniffs. 'I'm surprised to hear you say that.'

Leanne scans him. His surliness is amusing. He sees himself as a young gun who's going to change the world. He exudes high ideals and moral purpose. If he'd grown up where she did, he'd have realised that the world doesn't give a stuff for morality. It's survival of the fittest, and you need to join the tribe who wield the biggest sticks and get the biggest share of the pie.

She shrugs. 'What surprises you? That I think she was one of the best? She was absolutely unique. And let me tell you, Theo, I realised that twenty-five years ago. Coffee?'

He nods. She pours and places the ceramic mug on the table in front of him.

He gets out his phone, puts it on the table, and presses record. 'I assume this is okay?' he says as an afterthought.

'Why wouldn't it be?' says Leanne. 'I just wanted to reach out. I don't want any misunderstandings.'

He absorbs this for a moment.

'Okay, well, nor do we,' he says. 'I've been talking to Kieran Morgan, one of your husband's special advisers. And he said he couldn't tell me anything. I should speak to you.'

At least Kieran's on message.

'I can't imagine why,' says Leanne. 'SpAds don't like political wives as a general rule. And I'm sure Kieran could've answered your questions. To be honest with you, I expect he was just being lazy.'

'You know he used to hang out with Ella Naylor, the girl who topped herself?'

Leanne tilts her head and raises her eyebrows to feign surprise.

'What?' she says. 'Kieran was seeing her? That's news to me.'

Theo smiles. He thinks the hook is in.

So far, so good.

'Well,' he says. 'That was what I was working on with Mel. She talked to Ella Naylor's mother, who reckons they bullied Ella.'

'Robert is not a bully. I can state that categorically,' says Leanne. 'He has an excellent relationship with all his staff.'

'Yeah,' says Theo. 'Mel didn't really think that would fly either. That's how we got to Kieran. Her theory was that Ella was shagging a SpAd. She was a vulnerable intern and she was exploited when she should've been protected. I did some digging and I've found two sources who work in your husband's department. They both confirm Ella was in a sexual relationship with Kieran.'

Is this really all they've got?

Leanne sighs. 'I don't really think we can hold any minister responsible for the complicated sex lives of his younger members of staff. They are all adults.'

'Yeah, Mel said that would be your line. We had a couple of conversations on the phone about it.' He takes another phone out of his bag. 'Then she sent me a text late on Saturday night. Shall I read it to you?'

He thinks he's got a trick up his sleeve.

She smiles. 'By all means.'

He clicks the phone on and reads from the screen. 'I've

badgered Leanne. She's finally agreed to talk to me about this. I'm just about to meet up with her. I'll keep you posted.' He clicks the phone off. 'She sent that at 11.35 on Saturday night. I'm just wondering if you did meet her? Because you must be the last person to have seen her alive.'

Leanne inhales.

Deep breaths.

'Okay,' she says briskly. 'And this is for the record. Melissa approached me. She was quite drunk by then, and I'd also say pretty coked up. I'm sure the post-mortem will confirm this. I discussed with Robert whether to go and meet her. We decided she was not in a fit state to have a proper conversation. I remained with my husband in our rooms in the college. And there are two metropolitan police officers from my husband's close protection detail who were outside the door, and can confirm that.'

He looks a little crestfallen.

Leanne sips her coffee and smiles. 'I think your editor will want to play that to the lawyers before you proceed any further in this direction.'

She gives him a steely glare.

Now you can fuck right off, mate!

She stands up. 'I have another meeting. Caspar will show you out.'

48

Monday, 9.30am

Adrian has been expecting the police to come calling. He alerted his London lawyers on Sunday as soon as he was back from Cambridge. This was the first hurdle to overcome, then the PR people could pick it up and deal with any reputational fallout.

The senior partner put him in touch with their top crime specialist, a rather austere and fearsome woman called Beatrix Finborough. She made a house call on Sunday evening. Any approach from the police was to be referred to her immediately, she said.

As a result, two members of the Major Investigations Team are coming to interview him by appointment.

Beatrix arrived ten minutes ahead of time. She positioned herself in the middle of one of the large sofas, laptop open, and advised him to behave normally and not to disrupt his routine or seem in the least bit put out.

So he and Jermaine are lifting a few weights when the

cops show up. The idea is to throw them on the back foot and overawe them with a display of money and power. After all, he is a movie star.

One of his assistants escorts the two police officers in. Adrian picks up a towel, wipes his sweaty hands and comes straight over to greet them. He's still flanked by Jermaine.

'Adrian Cardello,' he says with a smile. Then he realises his hand is being shaken by the female cop who put him in an armlock and dragged him off Rob Gerrish.

She has an unnervingly direct stare. 'DS Boden,' she says. 'And my colleague, DC Mackie.' She doesn't mention their previous encounter.

He's huge, easily as tall as Jermaine, has a twinkle in his eye and the battered ears of a rugby player. He gives Jermaine a friendly nod. The cops are making a point here. They don't give a toss who you think you are.

But Beatrix steps forward. More introductions.

Beatrix has already explained that this is a 'trace and interview'. He isn't a suspect, but they want to ask him some questions.

'Well, have a seat,' says Adrian. 'Can we get you any juice, water, coffee?'

'We're fine,' says Boden.

He had little chance to look her over before. But she's certainly fit and would make a great role model for an edgy thriller. The tough female cop who'd look super sexy holding a gun and could stab the villain using her stiletto shoe. He muses on all the possibilities of this and her.

Umm, a real live cop? What would that be like?

He gives her an engaging smile. She half smiles back. The gorilla sits down next to her, making a large dent in the sofa and gets out his phone.

Boden looks at the lawyer. 'Do you mind if we record this?'

'No,' says Beatrix, getting her own phone out and placing it on the table next to the cop's.

And we're off to the races, thinks Adrian. He gives her another smile.

Would she fancy getting it on with a movie star? You never know.

'On the evening that Melissa Rowe died, you and Claire Naylor went to the hospital,' says Boden.

He dips his head. 'We did.'

'Can you recall any of your conversation with Claire?'

'We were both shocked and upset. But I really couldn't tell you what was said.'

'I'm sorry,' says Boden. 'I'm sure it was very upsetting for you.'

He shakes his head. 'Don't apologise. I just want to help in any way I can.'

'Can you tell us a bit more about your relationship with Melissa?' says Boden.

Adrian takes a moment, blows out his cheeks and gets into the part. 'Okay,' he says. 'She's…' he pauses, pinches the flesh between his brows and tears up. 'Sorry,' he says. 'She was an old friend. We were at university together. And for some of that time, we were a couple. She dumped me shortly after graduation.'

Only really half a lie.

'Was there a reason for that?' says Boden.

He sighs. 'Well, probably. But that's lost in the mists of time now. It was twenty-five years ago. We just went our separate ways and became grown-ups. As you do.'

'And when did you next see her?'

'This weekend. Perhaps in the early years she came to a couple of my plays. I don't really remember.'

'But you hadn't seen her for many years before this weekend's college reunion?'

'No, I hadn't.'

'And what happened?'

'Well, we said hello. All a bit awkward. So we all got pissed. Pretty much your standard college reunion.'

'Tell us about what happened with Robert Gerrish?'

He chuckles. 'Rob Gerrish is a twat. Excuse my language, but that's what he is. We were roommates in our first year. I just thought he was being a big lairy with Claire.'

'Claire Naylor?'

'Yes.'

'Another old friend?'

'Yes.' He leans back in his chair, gazes over the cops' heads and out of the window. 'Life hasn't been too kind to Claire. She's a bit of a mess.'

'What do you mean by that?'

He sighs. 'She had a grown-up daughter who committed suicide a few months ago. I only discovered this on Saturday. I've got kids myself. I'd just be wrecked if that happened to me.'

'And what was your relationship with Claire Naylor's daughter?'

This comes straight out of left field. He glances at Beatrix. 'That's a bit of a curve ball,' he says.

Beatrix jumps in. 'I don't see how this question relates to Melissa Rowe's death.'

'Well,' says Boden. 'It's been alleged, Mr Cardello, that Claire told you on Saturday that you were the father of her daughter, Ella.'

Leanne has been a busy little bee.

'This has absolutely no relevance,' says Beatrix fiercely. 'And is a private matter.'

'Okay,' says Boden. 'Moving on. When did you last see Melissa Rowe?'

Adrian sighs. 'I'm not sure. Elevenish?'

'Not later than that?'

'It was a party. I wasn't clock watching.'

'Did you go to the chapel at 11.43 to meet her?'

WTF?

'I don't know. That's a bit precise.'

He glances at the lawyer. He knows what she'd advise, but this is his call.

He stands up. He always performs better when he's moving. 'Okay,' he says. 'Well, I'm not going to lie about this. I went looking for her.'

'You went to the chapel at around that time?'

He looks at the cop. So formal. But he wouldn't mind seeing what she's like off duty.

C'mon, let's play.

'Yes. I was worried about her. She was drunk. She'd also been snorting some coke.'

'You went to find her in the chapel and then what happened?'

He flings his arms akimbo. 'She wasn't there. Place was empty.'

'Then what happened?'

'Someone had told me they saw her going in there, so I figured she must've gone out the back door. I followed.'

Boden looks at him.

Gotcha! She looks even better when she's annoyed.

'There's a back door?' says the cop.

'Well,' he says. 'Sort of. There's a door that leads down into the crypt. Looks like it goes nowhere. But if you go down there, and it is pretty spooky and dark, you'll find a short passage, and there's another door, which leads out into the Master's Garden.'

'A secret passage?' The cop definitely looks pissed off.

'Yeah, if you like. I went down there. Came out in the Master's Garden. Still no sign of Mel. So I went back to the bar.'

'Who do you think knows about this other exit through the crypt?'

'Loads of people, I should think. You'd have to ask the Bursar. Parts of the college are really old. It's a complete warren. As undergrads, we loved all that. Places to hide, hang out, smoke a bit of weed. You know what students are like.' He smiles.

The cop is processing this. They obviously thought they had him in the frame. Well, serves her right for practically breaking his arm. Now they're even. He likes that.

He tilts his head, gazes straight at her and smiles. This is his magic power with women. And it rarely fails him.

49

Monday, 2.15pm

Claire lies full length on the squidgy old sofa, staring at the cracks in the ceiling. She has a pulsing headache. She suspects she's taken too many of her tablets.

After she told the police about Gerrish, they didn't question her anymore. They released her under investigation? Was that the term? It meant their inquiries were ongoing and they might want to question her at a later date; that's what they said. It was the Asian girl who looked too young to be a police officer. The entire experience was just weird. She had to get a taxi home.

But that was last night, wasn't it?

Have you just been lying here since then?

She can't recall. She hasn't eaten. There's a queasiness in her guts. Her thoughts are illusive and hard to grasp. This probably means she's not well. Maybe it is the tablets, or even some kind of breakdown? She's not sure. How do you even tell? She should call the doctor's surgery and try to make an appointment. But the effort of it is just too much. Later maybe.

Where's Ziggy? No sign of him.

She's been racking her brains to remember what she actually said to Adrian at the hospital. But it's completely gone. She has no memory of it, which is worrying. She wonders what else she's forgotten.

They thought she killed Mel. But she didn't. Is she even sure about that?

The knife? That was real. The knife was in her bag and then in the palm of her hand. She was seconds away from stabbing Gerrish. She remembers that. If she'd succeeded, Mel would still be alive.

This thought hits her like a bullet. She could've saved her friend. She was so close. She wants to cry out, but she can't. Her lungs are frozen. The pain is paralysing.

Because of you, Mel is dead.

That's still hard to grasp. How? It all happened so quickly. But now she realises it's doubly her fault. She should've dealt with Gerrish when she had the chance. But Adrian stopped her.

Why did he do that?

She thought she was glad he did. Now she's not so sure. And did he really do it for her?

A suspicion creeps into her mind, and within seconds it explodes.

Adrian and Rob. You're such a fool. You should've seen that.

In their first year at uni, Adrian and Rob were roommates. And throughout their time as undergrads, they remained friends. Of course they did! Adrian was popular, the blue-eyed boy. But Rob Gerrish was his nerdy sidekick, always hanging around. And Adrian used to tease Rob, who never seemed to mind. Did Adrian have any other particular friends? Not that Claire can recall. It was always him and Rob. They were like best mates.

And maybe they still are. Somehow, she'd forgotten all this.

You trusted him!

Now she can see the horrible logic of it all. She'd confided in Adrian. He also knew that she'd asked Mel to help her. Adrian acted to protect Rob, not her. He only ever pretended to be on her side. They're both rich and successful men now. Still mates, still covering for each other. It's what men do. That's how the world works.

She feels wretched and naïve. And totally alone.

She needs another tablet. She probably shouldn't. But she's going mad with all this. What's she supposed to do? She has nowhere else to turn.

Getting up from the sofa, she searches for her bag. But she can't see it anywhere. A feeling of dread stampedes through her brain. It's gone. It's been stolen. For several moments she searches frantically and suddenly there it is, on the floor under the table. She grabs it, pulls out the blister pack.

Her hand shakes as she fills a glass with water. She takes just the one.

It'll be alright now.

She returns to the sofa and lies down.

Let the tablet do its job. Relax.

Random thoughts skitter through her mind. She dozes.

Opening her eyes, she becomes aware of her phone buzzing on the kitchen worktop. She struggles to her feet, goes over to it and picks it up. Six missed calls from her mother.

She answers. 'Mum?'

'What's happening, Claire? You said you'd call me.'

'I don't know. The police let me go.'

'They let you go?'

Why is she just repeating things?

'Mum, they're saying I killed Mel. That's what they think.'

'Did you?'

'What? No!'

'Well, I had to ask and—'

No, she didn't! She should've known the answer.

Claire clicks the phone off and tosses it back on the counter. It rings again immediately. She ignores it.

Where's Ziggy? Has he abandoned you, too?

She walks over to the French doors that open into the garden. The light is fading. Soon it will be dark. No sign of the cat. She's spent the whole day in limbo. Her mouth is dry and sticky. She has a painful crick in her neck.

Picking up the glass from the draining board, she fills it with more water. Why would her mother ask her that?

Because of Gerrish? Because she thinks you're crazy? Because you are crazy?

She needs to pull herself together. She needs to get a grip.

The water is cold and refreshing. She swallows it down.

In the main room, the shadows are deepening. A street-light has come on outside and its beam filters through the front window.

As she drinks her water, a stillness gradually settles in her mind and body. Her niggling thoughts and anxieties have slowed. She closes her eyes and inhales.

Stay in this moment. Just be.

She puts her left palm on her chest to comfort herself and focuses on her breath. In and out.

Wham!

It comes out of nowhere like the crack of a rifle, a sudden hammering on the front door. She jumps. Her anxiety skyrockets. Is it the police? Come to drag her back to their little box of a room?

You told them the truth about Gerrish.

Her heart is thumping, but she walks over to the door and opens it.

Then she does a double-take.

Adrian Cardello is wearing a baseball cap and his trademark grin. He leans on the doorjamb. 'Hey, Claire.'

Confusion envelopes her. Should she panic?

'Adrian?' she says, trying to sound normal. 'How did you find me?'

He just taps the side of his nose.

Leanne must've given him the address.

'Can I come in?' he says, removing his cap. 'I think we need to have a talk.'

She nods; there seems little choice.

'You're all in the dark,' he says, as he enters.

She reaches over and flicks the light switch. Only then does she realise there's another man with him. He's massive, dark cornrows across his scalp and expensive sports gear. He follows Adrian into the house.

'This is Jermaine.'

Claire gives him a nod; he smiles back. But she's at a total loss. What the hell do they want? Coming here, just as it's getting dark. Should she run? Perhaps she should run. Only one thought is roaring through her brain.

Adrian and Rob. In it together. Adrian and Rob.

50

Monday, 9.30pm

Boden perches glumly on a stone sarcophagus in the musty crypt of the college chapel. It smells of rotting wood, dead vermin and dust.

'I'm sure no one's been down there for years,' said the Bursar.

Turns out he was wrong.

The whole place has now been forensically examined, which has taken a team of suited and booted crime scene investigators all day. No one seems to know why this was missed in the initial sweep. Once they'd finished upstairs in the chapel, they moved down here. They've only just finished.

The preliminary conclusion is that several people have been through the place recently. There are fresh footprints which have been photographed. The door to the Master's Garden was left ajar. Numerous samples have been taken.

And Melissa Rowe's clothes will need to be examined in the lab to see if any particles of dust or debris from the chapel can be found on them, or whether her footwear can be matched to any footprints.

'I don't understand why any of them would come down here,' says Chakravorty, wrinkling her nose.

'For old times' sake?' says Boden.

'It's grim and manky and it smells,' says Chakravorty.

'Where's your sense of youthful adventure?' says Boden.

'I am youthful. And if I wanted to smoke dope or have sex, I'm sure I could find somewhere better.'

Boden sighs. 'I agree. I think we've been fed a load of lies to deflect from what really happened here?'

'Was she chased down here?' says Chakravorty. 'Or did she hide down here?'

'Or was she even here? We've only got Cardello's say-so. She was attacked upstairs in the chapel, sitting in a pew. Doesn't make a lot of sense.'

Boden gets up and brushes the stone dust off her trousers.

Her day began early, way too early, on a London-bound train with Mackie, and it still wasn't over.

When they returned with the news that Adrian Cardello appeared to have an alibi, or rather an explanation, DCI Knight seemed almost relieved. It's clear she didn't relish the idea of trying to bring such a high-profile case to trial. The opportunities for it to blow up in your face and wreck your career were legion, and Knight's career is already on life support. Boden understood why she didn't want to entertain it.

Knight is still hoping to nail her drug dealer. A straight-forward villain, the police praised for doing their job, and not too big a dent in the budget. Plus, the TZ gang were a nasty bunch who needed to go to jail, anyway. Cost-effective criminal justice. Everyone would be happy.

To this end, a team of officers, backed by civilian analysts, are working flat out to examine every inch of the college's fractured and archaic CCTV footage, hoping to find enough evidence to establish the guilt of Leon Davison. Digital forensics also have all the gang's phones that they've seized, plus data from the onboard computer of the Range Rover Discovery Leon was driving.

But the work at the murder scene is complete. The Crime Scene Manager and her team are packing up their kit. So Boden and Chakravorty head back to the office.

The incident room is still buzzing with quiet industry. Knight has ordered in pizza for the troops, and Boden and Chakravorty help themselves to a slice.

Mackie joins them. He gives Boden a wink. 'Has he texted you yet?'

Boden puffs out her cheeks. He's been teasing her with this since they left London. 'Mackie, give it up,' she says belligerently.

He throws out his palms in mock amazement. 'But Jo, a movie star? He could take you away from all this!'

Chakravorty giggles. Boden walks away to pour herself a cup of coffee. She knows what Mackie's like; this is his idea of humour.

She's well aware of the way Adrian Cardello was looking at her. It wasn't salacious; he's far too smart for that. He's a man who knows how to charm women with a subtle mix of gazing directly with those amazing blue eyes and adopting the wistful expression of an adoring puppy. This zeroing in carries a simple message: you are gorgeous and special. And you're so lucky that my gaze has fallen on you.

But Boden refuses to be fooled. And oddly, he reminds her of another man, equally charming but very dangerous. He's now serving a life sentence. Boden fell for him, but she was much younger then.

Cardello is too self-regarding for her taste. But the trip to London put Cal Foley squarely back in her thoughts. She's been trying not to dwell on that. And he has texted her. Several times.

She glances at the clock. Time she went home. Returning to her desk, she's finishing her coffee just as the DCI emerges from her office.

Rachel Knight looks worn to a frazzle. Boden watches her walk through the office. She's the boss, and people treat her with deference. But it's also obvious to Boden how isolated she's become. No one wants to get too close. Like the kid in the playground wearing the wrong brand of trainers.

Boden is struck by the gutlessness of most of her colleagues. They're keeping their heads down. Knight hovers at the shoulder of one analyst and asks a couple of questions. But her body language is insular and defensive, arms tightly folded.

Don't feel sorry for her. You'll regret it.

Gathering up her laptop and phone, Boden packs her bag. Chakravorty comes over. 'You off?' she says.

Boden nods.

'Word is,' says Chakravorty, 'that this could be done and dusted by tomorrow. If forensics can place Leon Davison in the chapel, CPS has advised the boss she can charge.'

'She's the boss,' says Boden.

Chakravorty gives Boden a quizzical look. 'You think she's got it wrong?'

'I don't know, Prish. How did Leon find her? How did he

even know what she looked like? Over fifty people milling around the place. And it was dark. There are too many unanswered questions.' Picking up her backpack, she loops it over her shoulder. 'See you in the morning.'

51

Monday, 9.55pm

Claire is in a car, travelling north. It's getting dark. She isn't even sure why she's agreed to this. Adrian sounded so convincing. He always did. She'd forgotten that about him. You ended up feeling he was on your side. But was it persuasion or coercion? It still felt like there was a threat.

'Just let me help you, Claire. That's all I ask. I owe it to you. For Ella's sake.'

He watched and waited, holding her in a steady, unwavering gaze. He was patient.

But he'd put his finger on the nub of it; she does need help. Desperately. She almost killed a man. And she has no one else. Her parents can do nothing. Her father is in hospital and her mother can barely look after herself.

What if it turns out to be a trap? Does she even care?

They've been driving for several hours. She sits in the passenger seat, deep soft leather, next to Jermaine, who's driving her.

'Jermaine will take care of you,' Adrian said. 'I have some things I need to do. And I'm asking you to just trust me.'

Those famous baby-blue eyes crinkling at the corners, cheeks dimpling as he smiled. It was probably all fake. He was lying. Or was he? He'd always been impossible to read.

For Ella's sake. He kept mentioning their daughter.

Jermaine turns out to be American; she deduces this from his accent. But he doesn't say much.

The car is something large and fancy. It purrs along, eating up the miles as they travel north. As darkness has fallen, punctuated only by the oncoming headlights and the soft glow from the dash, she's settled into a mood of dejection. Fear is still gnawing away below the surface. Where are they going? Where will she end up? Her body remains taut with anxiety. But it's all been taken out of her hands.

Could things get any worse? Maybe they could.

They stop at the services near Lancaster. Jermaine doesn't appear to be guarding her. He waits for her to return from the loos in the entrance area and hands her a bottle of water. If she wanted to run, she could. But she doesn't. What would be the point?

They head north over Shap Fell. The road signs flash by. The last time she came this way was when she and Ella went to Scotland for a holiday. It was a camping trip; she had little money back then. Her old second-hand Fiesta had wheezed and strained up the inclines. Ella was about twelve and excited to be in charge of navigation.

These are the best times she remembers. The times when it was just her and her daughter. But did she smother Ella? Was she too controlling? Is that what she did wrong? Perhaps it wasn't the best upbringing for Ella?

This is why she left you. Because you wouldn't let go.

They leave the motorway near Penrith and head into the North Pennines. Claire can see from the satnav that they're nearing their destination. The countryside is invisible, although the looming presence of the hills is near. Sharp curves in the road throw up walls of sheer rock in the headlights.

Jermaine nearly misses the turn; he brakes and has to back up to the gateway. They turn into a long winding drive between an avenue of tall horse chestnuts in heavy summer leaf; it's like a long, dark tunnel. At the end, the stark outline of the house appears. Lighted windows illuminate the intricate stonework of the facade. It's huge and imposing and the roof includes several turrets; a granite-built Victorian Gothic monstrosity. Jermaine pulls up at the massive front door.

He turns to her. 'You okay?' he says.

'Are you just leaving me here?'

'Nope, I'm staying.' She can't see his features properly in the dark, but she thinks he's smiling.

To reassure her?

She doesn't feel reassured. None of this feels right. Was it a mistake to trust Adrian?

As Claire gets out of the car, the solid oak door swings open and a young woman in pale pink medical scrubs appears. She comes trotting down the steps wreathed in smiles.

'Claire,' she says. 'We've been expecting you. Welcome to Stanfirth Hall. I'm Poppy. I'm one of the nursing assistants.'

Jermaine is getting the bags out of the back of the car. But Claire lets Poppy shepherd her inside. The outside may look like the Munsters House, but the inside is more like a lavish five-star hotel.

Adrian had described it to her as a private clinic where the wealthy go to rest, detox, get discrete medical care, and escape the prying eyes and stresses of the world.

'You'll be safe there,' he said.

She wasn't aware she needed to be safe. Standing in the palatial hallway with its domed ceiling, marble floor and sweeping staircase, she feels overwhelmed.

A young man, also in pale pink scrubs, comes round from behind the reception desk.

'Hey, I'm Karim,' he says. 'I'm going to be taking care of you, too. And, don't worry, we're very used to clients who have security issues.'

Does he mean keeping the world out or you in?

What on earth has Adrian told them? Is she a prisoner? The heavy front door has closed behind her. And, anyway, Jermaine is there to block her escape route. Any kind of resistance seems futile. She allows herself to be led towards the lift. She's glad there's a lift. The staircase looks magnificent but also hard work and she's exhausted.

Once out of the lift, Karim escorts her down a long, plushly carpeted corridor. Her small holdall follows on a large gold-plated luggage trolley pushed by Poppy. Jermaine has disappeared.

At the end of the corridor, Karim pauses. 'This is the Primrose Suite,' he says. 'Adrian mentioned that you'd like a view of the lake.'

Smiling, he opens the door and stands back to let her enter.

She's not sure what to expect. It's large. They step into a comfortable sitting room; a three-seater sofa, two matching armchairs, a polished wooden table with a couple of dining chairs. Just this room is bigger than her entire house. There's a wide screen television on a movable trolley. The door to the bedroom stands open. A king-sized bed with a neatly folded towelling robe on the end. Poppy deposits her bag on the wooden luggage stand next to it.

Karim hovers. 'If you need any pyjamas or other night-wear depending on your preference, Poppy can get something for you.'

Claire shakes her head.

'Poppy can unpack for you.'

She shakes her head again.

'Shall I show you the bathroom?'

'I'll manage.'

'Then we'll leave you to settle in and rest.'

Karim and Poppy head for the door.

Claire slips her mobile out of her pocket and glances surreptitiously at it. Just a weak signal. They must be surrounded by hills. She prays it'll be enough.

As the door closes behind her jailers, Claire hurries over to the window and pulls back one of the heavy drapes. Outside the tall window, it isn't entirely black. A rising moon is casting an eerie light over the undulating landscape. It shimmers on water; there is indeed a lake.

Claire holds up her phone and moves it around to improve the signal. Then she scrolls and clicks on the number.

It's answered after two rings. 'Hello.'

'Leanne,' she whispers.

'Claire? Why are you whispering?'

'Leanne, I think I've been kidnapped.'

52

Monday, 10.45pm

Leanne clicks her phone off and returns to the sitting room. Her husband is sprawled full length on one of the long leather sofas, television remote in one hand, irritably channel-hopping.

'Well, that was Claire,' she says. 'She's a bit upset.'

Robert gazes at her over his brandy glass. 'Where exactly is she?' he says.

'A private facility in the north. That's all Adrian told me.'

Robert exhales. His tone of voice is tetchy. 'I don't really see why you're doing this or how it helps us,' he says.

She's omitted to mention that the plan is to get her sectioned.

Leanne sits down on the other sofa. 'Darling, you've had an exhausting day. Leave this to me. Adrian and I have come to an understanding.'

'You trust him? I don't bloody trust him. Never have.'

'As I said, we've come to an understanding. And we both just want to help Claire.'

Robert scowls. 'The poor woman is bereaved. That doesn't make her crazy.'

He remains blissfully ignorant of the fact she came within inches of knifing him.

Tempting to just tell him. But, no!

Since they returned from Cambridge, his mood has been dangerously volatile. Robert, upset and reactive, is the last thing she needs.

'She's a schoolteacher,' says Leanne. 'She's got no proper money. Her parents are a nightmare. She's stressed out beyond belief. Now one of her oldest friend's has been killed. She needs professional help. And I've persuaded Adrian to pay for it. Surely that's a good thing?'

The rest? He doesn't need to know.

Robert drains his glass, adjusts his reclining position, and lets out an enormous fart.

Leanne wrinkles her nose. 'Darling, don't be gross,' she says.

'If a man can't fart in front of his wife, what's the point of being married?' he says sullenly.

She looks at him. Mondays are always bad. His workload is punishing. And this afternoon he had to endure two hours of being grilled by some stupid Parliamentary committee.

She smiles and holds out her hand. 'Let me get you a refill.'

Handing her the glass, he says, 'I just keep thinking, eventually, the police are going to get to Kieran.'

Leanne takes the glass over to the sideboard. 'Why?' she says. 'Who's going to tell them?' She pours a small measure of brandy from the decanter.

She hasn't mentioned her meeting with Theo Webber,

another sanctimonious hack the world could do without. But she's warned him off. Effectively, she hopes.

'I don't know,' says Robert. 'I'm just worried.'

'Melissa is dead. Everything is contained. You are protected. We move on.' She returns to the sofa and hands him the glass.

'Do you think I should contact the Chief Constable and ask how the investigation's going?'

'No, absolutely not. That displays anxiety. And it will make them suspicious.'

'But, Lee…'

'There were over fifty people at the reunion. We're just one of the crowd.'

'Except we're not. Are we? And if they get hold of Kieran. Stupid bugger! I never encouraged him, y'know. This is off his own bat.'

'I know that, darling.'

'Yeah, but they'll still come for me, won't they?'

Leanne perches on the arm of the sofa and grasps his hand. 'Stop it!' she says. 'You'll drive yourself insane. And that's when mistakes happen.'

She kisses the back of his hand. 'Trust me. I can manage this.'

He sighs. 'I know. You're extremely capable. I'm a lucky man.'

'You are,' she says. 'Now, I've got some calls to make.'

She gets up and walks towards the door. He returns to the television and his channel-hopping. She watches him for a moment, and it gives her a sense of warmth and ease.

Is this love? Who knows?

It's all just semantics. She knows how she feels about her children, but that's different. It's biological. For her, security was always top of the list. Never being left out in the cold.

Her own mother never held on to any man for long. Leanne was determined not to make the same mistake.

When she married Robert, she knew he was still hankering after someone else. He pretended not to be. He'd been turned down flat, and that had injured his pride. Leanne was just a substitute, but she went ahead because she knew she could make it work. And it has. In some ways, it was better, because she always understood the deal.

Now she's fiercely protective of him. Surely that counts as love? Far better than some romantic illusion that fades. What they have is a deeper connection built up over the years through the solid, day-to-day work that is any marriage. He's her husband. That's all that matters. And he needs her.

As for her own anxiety, it's there, bubbling just below the surface. The skill is to keep it firmly in check. And she's good at that. She learned it at Cambridge. You make a plan and execute it.

She heads down the hall towards the study. For the deflection strategy to succeed, she needs Adrian. The police need a suspect and a conviction. Claire fits the bill. Only when it all slots into place will everything be secure. But Robert doesn't need to know this.

Getting out her phone, she clicks on Adrian's number. He answers immediately.

'Leanne, hello,' he says brightly.

'Claire has just called me in a panic and told me she's been kidnapped.'

'Oh dear. That's rather awkward for you.' His tone is almost mocking.

Such a bastard.

'It is. Has she seen the psychiatrist yet?'

'Not yet. She's only just got there. Don't worry Leanne. Everything's in hand.'

He's being evasive. She can hear it in his voice, and it's bloody annoying.

'We agreed,' she says. 'Claire is dangerous. To herself and others. We need to get her sectioned. This is for her own good.'

'I know. And she's in a safe place. She's not going anywhere.'

'I'm relying on you, Adrian. To do the right thing here.'

He chuckles. 'I know. Be patient. The shrink will see her tomorrow. You've no need to worry. But I have to go now, because I've got a date with a girl.'

He hangs up.

Patient? Patronising fool.

If there was another option, she'd have taken it.

A date with a girl? Could he be any more shallow? He's behaving as if he's still twenty. She's so glad that Robert isn't some kind of immature man child like Adrian Cardello. Her husband may have his shortcomings, but he acts his age.

Leanne is frustrated. Has Adrian ever given a toss for anyone but himself? But she has no choice. She has to wait. She can't be the one to lead Claire down this road. That would be suspicious. She has to remain at arm's length.

53

Monday, 10.50pm

Boden has her pyjamas on. She stares at the screen of her entry phone and she can't believe what she sees.

WTF? Who does he think he is?

How did he even get her address?

She clicks the intercom on and says, 'I'll give you one minute to leave, then I'll call for some of my uniformed colleagues to come and remove you.'

Adrian Cardello tilts his head and smiles at the camera. 'DS Boden, I apologise. This is out of left field, I get it. But you are going to want to hear what I have to tell you.'

'I can assure you, Mr Cardello. I'm not.'

'I did see Mel in the chapel on Saturday night and I did talk to her. She told me what she was doing and why she was waiting there.'

What the hell is he playing at?

Boden can feel the hairs rising on the back of her neck.

She's got a bad feeling about this. She's in the hall. Her phone is on the table in the kitchen.

'Then why did you lie?' she says evenly.

Cardello chuckles. 'Okay, well, I had my suspicions, but I needed to look into a few things myself. I have a certain amount of resources at my disposal. And I believe I can point you in the direction of Mel's killer. You can't say you're not curious. Also, I don't bite. There's a bar down the street, the frog and something or other. I've just passed it. It's still open. Meet me there in five minutes and I'll tell you everything I know.'

He disappears from the screen. Boden curses under her breath. She runs back into the kitchen and grabs her phone.

This feels very wrong. Like a come-on from a narcissist who's playing a game. He lied. Now he's admitting he lied. He's trying to hook her. Tracking her down, approaching her at home at night? That's a red flag. But what does it mean? What does he want?

A chill runs up her spine.

Why is he doing this? The possibilities spiral through Boden's brain. He wants to frighten her? It's a power trip? He's an arrogant movie star who thinks he can outfox the police? But they all point in one direction. He's killed one woman and now he wants to kill another.

Is this Adrian Cardello revealing himself to be Melissa Rowe's murderer?

It could be. He's offering to meet in a public bar, but he could be waiting for her outside or lurking somewhere en route. And he could have help.

She picks up her phone and rings the DCI's number. It's busy.

She considers just having uniform pick him up. But on what grounds? This is just a hunch. A feeling. He hasn't done or said anything incriminating. Nick him and his lawyer'll be all over it. Then, if he is guilty, any chance to trap him is blown. He'll be on his private jet and gone.

She rings Mackie's number; he does pick up. She explains the situation quickly and succinctly.

'On my way, Skip. There in ten.'

Boden switches off the light, goes into the sitting room and peeps through the blinds. Her block is in a quiet cul-de-sac, but near to the main road. A neighbour is walking his dog. But apart from that, it's deserted. It doesn't mean he's not out there.

The flat is on the third floor and very secure. Boden upgraded all the locks when she moved in. The weak spot is the front door downstairs and the communal hallway; it's easy enough for people to blag their way in.

The minutes pass with glacial slowness. The DCI's phone is still busy and Boden leaves her a voice mail. With all the lights in the flat off, she opens the blinds to look out. Her nerves aren't as solid as they were when she started out in the job. Too many bad experiences. And one particularly bad. She checks her own pulse. Fast and shallow. The adrenaline is definitely pumping.

Then Mackie's car pulls up right outside. He jumps out and trots up the path to the front door. Boden rushes to the intercom, checks and buzzes him in. A couple of minutes later, she's opening her door to him.

She's tempted to throw herself in his arms, but she holds it together.

He's in his gym kit. 'Bloody hell,' he says. 'You're as white as a sheet.'

'Any sign of him outside?'

'Not that I could see. But I've called for backup.' Then he

laughs. 'Knight is going to have a fit if we nick Cardello for this.'

'But we've got no proof of anything. A verbal admission that he lied. He'll walk. We've got to be smart about this.'

'What now then?'

She looks down at her pyjamas. 'I need to get dressed. Go in the sitting room and watch out the front.'

He nods.

Returning to her bedroom, Boden changes into jeans, a hoodie and trainers. Her pulse is slowing and she has a few moments to think.

Are you overreacting?

She's been in the job long enough to know that in these situations, you err on the side of caution. Risky behaviour and ignoring your instincts can get you killed.

But what if Adrian Cardello is sitting in the bar down the road? Now she's got Mackie with her. She could check it out. Even if Cardello intends her ill, he's no match for Mackie.

They exit the flats through the fire door at the back, and cut through the gardens to the main road. The Frog and Donkey is a large bar popular with students. It has a late licence, a loud disco and plenty of hidey-holes for an intimate chat. It's a Monday night, so it's on the quiet side.

Mackie leads the way. The place is a warren, and they take a while to explore it. Boden is concluding that she was right in the first place, when a man in a booth at the side waves at them.

Cardello wears a baseball cap and a denim jacket with the collar up. He looks fairly anonymous and certainly no one seems to have recognised him.

Mackie slides into the booth opposite him and Boden sits down next to Mackie.

Cardello doesn't seem fazed. 'Thank you for coming,' he

says. 'Both of you. And I quite understand why you wouldn't trust me, DS Boden. In your shoes, I wouldn't.'

'What is this about, Mr Cardello?' says Boden. 'And if you're above board, why this clandestine approach?'

'Politics, Sergeant.' He has a backpack on the bench beside him. He reaches into it and pulls out a laptop.

Mackie gets out his phone, clicks record and places it on the table.

Adrian Cardello has a wistful look on his face. He also seems weary.

'Mel was a terrific journalist,' he says. 'And what made her so great was also what made her a hard person to be around. She was a little terrier, the sort of hunting dog that'll dig a rat or even a badger out of its hole and rip it to shreds. Ruthless.'

He opens the laptop. 'Mel thought she had a story on Robert Gerrish. While she was at the reunion, she had a junior colleague in London, Theo Webber, doing some digging for her. You can talk to him. He'll confirm this.'

Cardello turns the laptop round and shows Boden and Mackie the screen.

'Theo has shared with me the emails he exchanged with Mel on Saturday. When you read them, you'll understand what they were up to. To summarise, they had a story that would end the Minister's career.'

'I thought you were all old friends,' says Boden.

Cardello chuckles. 'Old enemies more like. You're the detectives, so you'll have to investigate this. But here's the theory I would like to offer you. I went to the chapel looking for Mel, and I found her. She told me she'd got Rob over a barrel and she was about to meet with someone. She was drunk. And quite coked up. But she was on a mission.

Insisted I leave via the crypt, told me she'd meet me in the bar after they'd talked and fill me in.'

'Did she tell you who this person was?' says Boden.

'No,' he smiles wistfully. 'She liked to ramp up the melodrama. That was Mel. But after I spoke to Theo, I'm guessing it has to be this guy.' He scrolls on the laptop and brings up another picture. 'Kieran Morgan. He's Rob's special political adviser and general Mr Fixit.'

'Why him?' says Mackie.

'Well, when you read the emails, you'll see that what they were investigating involved Kieran. It was his fault. And I know Rob. If he thought this was Kieran's mess, he'd force him to clean it up. But there's another piece to this puzzle which also points to Kieran.'

'What?' says Boden. There needs to be. She's already imagining the nightmare of selling this to the DCI, even if it is true.

'Leanne is Rob's wife. She's trying to suggest that Claire Naylor, an old friend who's been going through a tough time, is the person who most likely had a fight with Mel. This is nonsense. Leanne is doing this to keep suspicion away from Kieran, and to protect her husband. She figures you guys need an alternative suspect to pin it on.'

He's unaware they've got a suspect of their own.

Cardello removes the memory stick from the side of the laptop and hands it to Boden. 'The emails are all on here. It's a complicated story, but once you read them, you'll get it. And my reason for this unconventional approach is that Robert is good mates with the Home Secretary. So your bosses will be lent on.'

Boden exhales. He's right about that.

'And why did you lie when we spoke to you before?' she says.

'Because I knew as soon as Mel was attacked that Rob had to be behind it. I hoped she might recover and…but when she didn't, I knew that proving this would be a nightmare.'

Cardello wipes tears from his face with the back of his hand. Then he stands up and slots the laptop in his backpack. 'You want a statement from me, I'll be at my London apartment. You can contact me there. Oh, and I'm sorry if I freaked you out, Sergeant.'

'Why are you doing this, Mr Cardello?' says Boden.

He adjusts his baseball cap. 'Because Mel was my girlfriend once. I loved her. And that devious bastard had her killed to protect his fucking reputation. Excuse my language.'

He slips the backpack on his shoulder, turns and walks away.

'Phew!' says Mackie. 'Do you buy this?'

Boden turns the memory stick over between her fingers. 'Well,' she says. 'I went with Knight to question Gerrish and his wife straight after it happened, and that's exactly what the wife did. She tried to blame Claire Naylor. So he's right about that.'

54

Tuesday, 8am

Claire gets out of bed. She slept surprisingly well. Poppy brought her some herb tea, supposedly to help her relax. She suspects it was drugged.

Going over to the window, she pulls back the brocade drapes. The vista is spectacular; it takes her breath away. A panorama of lush green hills receding into the distance, their far caps turning to a misty blue against a cloudless sky. But immediately below her window, there's a lawn rolling down to a sizeable lake. Its surface sparkles, dark and mercurial in the morning sunshine. And at the waterside, on a short wooden jetty, there's a man on a mat, doing yoga asanas.

It's Jermaine.

Claire finds the towelling robe and puts it on over her pyjamas. Next to the bed, there's a pair of fluffy mules. She slips them on too.

When she gets to the door of the suite and turns the handle, she half expects it to be locked. But it isn't. She steps out into the hallway. Retracing her steps of the previous evening, she finds the lift. She takes it to the ground floor.

As the doors open, she peers out cautiously. This is most likely where she'll be stopped. There are two people behind the reception desk chatting. Pink surgical shrubs again. But not Poppy or Karim.

Can she slip past them?

The woman looks up and sees her.

Dammit!

She beams and comes forward to meet Claire. She's older than the others, dark hair drawn neatly back into a greying bun. 'Good morning,' she says brightly. 'You must be Claire. I'm Femi, one of the senior nurses. How did you sleep?'

'Okay,' says Claire.

Femi chuckles. 'I know. You first get here, it's all a bit confusing. Takes time to settle. How about some breakfast?'

'Umm, well, it's so lovely this morning. I thought I might…go outside.'

'By all means,' Femi points to a doorway. 'Go through there into the Orangery. The doors open onto the back terrace. It is a lovely morning.'

They're not going to stop you?

That's probably because she's in her dressing gown, miles from anywhere, and there's nowhere to run.

'Thanks,' she mumbles.

She finds her way to the terrace. Like everything else here, it's on a grand scale. Steps lead down to the lawn. On either side of the steps, rampant stone lions stand guard. But there are flowers everywhere. The wide bed below the terrace is bursting with colour. Dahlias, zinnias, blowsy peonies; they all look surprising well-watered and fresh. And the lawn is not sunburnt and dry, as in most other places.

There's a freshness in the air; no pollution. No traffic

noise. Just the chatter of birdsong. She has to admit; the place is idyllic.

Her phone call with Leanne comes back into her mind. It was rather odd. In the first place, her old friend didn't sound shocked when she said she'd been kidnapped. This morning, she feels a tad embarrassed. Perhaps she was being melodramatic, which is exactly what Leanne said.

She'd mentioned Adrian, and Leanne's response was that his desire to help her was genuine. She wonders how Leanne knows that. Have they discussed it?

The turf is soft and springy. Claire slips off her mules and buries her toes in the grass. It's cool and feathery on her bare soles. She strolls towards the lake.

Jermaine has his back to her. He's standing like a statue on one leg, hands straight up above his head. Tree pose? Is that what it's called? Claire did a yoga evening class for a while; she was persuaded to go by a friend, another teacher. For a large man, Jermaine is graceful. He releases the pose, dips slowly forward to touch the ground. Then he stands up and turns. Only then does he see her.

He picks up his towel. 'Morning,' he says with a smile.

'I didn't want to startle you,' she says. 'I used to do yoga.'

'My opinion, it's the best way to start the day. Learnt when I played football.'

'You mean like American Football?'

He chuckles. 'Yeah, NFL, not soccer.'

'Did you play professionally?'

He loops the towel round his neck. 'Oh yeah. I was an offensive lineman. Played through high school and college, went through the draft and got picked up by the Buffalo Bills.'

'I don't really understand how it works, I'm afraid. What's a lineman?'

'We're the big guys who tackle and block. I was much heavier in my playing days. Had to be. I've slimmed down a lot. Yoga is great for balance and core stability.'

'Why did you stop playing?'

'Injury. Smashed my shoulder. It's full of metal pins. When I go through the airport scanner, it really kicks off.' He laughs. There's such an ease about him. A gentle giant. Just standing here in the sunshine beside a beautiful lake; it seems ridiculous to feel threatened.

'Jermaine, I'm really confused,' she says. 'Why are you here?'

'Adrian asked me to take care of you.'

'Why? I don't really understand. I know I've done some crazy things—'

'Hey, who hasn't?'

'I mean really crazy.'

'Yeah, I know. I've seen the knife.' He smiles. He doesn't seem to be judging her.

'I probably should be locked up. Isn't that why I'm here?'

He laughs and tips back his head. 'No. Not at all. You want to go home, I can drive you. But this place is pretty cool. I'm mean, look at it. Adrian loves it here. They do all kinds of healing.'

She stares down at her bare feet and then out at the lake.

'Now I'm even more confused,' she says.

'Let's go get some breakfast,' says Jermaine. They walk up the lawn towards the house, side by side.

'So I'm not here because I'm crazy?'

'No. There's some stuff going on. Adrian'll explain when he gets here.'

'He's coming?'

'Yeah, this morning.'

'Oh.'

Claire considers this. Jermaine makes it sound like he'll be popping in, as if he's just round the corner. And what stuff? It must be to do with Mel. And what will happen when the police discover Claire's disappeared?

Jermaine stops and looks at her. 'I think it's tough for you Brits,' he says. 'I've watched this with Adrian. You're always trying to get everything right. Not upset anyone. Adrian's always apologising. He says it's habit. The way he was brought up. But, y'know, things happen that you never expect. The darkness moves in on you. Happens to everyone. No point resisting. You have to just push on through.'

He makes it sound easy.

'I suffer with terrible anxiety,' she says. 'I have for years.'

'What is it you're trying to control?'

'Control? I don't know. Everything?'

'When I busted my shoulder up, and I knew my career was over, I was twenty-three years old. Overnight, all my dreams, everything was gone. That was a very dark time. I thought about checking out.' He makes it sound such a casual thing.

Claire stares at him. It's weird, talking to a strange American like this. And yet it's straightforward and unchallenging. She doesn't feel judged.

'My daughter took her own life,' she says.

'Yeah, Adrian told me. That's a terrible thing to bear.'

'I worry it's my fault.'

'Why?'

'I'm her mother. I should've done something. Stopped her.'

'Sorry Claire, I don't agree. No one can carry the burden of another's soul. That's what my Grandma used to say.'

'I don't understand what that means.'

'She was a believer. Church every Sunday. And what she

would've said is the Lord gave us free will. We're not his puppets, which means we gotta be responsible for our own souls. Morally and spiritually responsible. Okay, I'm not real religious myself, but I've always interpreted it to mean we all gotta make our own choices. Your daughter made her choice.'

'That's very harsh.'

He nods. 'Yep. It is.'

'I still should've stopped her.'

'It's still her choice.'

'But…but she was my child.' A spasm of pure pain rises and catches in her throat. And from nowhere, the tears erupt as she sinks to her knees in the soft grass. Jermaine squats beside her and puts his hand on her shoulder.

And she sobs. She's cried for Ella before. But not like this. Her whole body and mind convulses with pure agony. Each time she tries to stop and take a breath, more tears come.

55

Tuesday, 9.15am

The helicopter swoops in low over the trees. Adrian Cardello always loves coming back to Stanfirth Hall. He gazes down at the lake and remembers the shock of early morning dips, icy cold, but the serotonin high afterwards is magic.

In the wake of his second divorce, he came here for a total detox and they got him off the booze and back on form, which led to a resurgence in his career. Money well spent.

The chopper circles the house and drops down to the small helipad on the other side of the kitchen garden. Flying time from Battersea heliport, which is a five-minute drive from his London apartment, is just over the hour. He's wearing his gym kit and a track suit so he and Jermaine can fit in a session while he's here.

But the primary object of the trip is to talk to Claire. It won't be an easy conversation, and it's twenty-five years overdue. But he has a debt to pay.

Adrian nods his thanks to the pilot, unclips his belt and

climbs out of the cabin. Dipping down to avoid any tilt in the blades, he heads through a stone archway into the kitchen garden. He knows the route well. The gardeners are busy. The Hall boasts five-star cuisine and lots of the produce is home grown. He bids a cheery good morning to a rather good-looking girl with a wheelbarrow. She gives him a lingering glance.

You still cut the mustard.

Adrian smiles to himself and shakes his head. He knows his weaknesses and his vanity. And he's learned the hard way that being in a position to indulge them is not necessarily a good thing. Often it's quite the opposite. Success and wealth produces its own form of ennui. In his way, he tries to be a good man, but what does that even mean?

Today is about proving it to himself. And it won't be easy.

His encounter with the police went fairly well, in so far as he could tell. DS Boden obviously found his approach deeply suspicious. But what else could he have done? Rob Gerrish, his nerdy, nervous sidekick, has turned into a force to be reckoned with, and Adrian is well versed in the back channels through which the rich and powerful protect their interests and get their own way. He read Boden as a woman who cared about what she did, and who might be prepared to go the extra mile to see justice.

Maybe.

He finds Claire and Jermaine sitting at a table on the terrace, having breakfast. They look comfortable together. But it doesn't surprise him. He needed someone to keep her safe, and he knew Jermaine was the perfect, although perhaps not the most obvious choice.

Jermaine radiates a stillness and calm, almost like a monk. His official job title is Adrian's personal trainer, but in the years they've been together, it's turned into something far more than that. Jermaine is his shadow and, at times, his conscience. He never says anything overtly critical; he doesn't need to. He's known success and failure on life's unending rollercoaster and learned to rise above it. In the world of extravagant fakery in which Adrian operates, Jermaine's the one person who keeps him grounded. He's also one of the most contented people Adrian's ever met, and it's hard not to envy that.

As Adrian approaches their table, Claire is refilling their coffee cups from a cafetière.

'You got a cup of that for me?' says Adrian.

Claire looks up. She smiles. Her eyes are red-rimmed and puffy, but the jittery tension has gone out of her limbs.

Jermaine stands up. 'I'll get another cup. You want some fruit or pastries from the buffet, man?'

Adrian laughs. 'See Claire, you're around and he offers me pastries.' He pats his belly.

'Couple of extra circuits to burn them off,' says Jermaine with a shrug. He heads inside to the breakfast buffet, but really it's to give them space.

Adrian sits down at the table. 'How you doing?' he says.

Claire sighs. 'Better than I was.' She hesitates. 'I've got a confession to make. Last night I freaked out. I thought you'd kidnapped me.'

Adrian looks around him and smiles. 'Yeah, understandable. This could be mistaken for a dungeon.'

'You're mocking me.'

'Sorry. Only a little.'

'No, I'm sorry. I phoned Leanne and told her that.' She frowns and reddens.

'Yeah, she said.'

Claire still has those Bambi eyes wrinkled with bags

underneath now, but the expression is still one of puzzled innocence that blokes find so compelling.

'What?' she says. 'I don't understand what's going on.'

'Well, Leanne wants you to be sectioned under the Mental Health Act, so you can then be blamed for killing Mel. Her scenario is that you're crazy. You and Mel had a fight, you whacked her. She thinks I've brought you here so a psychiatrist can do the deed. I've let her believe that.'

Claire's jaw loosens. She stares at him in disbelief.

'But…I don't understand…' she says.

'She needs to deflect any whiff of suspicion that might derail her old man's career. Plus, she noticed you start to pull the knife from your bag.'

'Oh, God!' Claire's shoulders slump. She dips her head.

'The thing is, Mel was doing what you asked. Trying to find out about what happened to Ella. She uncovered a can of worms, and one worm in particular, Rob's special adviser, Kieran Morgan.'

A frown of recognition. 'Kieran?'

'You know the name?'

'When Ella came home after she was sacked, I eavesdropped on a phone call. She was upset, crying and begging. It was awful. The person she was talking to she called Kieran.'

Adrian steels himself. He's used to playing the action hero, but the reality is he usually avoids conflict. But he has to do this.

Okay, let's rock and roll.

Adrian reaches out and takes her hand. 'There's something else we need to talk about,' he says. 'Why did you tell me Ella was my daughter?'

'Because…' Her head goes down and her eyes brim with tears.

'I don't think she is, Claire.'

She looks puzzled. Her lip trembles.

'C'mon,' he says. 'Let's go for a walk by the lake.'

Adrian takes her arm and helps her to her feet. She's still in her bathrobe, with fluffy mules on her feet. But the sun is already warm. He pulls his sunglasses out of his pocket and offers them to her. She puts them on and takes his arm.

They walk down to the lake. The moor hens and a couple of ducks are cruising round in leisurely circles, creating soft ripples on the surface.

'The party,' he says. 'After finals. You said that's when we had sex. How can you be sure it was then that you got pregnant?'

'Before that, I was a virgin.'

He glances at her. That's something he's never considered. Yet, it makes a strange kind of sense. There always was an aloofness about her. She held herself apart.

'But you had loads of boyfriends,' he says.

'I never slept with any of them. I suppose I was waiting for the fairytale. To be swept off my feet and to fall madly in love. It never happened.'

As he watches her, he realises what naïve children they all were back then. Each with a head full of hopes and fantasies, which turned out to be wildly inaccurate.

She gives him a wry look. 'How stupid was I?' she says.

'No more than any of us,' he replies. 'But what do you actually remember about that night?'

'I remember us dancing together at the party. I was idiotic and drank far too much. Then later, I felt awful. Don't think I've ever been so pissed. Could hardly walk. You carried me back to my room.'

'I did,' he says. 'And later, when you realised you were pregnant, you figured that's when it happened?'

She sighs. 'Yes. But I couldn't tell you. Because of Mel. Because you'd already left for London. You were going to RADA.'

He takes a deep breath. The blissful freshness of the morning air. The warm sunshine on his back. He knows how lucky he it, and it is dumb luck. But he's grateful for all of it.

'Let me tell you about my memories of that party,' he says. 'You weren't foolish. It wasn't your fault you got so drunk.'

'What d'you mean?'

He turns to look at her. 'Rob was besotted with you.'

'He always gave me the creeps,' she says, pulling the bathrobe round her.

'I know. He was just rubbish with girls. But he got the idea that the reason you kept rejecting him was you were uptight and you just needed to relax. Finals were done. He thought it was his last chance to hook up with you. So he spiked your drink. I saw him do it. And I should've stopped him.'

Claire stares at him in horror. She doesn't speak.

'I didn't see what happened after that. But later, he came looking for me, and he was freaking out. Said you'd had sex but now you were unconscious. He couldn't wake you up and he didn't know what to do. He begged me to help him. He showed me where you were, passed out in the college gardens. He was paranoid he'd get in trouble. I asked him if he'd forced you to have sex with him. He didn't answer, just insisted he hadn't done anything wrong. I tried to bring you round, but you were out cold. So I carried you.'

Her eyes are filled with dismay. Tears are welling. She's speechless.

He waits.

Finally, she splutters, 'What did he do?'

'Ran off basically. I took you back to your room. That's when you came round.'

She shakes her head rapidly, as if this is all too horrible to absorb. Then she inhales sharply. 'I remember you carrying me.'

'I stayed with you until dawn to make sure you were okay. I felt bad because I knew I should've stopped him. I just slept on the floor. Next day, I thought about telling you.'

'Why didn't you?'

'Rob turned nasty. He said if I did, he'd say he'd seen me raping you. And various people saw me carrying you back to your room when you were out cold, so he'd be believed. And you had no idea what happened to you. So you'd believe it too.'

Claire seems stunned. She takes off the sunglasses and wipes tears from her eyes. Her hand is shaking. She drops the glasses and buries her face in her hands. He picks them up for her.

Her body shudders. He watches her. This was never going to be easy.

After a couple of minutes, she raises her head. Her voice cracks with pain. 'He told you I had no idea what had happened? He said that to you?'

'Yes.'

'You mean he actually admitted he had sex with me when I was unconscious?'

'Yeah. He raped you.'

She shakes her head. More tears come. They course down her cheeks.

Wait. Let this take its course.

He wants to hug her and comfort her, but this probably wouldn't be welcome.

He says nothing.

She wipes her face with the sleeve of her bathrobe. He pulls a tissue from his pocket and offers it. She accepts it.

She blows her nose, then she says, 'Y'know, about a week after the party, I was packing up my stuff to go home, and he just appeared out of the blue and proposed to me. It was totally bizarre. I told him he was being ridiculous and he was the last person I'd marry. It didn't make any sense to me at the time. But I suppose I should've wondered more. A few days after that, I missed my period. And I just freaked out.'

'You never thought it was him?'

She gives him a sorrowful look. 'No, it never occurred to me, because I thought it was you.'

Adrian takes her hand. She allows it. 'Claire, I'm so sorry I didn't tell you,' he says. 'That I covered for him. I was young and self-centred. And scared. I believed he would point the finger at me. And I'd lose my place at RADA. But that's still no excuse.'

Her voice descends to a whisper. 'I can't believe he's Ella's father.'

'Do you think he knows?'

She shakes her head. 'No, he couldn't. After I turned him down, I didn't see him again. I went home. Ella was born. Then, months and months later, I heard he was marrying Leanne. She invited me to the wedding. But I didn't go. I didn't see them for years.'

'But Leanne got back in touch?'

'That was a few years later. I think she enjoyed feeling sorry for me. Poor old Claire. The struggling single-parent. Did you ever tell Mel what happened?'

'No. I told no one,' he says.

What he doesn't mention is that he left Cambridge the next day. Dumped Mel flat and ran as fast as he could to grab his new life before it slipped through his fingers.

He inhales. 'I didn't know what to do. I was ashamed and scared. I just ran.'

Claire looks up at him. 'Adrian,' she says. 'Are you telling me the truth? Please don't lie. I couldn't bear that.'

He puts his hand on his heart and meets her gaze. 'I swear to you, Claire, to my eternal shame, it's the truth.'

Her head jerks a little. She turns away from him and stares out across the lake.

He looks back towards the house. Jermaine is standing on the terrace, watching them. He feels a measure of relief, but also a deep sorrow. For Claire, and for Mel. For himself. For his ex-wives and his kids, who he rarely sees. For the sorry mess he's made of it all.

56

Boden and Mackie stand in front of the DCI's desk. The boss has her elbows on it and her face in her hands. In front of her, the laptop is open and the documents from the file given to them by Cardello are displayed on the screen. Boden knew this wouldn't be easy. She glances across at Mackie; he raises his eyebrows.

Abruptly, the DCI throws out her hands. Her eyes are bloodshot. She looks like she's been up most of the night, and it shows.

'Jo,' she says, with some exasperation. 'It's a theory. There's absolutely no proof. The victim was a journalist working on a story with a colleague. So what? Getting from that to the Minister's special adviser murdering Rowe is a bit of a stretch. And look at it, there are reams of this stuff. Plus, journalistic privilege covers this, so we'd need a section 9 warrant under PACE.'

'I know that, boss,' says Boden. She knows because she's

spent half the night reading and re-reading it. Rowe's emails were rambling and repetitive. Probably dictated into her phone. But it's obvious she was drunk.

Rachel Knight sighs. She reaches out for her mug of coffee. Boden notices her hand is shaking. 'We don't know what Cardello's agenda is here, do we?' she says. 'He freaked you out. You had to call for backup.'

Here we go.

As soon as Boden arrived at the office, she got an update from Chakravorty. Everyone was feeling the pressure. The analysts had been working in shifts all night. All that can really be established with concrete evidence is that Leon Davison, the drug dealer, entered the college through the kitchen porter's entrance. But that was forty-five minutes before Rowe was discovered. There are also witness statements about his attack on Tony and threats to the chef. They were still waiting on forensics; everything was frustratingly slow.

'Boss,' says Boden tentatively. 'Why don't we get a section 9 warrant and I just go and talk to this journalist, Theo Webber? See what he has to say.'

'If he's got information, why hasn't he come forward?' says Knight.

A good question.

And one Boden would like to ask him.

'I'll tell you why,' says Knight. 'Because it's just a story with no evidence to back it up. He knows that.'

Keep your mouth shut.

She doesn't. 'Due respect, boss,' she says. 'Leon Davison is just a story. It's the drug-dealer-did-it story. And we haven't got the evidence to prove that yet either.'

Boden can feel Mackie shifting nervously beside her. The

DCI purses her lips and inhales. An explosion seems imminent.

Boden wonders why she lobbed that hand grenade into the mix.

Foolish.

The DCI shakes her head sharply, as if a wasp has just landed on her nose. 'Alright, Boden,' she says. 'Have it your way. Talk to this bloody journalist. But you'll have to go on your own. I need Mackie here to do the real work of making this case.' She waves her hand to dismiss them.

'Thank you, boss,' says Boden.

She and Mackie walk out of the DCI's office.

'Stone me,' mumbles Mackie. 'She's running scared.'

He's right, which is bad news for Boden.

She spends a solitary train journey to London, in a packed, sweaty carriage, wondering why she's picked up this baton. Adrian Cardello described Melissa Rowe as a little terrier; perhaps there's a bit of a ratcatcher in Boden too.

On the other hand, if Melissa Rowe wanted to ruin the Minister's career for reasons of a personal grudge, maybe Cardello hopes to finish the job, for the same reason? But it doesn't mean that's why she was killed. It's still an assumption. She wonders if Cardello's playing her. Protecting Claire Naylor?

That's a possibility. Naylor has fallen out of the equation as far as the DCI is concerned.

Her train gets into King's Cross around eleven. She takes the Northern Line to London Bridge and the Jubilee to Canary Wharf. Trips to London always lift her spirits. It's another day of blue skies and baking hot pavements. But she's back on home turf.

The offices of Melissa Rowe's newspaper are in a modern air-conditioned tower high above the Thames. Boden takes the lift to the fifteenth floor. She's greeted by a junior and escorted to a large meeting room, where they're waiting for her.

Mob-handed. So that's how they're playing it.

A slight, balding man in an immaculately laundered shirt and neat tie steps forward and holds out his hand. 'Brian Hooper,' he says. 'Acting political editor.'

Handshake dry and firm. Good eye contact.

'DS Jo Boden,' she replies.

The rest of the room is introduced. Theo Webber, young, slightly pink cheeked with embarrassment and extremely sheepish, plus two lawyers, one male, the other female. The Rottweilers.

They offer Boden a chair facing them all; an effective way of turning the tables and making her feel she's being grilled.

'First,' says Boden. 'I'd like to offer my condolences for your loss.'

Hooper dips his head. He seems genuinely upset. 'Thank you, Sergeant. Mel was…an esteemed colleague and a personal friend.'

'I'm seeking background information that might assist our investigation and—'

Brian Hooper raises his palm. 'Can I stop you there, Sergeant? Obviously, we want to do anything and everything we can to help.'

'Of course,' says Boden.

'But I understand that my colleague, Theo, has passed some emails to a third party, which he absolutely shouldn't have done.'

Boden glances at Theo Webber, who's reddening even more.

'Okay,' says Boden.

'This was a private correspondence between Mel and a junior colleague. A purely speculative exchange of ideas of the sort we journalists indulge in from time to time. Also, this is privileged information under the Police and Criminal Evidence Act.'

'And we have the appropriate section 9 warrant,' says Boden. 'But all I'm asking is were Melissa Rowe and Mr Webber looking for material concerning Robert Gerrish?'

Hooper glances at the lawyers, then he shrugs. 'We review material concerning politicians and their activities all the time.'

'I have read the emails,' says Boden. 'And the story that seemed to interest them concerned Robert Gerrish's special political adviser, Kieran Morgan, and his attempts to deflect blame for some kind of leak on to an intern called Ella Naylor. Is that a fair summary, Mr Webber?'

Theo Webber looks like a frightened mouse. 'Umm, yeah, sort of. I guess.'

Hooper sighs. 'What we know, and can say for sure, is that Mel was an old friend of Ella Naylor's mother. Ella Naylor took her own life. And Mel was probably hoping to bring her friend some comfort by making a few general inquiries. It was a reunion. Mel was drinking. We must read the emails and the speculation in that light.' He glares at poor Theo. 'And if this were a more serious endeavour, Mel would've been working with more senior colleagues.'

They're shit scared that if any of this comes out, they'll get sued.

Boden nods. 'Did you give copies of the emails to Adrian Cardello, Mr Webber?'

He exhales. Sweat is beading on his forehead. 'Well, yeah…he tracked me down…and…'

'He shouldn't have,' says Brian Hooper. 'It was private speculation.'

Boden ignores this and focuses her gaze on the hapless Theo.

'Did you and Mr Cardello discuss who you thought might've attacked Melissa Rowe?' she says.

Theo can't make eye contact. 'I can't remember what I said. I was in a bar and frankly, I was pissed.'

Boden lets her gaze travel across the four of them, facing her across the table. Theo has been reined in and smacked. This is a damage limitation exercise. Whatever they might think or even know about what Melissa Rowe was up to the night she was killed, they're really not going to go there.

Boden gets it. Unless they're very sure of their facts, pointing the finger at a Cabinet Minister is, for them, a risky and potentially expensive business.

She's being stone-walled.

'Thank you for your time,' she says.

As she's escorted through the plush, high-tech offices to the lifts, she wonders where she's going with this. If there is something suspicious here, no one wants to admit it. Everyone, including her own boss, is focused on their own self-interest. Who killed Melissa Rowe is not top of any of their agendas.

57

Tuesday, 3pm

The heat is stifling and oppressive. Claire lies on the bed in her room, wearing only her underwear and with a damp flannel across her forehead. She has no energy. No willpower. Her thoughts are drifting like leaves on a stream as she slips in and out of consciousness. The large sash windows are all wide open to catch any breath of breeze coming up from the lake. But there's a sudden sharpness in the air as the atmospheric pressure drops.

A low rumble gathers in the distance, then an enormous thunderclap shakes the window frames.

Claire opens her eyes. The heavy curtains sway. Another crack of thunder and the heavens open. The slow pitter patter on the scorched ground quickly turns into a pounding deluge. Lightning flashes across the darkening sky.

Claire doesn't move. She just stares out at the storm clouds from her bed. There's a faint tap on the door to the suite. It opens and Poppy appears. She rushes over to the open windows and closes them one by one. The heavy wooden sashes descend with a thump. Claire watches her, immobilised.

As Poppy moves into the bedroom, she says brightly, 'It's what they've been forecasting. But it's such a relief. This heatwave is finally going to break.'

Yes. Finally.

The rain thrashes against the windows. More rumbles of thunder, then another enormous crack. Spurs of lightning streak across the hilltops, illuminating the sky. Poppy scurries out.

Adrian and Jermaine left for London in the helicopter, ahead of the storm. Claire is to stay for as long as she wants. It's all arranged.

'Spend the whole summer here,' said Adrian. 'Use it as an opportunity to heal and get back on your feet. They're brilliant and they can help you. They have all sorts of therapies.'

She said no at first.

But he insisted. 'It's what you need. Time out.'

And professional help. He didn't really spell it out, but she knows it's true.

Also, if the police approach her again, she has Adrian's lawyer on call to support her. But he doesn't think they will. Whenever she wants to leave, she has the car they came in, which turns out to be a Bentley Convertible, to drive wherever she likes. Adrian has even got his PA to arrange a pet sitter for Ziggy.

It takes about ten minutes for the storm to pass over. The rain abates. She gets up from the bed and pours herself a glass of water from the carafe on the table.

The sky in the distance is already brightening over the hills. She stands at the window, sipping the water and gazing out.

Should she believe what Adrian told her? Part of her is still resisting it, but in her heart she knows it's true. Her memories of the night of the Finals party are fractured. All she remembers is waking with the worst hangover ever.

Even before Ella died, whenever she encountered Rob Gerrish, and it wasn't that often, it made her feel extremely uncomfortable. There's always been something disturbing about him. She told herself the awkward vibe was because she'd turned him down. But if what Adrian said is true, it all makes sense.

He raped you.

She has no conscious memory of what happened. But maybe her body knew. Her body remembered. She was twenty-one and a virgin. He got her very drunk. Impregnated her. Did it traumatise her? It's hard to recall now if she was hurt or bruised afterwards.

You knew you'd had sex because you were sore and there was some blood. You thought it was your fault. You were ashamed.

When she returned home from university, she already knew she was pregnant. It just felt so unfair. The first time! And she was convinced it was Adrian. She tried to cover things up for as long as possible, but her mother noticed. Claire was petrified what their reaction would be, and how disappointed they'd be in her. It felt like a terrible failure.

Her father, in particular, surprised her. He took a pragmatic approach. We should not regard a baby as a mistake, he said. He would welcome a grandchild. They looked after Claire through her pregnancy and later moved house just so they could live nearer to where Claire had found a job.

Ella was precious to all of them. If anything, she was too cosseted. Did her sheltered upbringing make her naïve? She was a quiet, serious child, and once she had to go out into the world, perhaps she just wasn't tough enough?

Despite what Jermaine said, Claire knows she'll never stop blaming herself.

The rain has eased to a fine drizzle. She opens one of the windows again and the fresh breeze flows into the room with the pungent smell of wet earth. She looks out. The lake is sparkling and enticing. And it's much cooler.

She rummages in her holdall and finds a T-shirt and some leggings. She dresses, slips on a pair of flip-flops and heads out.

Instead of the lift, she takes the magnificent sweeping staircase, although she clings on to the banister. The staff she's noticed in their uniform of pink scrubs, but the other guests haven't really registered on her radar. There don't appear to be many. Some in dressing gowns. An older woman who looks familiar from television in a tracksuit. It's exclusive and her guess is extremely expensive. Adrian's gift.

And his penance.

She encounters Femi in the downstairs hall.

'You look a little better,' says the nurse.

The woman is a total stranger, but her gaze is direct and full of kindness. It brings a tear to Claire's eye. Femi touches her arm gently and smiles.

'I thought I'd go for a walk,' Claire says.

Femi nods. 'The rain's practically stopped. They'll be tea and homemade scones in the lounge at four.'

As Claire walks across the wet grass and down towards the lake, she reviews the painful events of the weekend in her mind.

The horror of Mel's death is raw. She can barely consider it, but she knows she must because she played a part in it. Her craziness kicked off a chain reaction. But it all comes back to him.

Rob Gerrish.

After Ella's suicide, it was easy to slip into blaming him and hating him. And it was hatred, a visceral and obsessive loathing. She simply couldn't let go of it. Sometimes she knew how irrational she was being. But she thought of nothing else. It lurked in the back of her mind every single day and filled her sleepless nights. She wanted to kill him. There's no doubt in her mind about that. And she would've done, if Adrian hadn't intervened.

The muscles in her belly are rigid, and her chest is so tight she can hardly breathe. A corrosive anger grips her. It travels from the gut upwards. She feels as if she might vomit.

She picks up the pace and walks faster. Kicking off the flip-flops, she runs across the grass. And suddenly the thought is there, pristine and fully formed.

But it was what he did to you. It was always about that. You just didn't know it.

Reaching the shore of the lake, she stops dead, tips back her head, opens her mouth and screams. A full-throated unrestrained howl of agony and despair.

Two mallards rise up from the water with a furious flapping of wings.

The sound echoes out across the lake towards the far hills.

She inhales a fresh lungful of storm-washed air and squats down on her haunches.

This is what it always was. She had every right to hate him. He raped her.

58

Tuesday, 4.30pm

The day has been hot and humid. And instead of getting the train back to Cambridge, Jo Boden has indulged herself. She spent some time sitting in Greenwich Park, at the top of the hill, looking down on the city spread out in the shimmering heat below her. Then she paid a surprise visit to her mother and had a cup of tea and a chat.

Now she's on the South Bank on the outdoor terrace of a bar. The sun is still fierce enough to make the huge sunshades essential. The bar is busy, people are bunking off work just like her and making the most of the alfresco lifestyle, which is not that usual in London.

Her phone buzzes. Chakravorty.

'Hey, Prish,' she says.

'Good news or bad news?' says Chakravorty.

What would good news look like? she wonders.

'Hit me,' she says.

'We've identified the murder weapon,' says Chakravorty.

'The heavy gold-plated crucifix that was on the altar in the chapel. Lab has tested it and found traces of the victim's blood in the piece of felt that's stuck to its base.'

'Okay,' says Boden. 'And?'

'No fingerprints. No traces of Leon Davison's DNA on it.'

There's a surprise.

'What's Knight saying?'

'Well,' says Chakravorty. 'She's still looking for the evidence to charge Davison. Hopes to make the case by placing him at the scene. The theory is he hit the victim with the crucifix, but then he cleaned it.'

'What with?'

'Knight's sent a team back to the cottage on the Fens that you raided to look for any clothing or something that Davison had with him that could fit the bill.'

'Any blood traces in his vehicle? Like on the steering wheel from his hands?'

'No. One theory is that if he exited through the crypt and into the Master's Garden, he could've washed his hands under the garden tap.'

'So could anyone else,' says Boden.

'I suppose,' says Chakravorty. 'You want the bad news?'

'Probably not.'

'The boss says you are not to approach the Minister's special adviser yet.'

'Yet?'

Ever more like.

'She was pretty emphatic,' says Chakravorty. 'It's a no.'

'Okay. Thanks, Prish.'

Boden orders herself another beer.

Questioning Kieran Morgan would certainly open a snake pit, and Boden understands why the boss doesn't want to go down that road unless she's forced to. Getting Theo Webber to talk would've helped. But unlike the boss, Boden doesn't expect the case to be solved in a few days. Knight has her own set of priorities.

And she's the Senior Investigating Officer, meaning she runs the case.

Nothing you can do.

Boden decides to kick back, enjoy being in London, and the beer.

She sees him walking towards her through the crowd; Cal Foley is always an impressive figure. He's off duty, so no slick suit. He wears Bermuda shorts just above the knee and a T-shirt, which shows off his pecs to full advantage.

He approaches her table, gives a brief two-fingered salute to his forelock and sits down opposite her, folding his arms. 'Hey, Boden. How's it going?'

He's as nervous as you.

She has the protection of her sunglasses. 'On a scale of one to ten,' she says. 'Minus five.'

'That good, eh?'

He laces his fingers and smiles. 'Your text said help. So I got on my trusty steed, AKA the Northern Line, and here I am. What's up?'

'The Rowe murder inquiry. I followed a lead up a blind alley. The intel is unreliable. I've got questions I can't get answered. I've pissed my boss off. And I've got nowhere to go with it. I was hoping for some sage advice.'

'I see.' He grins. 'Advice, I do. Sage? I dunno.'

He waves at the server and orders himself a beer.

'Another?'

She shakes her head.

'Okay,' he says. 'Between you and me, what's the central question?'

'Motive and killer. It was a savage attack from behind. Post mortem confirms that. The intention was probably to kill her. Was Melissa Rowe murdered to shut her up? That's the question.'

'Sounds plausible. So start with the why.'

'She was after Robert Gerrish, digging into a story that had the potential to ruin him.'

'You think it was him? Unlikely. We had him tucked up pretty tight in his rooms.'

'I know that. My intel is pointing the finger at Kieran Morgan, his special adviser.'

Foley chuckles.

'Why are you laughing?' says Boden.

'Because,' says Foley. 'I can quite believe it. The guy is an unpleasant, lying, vicious little toe rag. And that's on a good day.'

'You think he's a plausible suspect, then?'

'Absolutely.'

Boden takes a draft of beer. 'Well,' she says. 'That makes it doubly frustrating. I contacted my boss, asked if I could approach him. Got a resounding no.'

Foley exhales. 'That's bosses for you.'

'They're trying to make a case against a drug dealer who Rowe had a row with.'

'Course they are. So what are you going to do?'

She takes another drink of beer. 'Give up? Go home.'

Foley ponders this for a moment. Then he says, 'Let me make a couple of calls.'

A half hour later, Boden and Foley walk into a pub on a side road off Victoria Street in Westminster. The sun has gone in.

The heatwave is about to break with a storm forecast which is moving down the country.

The bar is heaving and hot as a sauna; the noise level is just below deafening. Foley points towards the back door, which stands open and leads into a small walled garden. She follows him out there. He makes eye contact with a tall, ginger headed woman, to Boden's eye another cop, but dressed in civvies. The woman lets her gaze travel across the yard to a loud gaggle of drunken twenty-somethings in one corner.

Foley leans down to speak in Boden's ear. 'We're in luck. This is a regular SpAd hangout. But let me do the talking.'

Foley pushes his way through the crowd towards the group, Boden tucks herself into his slipstream. Coming up behind them, he claps his hand on the shoulder of a medium-sized bloke who's waving a cigarette around in a circle above his head.

The man turns; he's small compared to Foley, but wiry. Dark hair, a baby face accentuated by his round glasses.

'Alright, mate,' says Foley.

Kieran Morgan beams at the sight of him. 'Foley, my man!' he exclaims and attempts to bump fists. He misses. He's drunk.

Foley steadies him. 'You've had a skinful,' he says.

Kieran totters a bit. 'Why aren't you guarding the citadel?' he says. The words are slurred.

'Day off,' says Foley. 'Bit early in the week to be getting wasted, isn't it?'

Kieran sways. 'Never too early when you work for a total bastard,' he replies.

'I always thought you and Gerrish were pretty tight.'

'So did I.' He shakes his head wearily. 'I need another shot. More tequila, eh!'

'Hang on, Kier,' says Foley, grasping his shoulder. 'What's up? You seem upset.'

'I can't say.'

'Course you can. We're mates.'

Kieran exhales. 'They got me in the crosshairs. I tell you, man, I'm seriously fucked.'

'Sounds bad, mate. Anything I can do to help.'

'You're a cop.'

'This is true.'

'Nah, but they just run you lot. You jump to their tune.'

'Not always. Tell me what the problem is. I might be able to do something.'

Kieran seems to consider this. He takes another swig from his beer bottle. Then he says, 'I can't give you any details. But I'm being thrown under the bus. And I wasn't even there! I hooked up with this girl on Bumble. I was at her place shagging her, five bloody miles away. She was alright. Got her number so I can prove it. And I will, when your lot come calling. Gerrish doesn't believe me.'

Foley glances round at Boden and raises his eyebrows. Kieran notices her for the first time.

'Who's she?' he says with a leery smile.

'Friend of mine,' says Foley.

'You shagging her?' He looks Boden up and down. 'I'd shag her.'

Foley bats him round the ear, but gently. 'Mind your manners.'

Kieran shakes his head wearily. His shoulders sink. 'She'll get away with it, y'know,' he says. 'She bloody will. That woman is a gorgon. Na, delete that. She makes your average gorgon look like a pussycat. She is evil.'

Boden and Foley exchange covert looks.

'Who we talking about here?' says Foley.

Kieran sways and nearly trips over the table behind him. Foley grabs his arm.

'I think maybe I'm going to chuck up,' says Kieran.

'Deep breaths, mate,' says Foley. 'You'll be fine.'

Kieran inhales a couple of times.

'So who we talking about here?'

'What?' says Kieran. He's looking deadly pale.

'The gorgon?' says Foley. 'Who's the gorgon?'

'Bloody Leanne,' says Kieran. 'Who else?'

He turns round and pukes. The sick splashes two women seated at the nearby table. They jump up in horror.

Foley turns to Boden. 'Let's get out of here,' he says.

She nods. It's starting to rain.

59

Tuesday, 5.15pm

Leanne is tense. She stares out of the sitting-room window. The rain is teeming down, running in a torrent down the road. The gutters and drains are overflowing. She left the office early to get ahead of the storm.

She's tried calling Adrian Cardello several times during the afternoon. He didn't pick up. Now she's left wondering if he might be avoiding her. Trusting him was always a high-risk strategy.

When she spoke to Claire on the phone yesterday evening, all Claire knew is she's somewhere hilly near the Lake District and off the M6, possibly the Pennines. Leanne got her assistant Caspar to trawl the net for every upmarket private clinic and health spa in the north of England. But blagging any information out of these places is near to impossible. If they're any good, and Adrian would pick somewhere good, then they'd be used to dealing with all the tricks used by the media to get information on their celebrity clients.

Leanne knows she must just wait and see how the situation unfolds. She's been meticulous and done her best to cover all bases with this. The police need a suspect. Claire is obviously her preferred option; she's off her head clearly. Her attempted attack on Robert proves it. The best place for her is Rampton, detained indefinitely.

She turns away from the window and examines her fingernails one by one. They're immaculate. The girl did an excellent repair job. Leanne also knows she can rely on her discretion. She didn't ask any silly questions about what had happened to them.

Once less thing to worry about. Tick that off the list.

But the possibility is emerging here that Adrian may have been lying to her. Would that really be such a surprise? The Claires and Melissas and Adrians of this world stick together. It all comes back to class. Where you grew up, and if you went to the right sort of school. The one-of-us club she was always excluded from. But now people like her have formed their own club. It's even more exclusive; to join you have to be clever and ruthless and rich enough to have beaten the bastards at their own game. Leanne knows she's all those things.

She learned early on that you should always have a fall-back position. It's basic strategy; every military commander knows that. And hers was quite easy to put in place. Kieran. If the police find evidence of what Melissa was up to or at least planning, then Kieran moves into the frame. His conviction would lead to some collateral damage for Robert, but nothing that couldn't be managed.

Robert would have to resign from the Cabinet initially, but political careers have recovered from far greater calamities. A year on the back benches, speaking up for all the causes that press the electorates' buttons, and they could turn it into a launchpad for a leadership bid. Second best often turns out best.

Her mind strays back to Claire. It's a niggling irritation.

She tried to attack Robert! If she ends up in Rampton with the rest of the criminally insane, it's what she deserves.

Leanne considers her nails again. She stopped biting them when she was fourteen. It was her first act of pure willpower. She'd read an article telling her it was just a bad habit, and a habit takes between thirty and sixty days to break. She relapsed only once and punished herself by drinking half a pint of salt water. Then she threw up. But it taught her a lesson in self control that she's never forgotten.

She checks her watch. The children are up in their rooms doing homework, but it'll be their teatime soon. She decides to sit down and chat to them while they eat; it will also be a useful distraction. They remind her of what matters and why she's doing all this.

She has two lovely daughters, several beautiful homes, a husband who could end up running the country, and a highly successful and lucrative business of her own. Any of those silly girls from her college days, with their superior attitudes and their skiing trips and their boyfriends with sports cars, would have to admit that she's the winner. Hands down, the outright winner. She's beaten them all. She worked the hardest and made the smartest choices. When it came to the game of life, those spoilt bitches didn't even come close.

That's the truth. No one can take that away from you.

But Melissa tried. Oh, she tried. And she still thought she could call her names and get away with it. She soon learned that was a mistake. When Leanne went to meet her in the chapel, she was tanked up on booze and high on coke, but all that did was loosen her tongue.

'He's fucking going down,' she sneered. 'I've got you in

my sights, Miss Piggy. You and your billionaire buddies and your whole greedy crew.'

It was pathetic. The usual bullshit.

'…. the Americans have got a name for people like you. You're white trash, Leanne. All the designer clothes, all the dosh and the famous friends, it'll never change that. Never change who you are.'

'I wonder if your left-wing paper knows what a class snob you are?' Leanne replied. She kept her cool.

Melissa ranted. 'It's not about class. It's about underlying values. It's about responsibility and caring for other people. It's about sharing things out, so everyone gets at least something. So kids in refugee camps aren't born to starve.'

'Let me see if I understand you, Melissa. In your lovely paternalistic world, you look after all your people, all the poor, everyone gets a little bit. So long as they all know their place, and don't get above themselves, and realise who's in charge. Who the bosses are. Which is your lot, isn't it? The ones that have always lived in the big house and had more. Loads more.'

Melissa tried to get up, but she could hardly stand. Her face was sweaty and flushed. She was spitting venom. 'That's not what I'm saying. You're twisting it. Like you twist everything.'

Leanne gazes out at the rain and sighs. Hindsight is a wonderful thing. She always makes a point of being honest with herself. And she has to admit that was the moment it got out of hand.

You let her get to you.

They were face to face at this point. Melissa towered over her, but Leanne stood her ground. 'You never thought I was as good as you,' she said. 'You always treated me like dirt under your expensive shoes.'

'Only because you were two-faced and manipulative. Whisper in this one's ear, then that one's. You were always trying to turn Claire against me. You're devious and dishonest. But here's something you don't know, Miss Piggy. You know Rob always wanted Claire.'

'That's old news.'

'But when she wouldn't give him what he wanted, Rob and I started to have a thing. Didn't know that, did you?'

She was lying. Clearly she was lying.

But it felt real. Melissa was in her face and she kept talking. 'Went on for quite a while,' she said. 'He wanted to get one over on Cardello, and frankly, so did I. For a weedy little guy, he was an okay fuck. But he comes a bit too quickly. Do you find that? I could've had him. He certainly would've chosen me over you. I could've been Mrs Gerrish. I think I would've made a better job of it.'

She was laughing. She thought she'd won. She slumped back down in the pew.

What did she expect? That you'd just slink away defeated?

Reflecting upon it now, Leanne realises Melissa was just being Melissa. She wanted to wind her up. Melissa was always a bully.

You shouldn't have let her get under your skin.

But it's easy to be wise after the event. She'd probably drunk a little too much herself and should never have agreed to the meeting.

Anger is a strange experience. Things can happen when you're in its grip, and afterwards, once it's gone, you feel completely different. She regrets what happened. Obviously she does. But it was only a momentary loss of control, under extreme provocation. She's not a killer. She can't be placed in the same category as Claire

Naylor, who was mental enough to have a knife in her bag.

Fortunately, she regained her composure almost immediately. And then the survival instinct kicks in. Robert thought she'd gone running. He'd had a stressful evening and she didn't think he needed to know she was meeting Melissa. This turned out to be a lucky decision.

She went back through the crypt and washed the heavy gold-plated crucifix and her hands under the outside tap in the Master's Garden. She dried the crucifix on her running top, returned to the chapel, polished it up with the altar runner, and replaced it. A forensic analysis might find minute traces of blood, but as long as there were no fingerprints or DNA, it was the best she could do.

When she got back to the college room, she put her running gear in her drawstring kit bag. It all went into the garden incinerator as soon as they got back to London. She cleaned under each fingernail with a cocktail stick and scrubbed her hands with a nail brush.

There were a few anxious hours when it looked like Melissa might survive, although Leanne thought it unlikely. With severe brain damage, any testimony she might give could easily be discredited. In the event, it all turned out well.

Since it happened, she's been wondering if she'd feel any remorse or guilt. After all, she's not a monster. She's a mother and a wife, and she was just protecting her family. But she hasn't. Nothing at all. And why should she?

It was Melissa's decision to take Leanne on. She was the victim of her own weakness and arrogance, and what Melissa got was exactly what she deserved. There's nothing to regret. It was self-defence.

Leanne hears her daughters coming downstairs for their tea. She's heading to the kitchen to join them when the front door opens and her husband appears. It's still pouring with rain; his driver is holding an umbrella over him.

'God, what bloody awful weather,' he says.

'You're home early, darling.'

He thanks the driver and closes the front door. He's grinning from ear to ear.

'And that's because I'm the bearer of good news,' he says. 'Got a call from the Home Office. A heads up. The police have charged someone with Mel's murder.'

She holds her breath and a shiver runs through her.

'Who?'

'This is the best part. A drug dealer called Leon Davison. Apparently, she bought some cocaine from him and they ended up in some kind of row. How brilliant is that?'

She flings her arms round him and hugs him.

'It's perfect. I'm so pleased for you, darling. But you'll still get rid of Kieran.'

'He is off the hook.'

She huffs. 'Oh, come on, Robert...'

He smiles. 'Just a little tease,' he says. 'Of course I will. For you, my darling. Because it's what you want.'

He lifts her hand to his lips and kisses her freshly painted fingertips.

60

The office feels half empty after the bustle of the last few days. Boden wanders through it to her desk. She came back from London this morning, feeling slightly the worse for wear. She spent the evening in a bar with Foley. They caught a brief glimpse of DCI Knight on the Ten O'clock News facing the cameras and announcing that Leon Davison had been charged.

She sits at her desk and stares at her laptop. She wonders if Kieran Morgan's supposed alibi would've stood up to any scrutiny.

Unlikely you'll ever know.

Chakravorty appears. 'Hello, stranger,' she says.

'Oh,' says Boden. 'Is it that bad?'

'DCI spent most of yesterday afternoon asking where you were. We tried to cover for you.'

'Thanks.'

Chakravorty tilts her head and considers Boden. 'Where have you been? You look a bit...I dunno.'

Boden smiles to herself. The young DC is sharp as a tack. No point trying to fool her.

'I stayed over with an old friend,' she says, as casually as she can.

Chakravorty grins and raises her eyebrows. 'Oh,' she says. 'Was it fun?'

Boden can't help grinning. 'Yes. But say nothing to Mackie.'

Chakravorty zips her lips with her finger. Then she says, 'It was the close protection guy, wasn't it? He's hot.'

Boden shakes her head in weary amusement. 'You'll be running this place before long, Prish. So tell me, how the hell did Knight get enough to charge the drug dealer?'

'Forensics can place him in the chapel. He definitely went there. Plus, we've found two witnesses. Someone looking for Melissa Rowe accosted both of them. One of them admits he told this person he saw her going into the chapel. They've both IDd Davison.'

'You've got no CCTV though?'

'A couple of clips. One of him running back to his vehicle. There's nothing covering the Master's Garden at the back. He could've come and gone undetected. And washed the crucifix under the garden tap.'

Boden sighs 'Still doesn't explain why he didn't just knife her.'

'When the evidence was put to him, he got rattled. Then his story was to admit he went there. He says she was already dead.'

'What if he's telling the truth?'

'Well, she wasn't dead, was she?'

'Dead? Unconscious? He probably didn't stay long enough to investigate.'

Chakravorty gives her a quizzical look. 'What are you thinking?' she says.

'I don't know. Probably nothing.'

The Gorgon? Was Kieran just mouthing off?

Most investigations turn on the questions you don't ask, not the questions you do ask. That's what an old boss of hers used to say.

She wonders about the questions they haven't asked. She wanders over to the coffee station and fills her mug.

A text pops up on her phone. Cal.

Hey, how you doing? Followed by a smiley face.

She replies with a smiley face and then adds *what did your guy say?*

They'd discussed the question of Kieran's veiled accusation against Leanne Brady. A close protection officer remained on duty outside the door to the Minister's rooms all evening. Foley was pretty certain Robert Gerrish never went anywhere, but he wasn't so sure about his wife.

Boden sips her coffee and waits.

Her phone flashes with a reply. *She went for a run.*

Boden stares at the screen.

There's no sign of the DCI in her office. Leon Davison is making his first court appearance. No one seems to know when the boss'll be in.

Boden goes out to the sandwich shop round the corner and buys herself a salad box for lunch.

They've found a thread. What will happen if she pulls it? She suspects the entire case might unravel, but first you have to pull it. And she doubts the boss will countenance any sort of approach to the Minister's wife.

And she's right. It's after two when she finally speaks to Rachel Knight.

The DCI stares at her. 'You are kidding?' she says. 'I know I'm not liked round here, but is it your mission, Boden, to make my life difficult?'

Boden sighs. 'No,' she says. 'Of course not.'

The DCI throws up her hands in horror. 'You want to ignore a violent drug dealer who threatened Rowe and we can prove was looking for her and we can place at the crime scene, because the Minister's wife went for a late night run?'

'I just think, boss—'

Knight puts her hands on her hips. 'I'm beginning to realise, Jo, why a woman of your undoubted ability has failed to rise through the ranks. You'll never make Inspector if you continue to behave like this. You just don't know when to let go.'

Why make it personal? A low blow.

This gets Boden's goat more than anything else.

She fixes Knight will a steely glare. 'I'm just trying to do my job, boss. We can't connect the suspect to the murder weapon.'

'He's a violent criminal and he threatened her.'

'Blunt force trauma to the head? Why that? Messy. Especially when we know he was carrying a knife.'

'Criminals don't always think or behave rationally. So he didn't stab her? That doesn't prove he didn't kill her.'

Boden knows she's on a hiding to nothing. She dips her head to control her temper.

There's a heavy silence in the room.

Let go. Leave it.

Knight sighs. 'Davison appeared in court this morning.

He was committed for trial. He'll have every opportunity to argue for his innocence. And a jury will decide. We've done our job. Move on.'

Half a job. Full of loose ends.

Boden says nothing. For a moment.

Then she says, 'It just pisses me off that we're drawing a line under this. Why? Because it's easier. Because it's convenient. Because you know and I know if we go after Leanne Brady, question her, search her house, try to break down her supposed alibi, check her DNA to see if we can place her at the scene too, then there'll be phone calls to the Chief Constable.'

'All you seem to have against her is the vaguest suspicion. You can't substantiate it.'

'But you won't even let me try to substantiate it, because you're not willing to take the flack.'

Knight glares at her; she appears to be shaking.

'Think about it, boss,' says Boden. 'What does this really look like? A drug dealer with a beef? The MO is all wrong. Or an old friend, who the victim had history with and whose husband she wanted to discredit? You said it yourself, old jealousies and resentments can become toxic.'

'I know what I said. It's still just speculation. On the balance of the evidence we've got, it's the drug dealer.'

'Surely that's the point. We haven't gathered all the potential evidence, have we? If Leanne Brady wasn't married to a government minister, we'd be questioning her. At least admit it.'

The DCI folds her arms. 'You're way out of line here, Sergeant. I'm the SIO of this inquiry. And I'm satisfied that the right person has been charged. I understand your frustration. You've worked hard. You're stressed. I'm going to put your aggressive and totally unprofessional attitude down to that. Take some time off. Forget about the job.'

Unprofessional attitude?

'I don't think I'm the one who's unprofessional here,' says Boden, and turning on her heel, she walks out of the door.

As she heads back through the office, her phone lights up.

A text from Cal. *When can I see you?*

She smiles to herself as her thumbs hit the keys. *Dinner tonight? I'll be in London by 5.*

61

. . .

Two months later

The memorial service is being held at St Bride's Church, just off Fleet Street. It's known as the Journalists' Church, although what's left of the newspaper industry has long since migrated elsewhere.

Claire stands under the trees, just inside the gateway. She gazes up at the spire; the Wren church, bombed and burned by the Luftwaffe, has been replaced with an elegant restoration which keeps faith with the original.

It's her first trip to London since she left Stanfirth Hall. Negotiating the crowds and the hustle of city life has been a little unnerving. But her seven-week stay in the rural peace and tranquility of the Hall has helped her find a new equilibrium. She's well aware of her continuing fragility. She has to pace herself. But this is an event she felt she couldn't miss.

Mel's funeral was held in Sussex and was a private family affair. Claire didn't attend. But the memorial has attracted a huge and diverse array of people. Friends, colleagues, admirers, it's hard to tell who they all are. Claire watches them file into the church.

A framed portrait of Mel sits on an easel next to the door. Under the image it says: A service of Thanksgiving for the life of Melissa Rowe. Award-winning journalist and author. It gives her dates. She was forty-seven at the time of her death.

And Ella was twenty-four.

Through the tight knot of people moving sedately towards the gateway, Claire catches sight of Adrian in his aviator shades, a white open-necked shirt, and a charcoal grey silk suit. He's in incognito mode and is passing largely unrecognised. It's hard to work out how he manages this, but he is an actor.

They haven't met since he left her at the Hall, but they've FaceTimed. Claire gets the feeling he's been monitoring her without wishing to intrude.

He comes up next to her, raises his glasses up on to his forehead and smiles. 'You're looking well,' he says. 'Nice dress.'

She's bought a new dress for the occasion, and has a light jacket draped over her arm. The weather is warm for the end of September. Another record-breaking year of heat.

'How's your filming been going?' she says.

He chuckles. 'Well, I'm doing my level best to rescue the President, defeat a worldwide criminal conspiracy led by an AI enhanced mastermind and get the girl. And the dailies don't look too bad either.'

'The dailies?'

'Each day's batch of filming. It's a tight schedule and we have to make sure we're getting the footage we need.'

'Sounds complicated.'

'It's just a job. You put one foot in front of the other.'

'How's Jermaine?'

'Good. He sends you his love. Did you get things sorted out for your parents?'

'They have a live-in carer now. My dad came out of hospital. He's frail, but he soldiers on.'

'And are you soldiering on?'

'Better than that, I think. I hope.'

He offers her his arm. 'Shall we?'

They link arms and join the procession into the church. Walking down the nave, with its distinctive black and white tiled floor, Claire gazes up at the high vaulted ceiling decorated with gilded flowers. The usher directs them to seats in the ornately carved wooden stalls to the side. The place is filling up fast.

A young man trots up the short aisle next to them. Dark, curly hair, handsome. He squats down next to Adrian. 'Just wanted to touch base,' he says.

Adrian turns to Claire. 'Claire, this is Theo,' he says. 'He worked with Mel.'

'Hello,' says Claire. Theo smiles and nods in acknowledgement.

Then he lowers his voice and leans in closer. 'Brian wants you to know that we're moving ahead. Our source is being extremely helpful. He's giving us chapter and verse. We have a contact at the National Crime Agency who's very interested in our findings.'

'That's great,' says Adrian.

'We're doing it for Mel,' says Theo. 'And because it's right.'

Theo stands up and heads back across the nave to his seat.

Claire glances at Adrian. 'What's that about?' she whispers.

Adrian turns his head and speaks softly close to her ear. 'They're going after Gerrish big time. Every dodgy financial deal. All his scams in and out of government. Their source is his former political adviser.'

'Kieran?'

'Yeah.'

Claire absorbs this.

The man who used and abused her daughter.

She dips her head.

'You okay?' says Adrian.

She nods.

There's no chance to say more. The organ strikes up and the choir processes up through the nave and into the chancel. Their voices rise up and flood the church.

Onward Christian soldiers!

Marching as to war,

With the cross of Jesus,

Going on before.

Adrian leans towards Claire and whispers, 'Very Mel. She was always fighting someone.'

The service is varied and in parts extremely moving. There's lots of music. A soloist sings Amazing Grace, a song that always brings a tear to Claire's eye. A niece reads a passage from one of Mel's books. Her editor and former boss speaks about the kind of journalist she was. Difficult to manage at times, demanding of her colleagues, but ruthless in her pursuit of the truth. There are some amusing anecdotes which raise a laugh. Her sister gives a touching personal account of the trials and tribulations of their shared child-hood, growing up in a military family. That provokes a few tears. There are prayers. And then it's all over.

The organ plays in the background, and the congregation moves towards the exit. But it's a slow process and people stop to chat.

This is when Claire sees him for the first time.

There he is.

Rob and Leanne were seated near the front. The power couple are immaculately turned out, meeting and greeting, no doubt saying all the appropriate and polite things.

Leanne is talking to Mel's sister. Claire watches her touch the sister's arm, then give her a hug.

Claire notices Adrian watching her.

'Are you okay?' he says. 'We can slip out round the back if you want.'

'No,' says Claire. 'I want to speak to them. I want to look him in the eye.'

'Then that's what we'll do,' says Adrian.

He takes Claire's arm and shepherds her down the steps, through the press of people and up the aisle to where the Gerrishs are holding court.

Leanne sees them first. The startled look in her eyes is momentary. She immediately paints on a smile and steps forward.

'My dear Claire,' she says. 'I didn't know if you'd be here.'

'Why wouldn't I be here?' says Claire. 'Mel was one of my oldest friends.'

'I'd...heard that you were unwell.' She turns immediately to Adrian. 'Adrian,' she says. 'I see that you're taking care of Claire.'

'Yes, I am,' says Adrian, meeting her gaze directly. 'And I've got to give it to you, Leanne. If you were on the list of nominees for an Oscar, I'd vote for you.'

Leanne looks slightly taken aback, but she raises her chin defiantly.

'I really don't know what you mean,' she says with an affected chuckle.

'Don't you?' says Adrian. 'That surprises me.'

Claire looks past Leanne to where Rob is standing, talking to the Vicar. Then he notices her staring at him.

A strange look passes over his face. Fear? Longing? A fox at bay facing the hounds, about to rip it to shreds?

But he seems to steel himself. He steps forward until they come face to face.

'Claire,' he says. 'This is a surprise. But I know how close you and Mel were.'

'We were,' says Claire.

He shifts uncomfortably and can't keep eye contact. 'Such a lovely service,' he says. 'A moving tribute to an amazing life.'

'I thought you didn't like her,' says Claire.

'Well,' he says with some bluster, 'obviously we had some political—'

'She hated you,' says Claire.

Leanne comes and stands shoulder to shoulder with her husband. 'Darling,' she says. 'I think we should go. We're running behind schedule and—'

'No,' says Claire emphatically. 'You don't get to walk away.'

Adrian stands next to Claire and folds his arms. This effectively blocks their way out down the aisle.

'I've got some questions I need answering first,' she says. 'I've been thinking a lot about the party that took place after Finals. Remember that, Rob?'

'It was a long time ago and—'

'Yeah, it was. But it was a momentous night for me. That's when I became pregnant with Ella.'

A look of incredulity springs into his eyes.

Has he really never thought of this?

'Are sure...I didn't...' He takes a neatly pressed linen handkerchief from his pocket and presses it to his lips.

'Yes, I am sure. I was a virgin before that. And I didn't sleep with anyone again until much later, after she was born. That was definitely the night she was conceived.'

For a moment, he's speechless.

Leanne tugs at her husband's sleeve. 'Robert, this is not a conversation we should—'

He pulls free from her. 'Wait a minute!' he says sharply.

Leanne steps back, a look of shock, as if she's been slapped.

Claire stares right at him. His eyes shine like pinpricks, but she can see the panic.

'I just want a straight answer, Rob. I want to hear it from your lips. What did you do to me that night? Because it was you, wasn't it?'

He dips his head and mutters, 'I didn't do anything. I adored you, Claire. But you just wouldn't give me a chance. You dismissed me. Dismissed my feelings. It wasn't fair.'

'But I didn't feel the same. You knew that. Because I told you.'

He sneers. 'A girl like you. Blokes were chasing you all the time. You really expect me to believe you didn't sleep with any of them? Why wasn't I good enough for you?'

'I told you. I didn't sleep with any of them.'

Rob glares at Adrian and stabs an index finger in his direction. 'What's he been telling you? Filling your head with a pack of lies? I did the right thing. I came and I proposed to you. And you just laughed in my face.'

'I didn't laugh. I just told you I didn't want to marry you. And why was proposing the right thing?'

He's snookered. He glances around him like a trapped rat.

'What?' he mumbles. The sweat is beading on his fore-head. He steps back. 'I need to get out of here. Get me out of here, Lee.'

Leanne grasps his arm. 'It's all right, darling. Calm down.' She swivels round and shouts, 'Foley! Get these people out of the way! They're threatening the Minister.'

She appears to be addressing a large black guy in a sharp suit with an earpiece. But he remains stock still, staring straight ahead of him, hands folded in front of him.

'Foley! Now!' she shouts. But Foley doesn't budge.

'Why was it the right thing, Rob?' says Claire. 'Was it because in your twisted view of things, having spiked my drink and raped me, you saw that as the decent thing?'

'It wasn't rape. You were just a bit drunk. I loved you Claire. How could it be rape if I loved you? You never gave me a chance. It wasn't fair.'

'I wasn't a bit drunk. I was unconscious. What about me? Didn't I get a say? You had sex with me when I was unconscious. Forced me. Is that fair? Just because you want something and you can't get it, you can't just take it.'

Rob Gerrish inhales. He stares at her. His chin quivers, but a steely look has come into his eye.

'Really?' he says. 'Why not? I find that's exactly how the world works. This is just a pack of lies. You can't prove any of it. If we had sex, it was totally consensual.'

He spins round and addresses the circle of astounded onlookers that have gathered around them.

'Any of you think you can publish any of this, I'll sue!' he shouts.

Foley steps forward. 'Sorry, Mrs Gerrish. Did you say something? I didn't hear you. Are you wanting to leave, sir?'

Rob rounds on him. 'Fuck you, Foley! I'll have your fucking job for this.'

The cop towers over him, face impassive. 'I'll tell your driver to bring round the car, sir,' he says.

Adrian stands back so Rob and Leanne can pass.

Leanne glares at Claire. 'This is a total lie. My husband is not that sort of man.'

'You sure about that, Leanne?' says Claire.

'Repeat any of these ludicrous accusations and we'll sue,' she spits.

Leanne takes Rob's arm and they scurry down the nave towards the door. Foley follows them.

The church has emptied out. But there are still at least a dozen people who have watched the altercation, mostly open mouthed.

Theo Webber clicks his phone off. He videoed it, as did several others.

Adrian turns to Claire. 'Are you alright?' he says.

She smiles at him. 'I'm not sure,' she replies. 'But I think now I will be.'

EPILOGUE

December

Claire sits on the sofa, her feet tucked up under her. Ziggy is in his usual spot, curled up beside her. The curtains are closed against the wintery darkness. Claire has her notebook in her lap and a pen in her hand. After many years, she's gone back to writing poetry again. She doesn't know if it's any good. Probably not. She hasn't shared it with anyone yet, except Ziggy.

In September she went back to her teaching job, but only part time. This feels manageable. She earns enough to pay the bills, and it frees up time for writing and walking; these are now her favourite pastimes. She's also joined a local book club. They're mostly women, a diverse bunch, with a ribald sense of humour.

A new GP has helped wean her off her medication. She still has a zoom consultation once a week with the therapist who treated her at Stanfirth Hall. She offered to start paying for this herself, but Adrian refused point blank.

There are good days and bad days. But aren't most people's lives like that?

The phone on the table beside her buzzes. She picks it up.

'Hello, Mum.'

'Are you watching the Six O'clock News?' says Sandra urgently.

'You know I never do,' says Claire. 'I can't stand it. It's just doom and gloom.'

'Well, turn it on,' says her mother. 'You'll want to see this.'

Claire has to search for the handset. She points it at the television in the corner. It takes her a moment to navigate through the options.

And suddenly there is Leanne, standing on what appears to be the doorstep of a rather large house with a piece of paper in her hand. She's caught in a ring of light from the TV cameras and photographers bunched in front of her and faces a phalanx of microphones, phones and other recording devices.

'…and he will continue to assert his total innocence. These charges are malicious and politically motivated. And we will prove that when his case comes to trial.' Her voice is high-pitched and shaky. She looks like a scared rabbit.

Robert Gerrish's fall from power has been rapid and spectacular. He was dumped from the Cabinet the day after Mel's memorial service. Footage of Claire and Adrian's confrontation with the Gerrishs went viral on social media.

Claire decided not to pursue rape charges against him. She'd spoken to a lawyer. It would be hard to prove. Did she need to put herself through another ordeal? She'd looked him in the eye, seen his guilt, and now she just wanted to put it behind her.

But Mel's newspaper had built a case against him for

financial fraud. The National Crime Agency had become involved. And now it seems they had brought charges.

'Do you expect to be arrested as well, Leanne?' shouts a voice from the crowd.

'I have nothing more to add,' says Leanne as she turns back towards the house.

'Do you deny that your PR firm acted on behalf of some of your husband's clients? That you helped funnel the cash?'

She disappears into the house. The front door closes behind her.

The footage cuts to a reporter speaking directly to camera. 'Robert Gerrish was taken into custody this morning,' he says, 'and faces a long list of charges related to his connections with various individuals and the alleged illegal financial transactions he carried out on their behalf. These activities go back many years and cover his time both in and out of government. A statement from Downing Street has made it clear that—'

Claire clicks the television off.

She picks up her phone. Sandra is still on the line.

'Mum?' she says.

'Looks to me like they both might go to jail,' says her mother. 'What do you think about that?'

Claire sighs.

What do you think?

'I actually feel sorry for Leanne,' she says.

'Why?' says her mother. 'I wouldn't.'

'Well, y'know, she had a tough start. She reminds me of many of the kids I teach.'

'C'mon, Claire. She won a scholarship to Cambridge. She had plenty of other choices.'

'Maybe.'

Choices? One bad choice can lead to another, and then another.

You made a bad choice and you got away with it.

'It's all just a lottery, Mum. I don't know that I'm about to judge Leanne. She was once a good friend to me.'

'You sure about that?'

'No. But I can't spend the rest of my life being angry. So let's change the subject. I've been thinking about Christmas. I'm assuming we want turkey with all the trimmings.'

'If you're going to cook it.'

'Absolutely.'

LEAVE A REVIEW

If you feel like writing a review, I'd be most grateful. The choice of books out there is vast. Reviews do help readers discover one of my books for the first time.

Scan QR code to review You Left Me

 tiktok.com/@susanwilkinsbooks

bookbub.com/authors/susan-wilkins

facebook.com/susanwilkinsauthor

instagram.com/susan_wilkins32

twitter.com/SusanWilkins32

A MESSAGE FROM SUSAN
PLUS FREE BOOKS TO DOWNLOAD

Thank you for choosing to read *You Left Me.* If you enjoyed it and would like two free downloads, plus keep up to date with my latest book releases and news, please use the address below.

susanwilkins.co.uk/sign-up/

*Your email address will never be shared, and you can unsubscribe at any time.

Scan QR code to go to Susan's sign up page

Do get in touch and let me know what you thought of *You Left Me.* I love hearing from readers. You can message me at:
susanwilkins.co.uk/contact/

Scan QR Code to go to Susan's contact page

BOOKS BY SUSAN

Detective Jo Boden Case Files:

She's Gone

Her Perfect Husband

Lie Deny Repeat

See Me Fall

You Left Me

Other Books by Susan:

The Informant

The Mourner

The Killer

It Should Have Been Me

Buried Deep

Close To The Bone

The Shout + The Right Side Of The Line (Free when you sign up to Susan's newsletter)

A Killer's Heart

ACKNOWLEDGEMENTS

Huge thanks to Colin James and Graham Bartlett for their expert advice on how the police would proceed. Some things have been altered slightly in the interests of drama.

In my career as an author, I've received the help and support of too many people to mention. The community of crime writers is friendly, welcoming, and nowadays global. Learning from those who have gone before is essential for any writer.

Big thanks to my Reading Team for their diligence and valuable feedback.

Thanks also to Jenny Kenyon for her unwavering support.

Last, but not least, thanks to Laura Wilkinson for her sharp editorial eye on the manuscript and her many suggestions for improvements.

But getting the books out into the world would be impossible without my partner in crime, Sue Kenyon. I just write the books. She does everything else.

Published by Herkimer Limited in 2023
Summit House
170 Finchley Road
London NW3 6BP

Scan QR code to go to susanwilkins.co.uk

ISBN 978-1-7392493-4-2

Printed in Great Britain
by Amazon